WINNIPEG
FEB 06 2013
PUBLIC LIBRARY

D0428457

Mercury Rests

Mercury Rests

A NOVEL BY ROBERT KROESE

The characters and events portrayed in this book are fictitious. Any similarity to real persons, living or dead, is coincidental and not intended by the author.

Text copyright © 2012 Robert Kroese
All rights reserved.
Printed in the United States of America.

No part of this book may be reproduced, or stored in a retrieval system, or transmitted in any form or by any means, electronic, mechanical, photocopying, recording, or otherwise, without express written permission of the publisher.

Published by 47North
P.O. Box 400818
Las Vegas, NV 89140

ISBN-13: 9781612185842
ISBN-10: 1612185843

07414 8278

For Climber.

Dramatis Personae

Alistair Breem: Physicist; Jacob Slater's mentor

Cain (Colin Lang): Biblical figure best known for killing his brother; cursed to walk the Earth until the End of Time

Christine Temetri: Jaded religion reporter and Apocalypse magnet

Cody Lang: Private investigator, actress, thigh model, conspiracy theorist; daughter of Colin Lang/Cain

Cravutius: An important seraph

Dirk Lubbers: Deputy Assistant Director of the FBI

Ederatz (Eddie Pratt): A cherub who was misplaced by the Mundane Observation Corps

Elihu: A young boy, contemporary of Job

Gamaliel: A fallen cherub (demon); servant of Tiamat

Horace Finch: Eccentric billionaire who built the Chrono-Collider Device (CCD) to uncover the fundamental secrets of the Universe; prior head of the Order of the Pillars of Babylon (OPB)

Izbazel: A fallen cherub (demon); servant of Lucifer

Jacob Slater: Forensic blast investigator for the FBI

Job: Biblical character known for his patience

Karl Grissom: Gaming geek; the Antichrist

Lucifer (Rezon): The devil

Mercury: A cherub employed by the Apocalypse Bureau

Michelle (Michael): Archangel; the general of Heaven's army

Nisroc: A dim-witted cherub charged with guarding the interplanar portal in Glendale, California; aficionado of SpaghettiOs

Perpetiel (Perp): A cherub who works as a porter/escort at the Planeport

Ramiel: Nisroc's partner in guarding the Glendale portal; servant of Lucifer

Roger Daltrey: FBI agent

Tiamat (Katie Midford): Demoness who is determined to rule the Universe

Travis Babcock: President of the United States

Uzziel: Former head of the Apocalypse Bureau

Wanda Kwan: Acquiring editor for the Finch Group's publishing company

PROLOGUE

To Your Holiness the High Council of the Seraphim,

Greetings from your humble servant, Ederatz,
Cherub First Class,
Order of the Mundane Observation Corps

First, allow me to apologize for the abrupt ending of my previous missive. We writers call such suspenseful endings "cliff-hangers" and generally employ them when we are worried about losing the interest of readers and consequently not being able to make our mortgage payments.

In this case, however, my concerns were more existential in nature. For reasons that will be clear to you if you've read the previous installments of this report, I was concerned that neither I nor the plane on which I currently reside would exist by the time I delivered my final report to you. So I sent the first two volumes ahead, in the hopes that even if the third didn't survive, you'd at least have a partial account of the story.

Considering the deference typically accorded my reports, of course, I put the odds of you having read either of them at about zilch. And then there's the possibility that by now, the space-time continuum has been annihilated, a contingency that entails that even if you did at one point read my previous two reports, you have no longer read them, because they will at this point have never existed.

On the other hand, if you're reading this report—and it seems that you are—we can reasonably assume that reality has not been annihilated, which is a pretty good start. This situation—you and the report both existing, and you reading it—suggests that Tiamat hasn't completely bollixed up the space-time continuum. That's good news, I suppose, although I think it's safe to say that Heaven's designs on the Mundane Plane have been, well, *disrupted*, to say the least. But then you know that. In fact, if you are reading this, it's probably because you're a little curious about how those pesky mortals managed to turn the tables on you and make a complete hash of your precious SPAM.

I took a few liberties with the end of the story. Obviously I wasn't there when Lucifer showed up in Heaven with his little surprise, for instance, so I had to guess at the details. You'll have to let me know if I got it right. If, you know, we all still exist.

"I really am beginning to think as I've restudied these matters that there's going to be no big display of any kind. The end is going to come very, very quietly."

—*HAROLD CAMPING, October 14, 2011*

"It isn't necessary to imagine the world ending in fire or ice—there are two other possibilities: one is paperwork, and the other is nostalgia."

—*FRANK ZAPPA*

ONE

Mercury awoke with a start, finding himself lying on an uncomfortable, molded plastic bench. He sat up and looked around. There was no way to know what time it was—or even *where* he was. It was pitch-dark except for the flicker of light coming from a fire that burned in a steel drum nearby. Around the fire, on makeshift mats of cardboard and blankets, lay seven very old and weathered-looking individuals, sleeping fitfully. Underneath them was a floor of concrete.

Angels technically have no need for sleep, but Mercury had been exceptionally tired—the sort of tired that you get from flying a hundred thousand miles into deep space to implode the moon. Well, not that *you* get, because you've probably never done that. But Mercury had.

Or had he? He was beginning to doubt his own memories. Why would he have thrown an anti-bomb at the moon? To prevent something worse from happening, he supposed, but he couldn't put his finger on what that was. There had been some sort of experiment in Africa involving the anti-bomb and…croutons or something. And then he had been imploded along with the moon, presumably, and reincorporated here—wherever *here* was.

He studied the group of people sleeping on the concrete around the drum. There were four men and three women. They had told him their names, but he had forgotten them. One of them was Arnie, or Ernie, something like that. He made a mental note to devise some sort of mnemonic device to help himself remember them. Maybe an acronym with the first letters of their names.

And the fire—there was something about the fire. He had looked into it and seen…what? That memory too was fuzzy. All he knew was that he didn't care to repeat the experience. His fingers went to his temples, as if he could somehow massage his memories into the right slots in his brain. Where was he? How did he get here? Who were these people? He could almost see the answers, but couldn't quite get to them, like a man with a hundred-dollar bill standing in front of a vending machine.

He stood up, blinking in the glare of the fire. He walked a few paces from the drum, but his vision didn't improve. The darkness was a palpable thing, enveloping him and threatening to extinguish even the very idea of light. And it was *cold*. It hadn't exactly been balmy on the bench, but it got noticeably colder with every step he took away from the fire.

Mercury felt in his pockets for something to provide some light. He found a deck of cards, three Gummi Bears, the decapitated head of a Cobra Commander action figure, a business card, a black Sharpie marker, and a package of dental floss (unwaxed).

He shuddered, thinking of the last time he had used unwaxed dental floss. "Why do they even make this stuff?" he grumbled to himself. But as much as he hated it, he couldn't make himself throw away forty-nine and a half yards of perfectly good dental floss. He put it back in his pocket, where it had resided for eight years, along with the rest of the jetsam—except for a single playing card. He held the card between his thumb and forefinger and concentrated.

It took more effort than he expected—the amount of available interplanar energy here was almost negligible—but after a few seconds the edge of the card caught fire, providing a modicum of light. Mercury held the card up and peered into the darkness.

"Good morning!" barked an unnaturally chipper voice behind him, causing Mercury to jump and drop the card. It fluttered down and lodged itself in his pants pocket, where it continued to burn with a supernatural flame.

"Gaaahhh!" howled Mercury, swatting furiously at the card, which refused to go out. "Gaaahhh!" he howled again, hopping around madly as the flames licked up his shirt. Finally, he mustered the presence of mind to grab hold of the card and toss it onto the ground, where it continued to burn with defiant indifference.

Mercury stuck his fingers in his mouth and glared at the man. It was Arnie or Ernie.

"Playing with the queen of hearts, I see," mused the man. Mercury was fairly certain it was Ernie.

" 'on't ay ip!" Mercury growled through his fingers.

"You know what they say," Ernie continued. "It only—"

"I 'aid, 'ON'T AY IP!" Mercury yelled.

"Don't say what?" Ernie asked.

Mercury removed his fingers from his mouth and studied them. "*You* know what," said Mercury. "If you say it, I'll have that song stuck in my head for the next five hundred years."

Ernie shrugged. "Where are you going?"

"Just exploring a little," replied Mercury. "Can you tell me where we are?"

"Well," said Ernie, "underground, for starters."

"OK," said Mercury, trying to be patient. "But what is this place? A basement? A bomb shelter?"

"It used to be a sort of train station," Ernie said. "A long time ago. So, I don't mean to be inhospitable, but where did you come from?"

"Er," Mercury started. "It's difficult to explain. There was a sort of science experiment that went wrong. I got, well, imploded, and I ended up here."

Ernie nodded sympathetically, as if that explanation made perfect sense. Or at least as much sense as anything else in his experience. Ernie gave the impression of somebody who had pretty much given up making sense of things.

"This may sound like a stupid question," Mercury went on, "but do you know what plane this is?"

Ernie nodded and smiled.

Mercury frowned. "Well?"

"Oh, I'm sorry!" replied Ernie. "I was just agreeing that it was a stupid question. We're not in a plane. I thought I mentioned this was a train station."

"Yes," replied Mercury, trying to remain patient. "But where *is* this train station?"

Ernie looked confused. He gestured with his hands and spoke slowly. "It's…*right*…*here*."

Mercury bit his lip in frustration. Is Ernie really this dense, or is he screwing with me?

He began again: "OK, how about this: how do I get topside?"

Ernie smiled and pointed. "Stairs that way. But there's nothing up there."

"What do you mean, nothing? There has to be *something* up there."

Ernie nodded. "No, not really."

Mercury sighed. "I have to hand it to you," he said. "You've got a gift for making a guy not want to ask any more questions."

He pulled another card from his pocket, squinting to read it in the dim light. "Six of diamonds," he said to Ernie. "Got anything you want to say about that?"

Ernie shook his head.

"OK, then," said Mercury, holding the card in his fingers. A flame appeared.

Ernie smiled the way one might smile at a cat trying to bat at a bird fluttering on the other side of a window.

Mercury shook his head and walked alone into the darkness.

Soon he found a staircase leading up. A dim gray light filtered down from somewhere above. He trudged up the steps.

He found himself on what must have been at one time a busy city street. The concrete sidewalk was badly cracked and littered with debris. An eerie horizon of dilapidated skyscrapers lay in the distance. The sky was a dark gray, and the cold air hung close, completely motionless. Beyond the skyscrapers an oppressive gray fog hung in the distance. Mercury shivered.

"Whatcha doin'?" barked a voice from behind him, causing him to drop the flaming card again.

Mercury spun around. "Damn it, Ernie. Stop doing that! I'm having a moment here."

"Sorry," replied Ernie. "There's nothing out here, you know."

"What do you mean, nothing?" Mercury said irritably. "This isn't *nothing*."

"Hmm," said Ernie doubtfully. Then something seemed to dawn on him. "Oh, wait, here's something!" Ernie took off on a sort of slow, loping run. He moved more quickly than Mercury would have thought, given his apparent age. Mercury followed him dutifully.

Ernie climbed a pile of rubble that seemed to be the remains of a collapsed brick building. "Check it out!" he said excitedly, pointing to something in the distance.

Mercury came up behind him and looked in the direction Ernie was pointing. Something was sticking up out of the ground in the distance. At first it looked to Mercury like a man holding an apple above his head. Then he realized what it was.

"Holy shit," he said. "It's the Statue of Liberty!"

"Oh," said Ernie, scratching his head. "Is that what you call it? We just call it the Big Apple Guy. You know, because of the big apple he's holding. Anyway, that's about all there is to see around here. Unless you like rubble. We have lots of rubble."

"It's not an apple," Mercury said. "It's a torch. And technically it's a she. She's pretty badly corroded." A light went on in Mercury's head. "Wait a second, this is *Earth*!"

Ernie gave him an odd look. "Well, of course it's Earth. Where did you think we were?"

Mercury shook his head in disbelief. If this really was New York, then many centuries had passed since he left. Somehow by setting off the anti-bomb hundreds of thousands of miles away from Earth, Mercury had opened a portal to the distant future. His heart sank as he realized that he would probably never be able to return to his own time. He had assumed that he would be transported by the anti-bomb to some backwater plane and that it might take some doing to get back, but this was something entirely unexpected. Not even the angels could make time run backward.

He turned to face Ernie. "I suppose next you're going to tell me that Earth is ruled by monkeys?"

"Monkeys!" exclaimed Ernie, shaking his head. "Of course not. I mean, I understand there were a few rough years a while back."

Mercury's brow furrowed. "Wait, are you saying that Earth *was* ruled by monkeys at one point?"

"Only very briefly," said Ernie. "It didn't really work out either time."

"*Either time*?" repeated Mercury incredulously.

Ernie nodded. "It was during the second term that we realized monkeys probably weren't the best choice. I say 'we,' although of course I wasn't around. This was many years ago. Our records aren't very good, but as I recall, it went Republicans, Democrats, Democrats, Republicans, monkeys, Democrats, Republicans, monkeys."

"Hmm," Mercury replied thoughtfully. He was starting to see the appeal of the monkeys.

"So," Mercury continued. "What year is it?"

Ernie seemed to cringe slightly at the question. "Maybe we should go back underground."

"Underground? Why?"

"It's not really safe out here. The fog drives people a little crazy."

Mercury wondered what might qualify as "crazy" in Ernie's estimation. As if in response, there was a shout in the distance. It sounded like "Hwaaaaaah!"

"What the hell is that?" Mercury asked. But when he turned back to Ernie, he saw that the old hobo was retreating back down the steps into the darkness. He heard the shout again.

"Hwaaaaaah!"

Mercury shrugged and walked toward the sound. After a few hundred feet, he rounded a pile of rubble to encounter a surprising sight: two men were playing Ping-Pong on a table set up in the middle of the street. They were engaged in an intense volley and appeared oblivious to his approach. The man on his left was sinewy and compact, with a stern expression on his face. His age was difficult to determine; at first glance he could have passed for thirty, but his sunken eyes and the lines worn in his face hinted at many more years. The man on the right was gray-haired and more sturdily built, but not much taller. His age too was difficult to determine. He had a bemused look on his face, as if he knew something that his opponent didn't. There was something familiar about him, but Mercury couldn't at first place where he had seen him before.

"Hwaaaaaah!" the gray-haired man howled, the ball caroming wildly off his paddle toward Mercury. Mercury caught the ball and smiled apologetically. The smile froze as he realized who the gray-haired man was.

"Any chance we can get our ball back?" asked the man amicably.

Mercury stood dumbly, staring at the man, still holding the ball in his right hand. *It can't be*, he thought. *It's impossible.*

"Seriously, the ball? We only have the one."

"Y-you're..." Mercury stammered. "You're *Job*. From the *Bible*."

"I am," said Job. "Say, I remember you. Aren't you an angel or something?"

Mercury nodded. "Mercury," he managed to say.

"I should punch you right in the nose for what you did to me," said Job.

Mercury nodded again.

Job laughed. "I'm joking," he said. "No hard feelings. You were just doing your job. So, ball?"

"Huh?" replied Mercury smartly.

"The ball, genius," growled the other man.

"Oh!" exclaimed Mercury, and tossed the ball to Job. "I'm sorry, I'm afraid I don't..."

"Name's Cain," said the other man. "I was in Genesis."

Mercury frowned. "Phil Collins Genesis or Peter Gabriel Genesis?"

"The first book of the Bible?" Cain explained impatiently. "I murdered my brother Abel and was cursed by God to wander the Earth?"

"Oh, thank God," said Mercury. "I thought maybe you had something to do with 'Abacab.' "

TWO

President of the United States Travis R. Babcock leaned slightly into the camera and smiled.

Actually, to say that he smiled vastly understates the effort that Travis was exerting. This wasn't just any smile. It was a smile that was perfectly calibrated to simultaneously reassure and disarm its recipients. It was, to be precise, Smile Number Fourteen, consisting of equal parts grim determination and youthful optimism. Smile Number Fourteen was tough to pull off, and Travis was a little out of practice. There hadn't been much call for Smile Number Fourteen for the first three years of his presidency. Privatizing Medicare had required mostly Smile Six (acknowledgment of sacrifice in the service of the greater good), and eliminating the capital gains tax had been a Smile Eleven job (faith in the ability of the American entrepreneurial spirit to overcome basic algebra). But for the sudden, unexpected implosion of a third of the moon, only Smile Fourteen would do. Travis pushed his lower lip forward while simultaneously furrowing his brow slightly and letting the right corner of his mouth curl upward three eighths of an inch.

Nailed it, thought Travis.

"My fellow Americans," he began. "Yesterday at four twenty-nine p.m. Eastern Time, Earth's moon came under attack. While

I cannot at present give you any details regarding the exact nature of the attack or the identity of the perpetrators, I can assure you that the full resources of the United States government are being used to address the situation.

"Our top priority is to deal with the aftermath of the attack, both here in the United States and abroad. FEMA has been dispatched to assist areas that have been hardest hit by earthquakes, tornadoes, flash floods, and hurricanes, and the National Guard is working closely with governors to maintain order. The State Department is actively coordinating efforts with the International Red Cross and other relief agencies in Brazil, China, Pakistan, and many other countries that have been hit by natural—that is, by disasters. Obviously, our resources are strained to their limits, but I am confident that our brave men and women will rise to the challenge.

"While relief work is ongoing, we are also working hard to determine the exact nature of the attack and identify the individuals responsible. As I said, because the investigation is in progress, I cannot provide any details, but our intelligence agencies are working in concert with the best minds at NASA to determine the exact means of attack and find whoever committed this heinous act.

"Make no mistake: we will find the folks who took a chunk out of the moon, and we will bring them to justice." Travis glanced at his watch, as if checking whether the time for justice had arrived. "I'll take a few questions," he said.

The room erupted in a flurry of shouts and waving hands.

"Deborah," he said, pointing his chin at a reporter near the front of the room.

"Mr. President," she said, "six weeks ago, you pledged that you would find the individuals responsible for the Anaheim Event and bring them to justice. My question has two parts: First, has any progress been made in that matter? And second, is Black Monday related to the tragic event in Anaheim?"

Monday, October 29, 2012. *Black Monday*. That's what they were calling it. It was an absurdly understated name for the day that a third of the moon simply disappeared from the universe, crumbling into oblivion and leaving behind an unstable clump of rock that seemed to be settling into a sort of grotesque mockery of a crescent. But what else could you call it? It was either ironic or fortuitous that the event had occurred on a Monday; Travis imagined there'd have been some serious hand-wringing about the name at the TV networks if the moon had collapsed on a Tuesday. There was no precedent for a Black Tuesday.

Black Monday is one of those terms that gets dusted off for reuse by journalists every few years to describe a Monday that has, for whatever reason, gone even worse than usual. The first Black Monday occurred in Dublin, Ireland, in 1209 AD, when a group of five hundred recently arrived settlers from Bristol were massacred by the Gaelic O'Byrne clan.

The next Black Monday was on April 14, 1360, during the Hundred Years' War, when the army of Edward III panicked after being struck by hailstorms and lightning, causing significant losses. In retrospect, Edward probably should have taken this as a sign that his men weren't quite up to the task of conquering France.

Black Mondays were particularly popular in the late 1800s, with Black Mondays occurring in 1865, 1886, and 1894—caused by sandstorms, riots, and a bank crisis, respectively.

The most significant Black Monday to date occurred with the Wall Street Crash on October 28, 1929. It was echoed by another Black Monday some fifty-eight years later, on October 19, 1987—

the largest one-day percentage decline in recorded stock market history.

This latest Black Monday eclipsed all the previous Black Mondays combined. Stock market crashes, riots, and hailstorms were just the *aftershocks* of this cataclysm. And on top of the practical consequences, there was something profoundly upsetting about looking up at the night sky and seeing what looked eerily like a partially constructed Death Star. "That's no moon," Travis remembered thinking as he took in the grim sight from the night before. "That's a *space station*."

"Well, Deborah," Travis replied with a practiced fatherly concern, "if you're asking whether the people who destroyed Anaheim Stadium are responsible for the attack on the moon, I can't give you a definitive answer. I will say, however, that this latest attack demonstrates the urgent need for America to act swiftly and decisively against its enemies."

Boom! thought Travis. Let's see the doves in Congress try to block my resolution to use force in the Middle East now.

"Sir, a follow-up, if I may," Deborah continued. "Are you blaming the antiwar contingent in Congress for the attack on the moon?"

Travis let slip the slightest hint of a smile (Number Three, used for implying an affirmative while delivering a more politic answer). "Let me be clear, Deb," he said. "The only people responsible for these events are the individuals who planned and executed the attacks. But a shepherd who lets wolves run free around his flock shouldn't complain when sheep start disappearing. Next question. Yes, Brian."

"Mr. President, you've intimated in the past that you believe Syria or Iran may have been involved in the Anaheim Event. Do you—"

"Let me stop you right there, Brian. I'm not going to speculate about the involvement of any foreign governments in these attacks."

"Mr. President!"

"Yes, Janice."

"I'm hearing reports that the moon is dangerously unstable—that it could split apart, causing a new round of tsunamis and hurricanes. Is anything being done about that?"

Travis was taken aback for a moment. "I'm sorry, Janice. Is anything being done about what?"

"The instability of the moon. Is the United States government doing anything to stabilize the moon?"

"Well, Janice," Travis said thoughtfully. "That's certainly an area of ongoing concern. We're awaiting word from NASA before we take any action." Stabilize the moon! thought Travis. I'm sure we'll get to that right after Afghanistan.

"What about meteors?" Janice asked. "There have been reports that fragments of the moon could break off and strike Earth."

Travis shook his head. "The people at NASA are telling me that there do not appear to be any large fragments heading toward Earth. I'm sure we'll see some fallout over the next few weeks, but I'm told that any fragments heading our way are likely to be small enough that they'll burn up in atmosphere. Any meteors that make it through the atmosphere will in all likelihood land harmlessly in the ocean. Our main concerns at this point are floods, tornadoes, and hurricanes. We've got enough to deal with without worrying about the sky falling. Last question. You, in the back." Travis didn't recognize the wiry, bearded man, but he liked to throw an occasional bone to the back row.

"Sten Brillig," said the man in a high-pitched, nasally voice. "Freedom Media Network. What is your response to the rumors that these attacks were extraterrestrial in nature?"

Travis began to laugh but was greeted only with stony stares from the press corps. It seemed that although Sten was the only one with the balls to ask the question, he wasn't the only one who had space aliens on the brain.

It was a tricky question: If the attacks were the work of some alien race, then it was possible that the US was dealing with a military force considerably out of its league. On the other hand, if the attacks were the work of ordinary human beings, it meant that a terrorist group had acquired destructive technology that put America's nuclear arsenal to shame.

Travis composed himself and spoke: "As I said, I'm not going to speculate regarding the identity of the perpetrators. What I can tell you is that whether these folks are huddled in a cave in Pakistan or cruising the galaxy in the Death Star, they are going to be hearing from the men and women of the United States military soon. Thanks, everybody. God bless America."

Travis flashed a quick Seven (understated pride in American military might) followed by another Fourteen, then turned and walked away from the podium. There were a few obligatory calls of "Mr. President!" followed by polite applause.

The press conference had gone as well as could be expected, given the fact that Travis's knowledge of what had happened on the moon was limited to what he had learned from FOX News that morning. The boys at NASA had been no help; all they could tell him was that roughly a third of the moon had suddenly disappeared without a trace. The top physicists at JPL were trying to sell him on the idea of some sort of extradimensional portal, which sounded like a lot of hooey to a straight-talking California almond farmer[1] like Travis Babcock.

Travis had been adopted at a very young age into a family of wealthy nut farmers in Modesto, California.[2] Modesto was located at the dead center of the California Central valley, which was sometimes charitably referred to as the California Heartland, and less charitably as Appalachia West. A dry, dusty, economically depressed city known primarily for its boxed wine and high incidence of auto theft, Modesto was on exactly no one's lists of likely origins of future US Presidents. But Travis found inspiration in another native son of Modesto (albeit one who left as soon as he had a chance): George Lucas.

One of Travis's uncles, in fact, had the dubious distinction of serving as the inspiration for the character played by Harrison Ford in Lucas's 1973 movie *American Graffiti*. That movie romanticized the fad known as "cruising," which was a cool-sounding name for driving around aimlessly because there was nothing else to do. Travis remembered when, in the 1980s, the Modesto city fathers addressed this dearth of entertainment options by putting up signs on main thoroughfares that read NO CRUISING.

Travis was ten years old when *Star Wars* was released. Every generation has its defining events, and *Star Wars* was Travis's Woodstock, moon landing, and D-Day, all combined into a single all-pervasive cultural wave of interstellar awesomeness. He was thirteen when *The Empire Strikes Back* came out and sixteen when *Return of the Jedi* premiered. His childhood was so infused with *Star Wars* that third-tier denizens of the Empire like Boba

---

1 Like all almond farmers in the California Central Valley, Travis pronounced *almond* to rhyme with *salmon*. When asked why, Travis would smile (Number Six) and say, "Because when they shake the nuts out of the tree, they knock the *l* out of them."

2 Almonds on his father's side, walnuts on his mother's. There were also some pistachios a few generations back, but the Babcocks didn't like to talk about that.

Fett and Admiral Akbar of the Mon Calamari were more real to him than most of his cousins who lived in Iowa.

Every kid Travis's age was crazy about *Star Wars*, but Travis identified with Luke Skywalker on a much deeper level. The desert planet Tatooine was clearly a thinly disguised version of the California Central Valley, and Modesto was the real-world Mos Eisley, that "wretched hive of scum and villainy." And that could only mean that Travis Babcock, the adopted son of simple farming folk, was destined to lead the rebellion against the forces of evil.

With that simplistic narrative always in the back of his mind, Travis graduated from high school with honors and went on to receive an MBA from Stanford. He returned to Modesto to work for his father's nut consortium (which at that time had the unfortunate name Blue Ball Nuts). He rapidly climbed the ranks, becoming CEO at the age of thirty-two, at which point he successfully lobbied to change the name of the company to Blue Sapphire Agricultural.

Travis got involved in politics, becoming a champion of smaller, more efficient government that would deliver millions of gallons of irrigation water without making him pay for it. At thirty-seven he became the governor of California, and at forty-three he was elected vice president of the United States. When President Alexis Friedman died of food poisoning after eating a tainted bratwurst from a Philadelphia street vendor, Travis ascended to the presidency.

So far, Travis's presidency had gone reasonably well. Sure, his approval ratings hovered around 45 percent, but he'd been taking a lot of heat lately on the Medicare deal and the mess in the Middle East, not to mention the Anaheim Event. If he played his cards right, this moon thing could be his ticket to a second term.

Of course, if the terrorists or aliens or whoever blew up Manhattan next, he'd have a tough time spinning it to his advantage. His plan rested on the assumption that whatever point the aliens/terrorists were trying to make, they had made it with their attack on the moon. If that was true, then it was just a matter of hoping FEMA didn't screw up the relief efforts too badly and riding Smile Fourteen to reelection. Still, he'd feel better if he knew what the hell was going on.

Gabe Horton, his chief of staff, was nodding in approval as Travis left the podium. "Nice job," said Gabe. "Vague but decisive and reassuring. That's exactly what we needed to do."

Travis grunted in reply. Smile Fourteen had left his face, replaced by the no-nonsense demeanor that was seldom seen by the press. He brushed past Gabe and fixed his eyes on a stocky, gray-haired man standing in the hall. The man's face reminded Travis of a bulldog—and not just the *face* of a bulldog. Somehow he gave the impression of having an entire bulldog sticking out of his collar. The man fidgeted nervously as Travis approached.

"Lubbers," said Travis, jerking his head to indicate he wanted Lubbers to walk with him. "What have you got for me?"

Deputy Assistant Director of the FBI Dirk Lubbers fell into a brisk walk alongside the president, trying to stifle his anxiety. Lubbers had been getting pressure from higher-ups to deliver some actionable intelligence about the Anaheim Event, but his team of scientists had come up with virtually nothing. The most likely explanation that he had heard so far was that Anaheim Stadium had somehow been sucked into another dimension. The notion had seemed like pure fantasy at the time, but then a third of the moon had gone missing, and coincidentally the theory's proponent—a forensic blast investigator by the name of Jacob

Slater—had mysteriously disappeared. Lubbers was starting to think that Slater knew more than he let on.

Before he could look into the matter further, though, Lubbers had been ordered to return to Washington. At first he had assumed he was being relieved of his authority, but in fact he had received a promotion of sorts: everybody assumed that the moon implosion was somehow related to what had happened in Anaheim, which meant that Lubbers was the closest thing they had to an expert in the matter. Of course, if he failed to deliver results, he'd soon find himself turned into a scapegoat. Fortunately, he had received some good news only minutes before.

"Mr. President," said Lubbers as they made their way down the hall. "We may have had a break in the Anaheim case. There was a report of a break-in at Katie Midford's house in Burbank two days ago. It isn't clear what happened exactly, but there was some sort of altercation. Shots were fired."

"Katie Midford? The woman who wrote those terrible children's books?"

"Young adult fantasy," corrected Lubbers. He would never admit it publicly, but Lubbers was a closet Charlie Nyx fan.

The president glared at him. "What does Katie Midford have to do with anything?"

"We're not sure," said Lubbers. "But the description of one of the suspects matches that of a missing FBI employee named Jacob Slater. Slater was on the Anaheim blast team."

"You lost an FBI agent?" the president asked, frowning.

"He's a forensic blast investigator," said Lubbers. "Not a field agent. Slater had some, uh, interesting theories about the Anaheim Event. Theories that in retrospect seem to be a little too accurate."

"You think Slater is a double agent? Working for Syria or somebody?"

"We're looking into it," said Lubbers. "A witness got a plate number of a vehicle that was seen at Midford's place. The plate is assigned to a BMW that was rented by Midford's publisher, the Finch Group. We've made some inquiries about who was driving the car, but so far no one in the Finch Group has been able to tell us anything."

"You said you had a break in the case," said Babcock. "This sounds like a lot of unconnected facts and innuendo."

It was true, thought Lubbers. He was starting to wish he had kept his mouth shut and waited until he had more information before talking to the president. But Babcock had demanded a briefing immediately after the press conference, and Lubbers was so relieved to have something to report that he hadn't considered that *something* might actually be worse than nothing. Still, now that he had gone this far, there was no point in being coy.

"Sir," he said, "how familiar are you with the Charlie Nyx books?"

Babcock gave him a pained look. "You're kidding."

"No, sir, Mr. President. The fact is that there are some strange parallels between the Charlie Nyx books and what is happening in Anaheim. The shafts we found below the stadium, for instance. In the Charlie Nyx books, there is a network of tunnels underneath Los Angeles, and our excavations lead us to believe that..." He was clearly losing the president. "The point, sir, is that Midford seems to have had access to some information that was not publicly available. We're looking into whether she or the Finch group may have had something to do with the destruction of Anaheim Stadium."

"Hmm," said Babcock. He was obviously not impressed.

Lubbers found himself blathering on, despite his better judgment. "We've located the car and we're following the driver. We haven't identified him yet, but he seems to be—"

The president held up his hand. "That's enough," he said. "I'm a busy man, Mr. Lubbers. I don't need to hear every detail of your operation. Get back to me when you have something solid."

"Yes, sir!" said Lubbers.

"And Lubbers?"

"Yes, sir?"

"It had better be soon."

"Yes, sir, Mr. President."

THREE

"Are you insane?" Wanda Kwan asked, her perfectly proportioned Asiatic features scrunching into an unsettling scowl. The way she paused, it didn't seem like a rhetorical question, but Eddie wasn't sure what to say in reply. He sat in glum silence, waiting for some kind of cue.

"Are you?" she demanded.

Eddie smiled weakly and shrugged. "No?" he ventured.

Wanda snorted in disgust. "It's a rhetorical question, Eddie. You know what a rhetorical question is, right?"

Eddie sat in silence, fearing a trap.

"It's a question posed in order to make a point, not to evoke an answer," Wanda explained, her words coated in condescension. "The reason I feel the need to explain this, Eddie, is that you don't seem to understand the first goddamn thing about being a writer."

Eddie cleared his throat. "Is there something wrong with the manuscript? If there is, I'm sure I can fix it..."

"Oh, I can't wait to hear about how you're going to fix it," snapped Wanda. "All you have to do is change the name of the Israeli general who gets killed in chapter four, remove the stuff about Harry Giddings, gloss over the part about Anaheim Stadium exploding—"

"Imploding, actually," corrected Eddie.

Wanda stared at him. "Oh, imploding. *Imploding*," she said. "Well, that makes it OK."

"It does?" Eddie asked, confused.

"No, you imbecile! Do you have any idea how many different parties would have grounds to sue us if we published this...this... *abomination*? Not to mention that it's in absolutely horrible taste. You can't just stitch together a flimsy fantasy story from the latest newspaper headlines, Eddie. I mean there's topical, and then there's...God, I don't even know what this is."

"I did try to warn you," said Eddie defensively.

She glared at him. "You told me you might have to do some rewriting because of the Anaheim tragedy. I didn't realize you meant you were having trouble incorporating *more* horrific real-life events into the book. Besides, that discussion was about the Charlie Nyx book, not this...*thing*." She looked distastefully at the thick stack of paper on her desk. "Eddie, there isn't a publisher on Earth who would touch this manuscript. Maybe you could"—Wanda's nose crinkled in disgust at the thought—"*self*-publish it." She shook her head grimly. "What a waste."

Eddie was pretty sure she meant the money the Finch Group had spent retrieving him from Ireland and putting him up in a hotel for two weeks, not the time and effort he had put into his manuscript. Still, he silently agreed. Why did he keep doing this to himself? Why did he persist in the delusion that he was destined to be a successful writer?

"You can see yourself out," Wanda said, not bothering to look up from her desk.

Eddie got up and made for the door.

"Forgetting something?" she asked, still not looking up.

Eddie shuffled back to the desk and scooped up the manuscript.

"Leave the keys to the Bimmer," said Wanda. "We'll cover the hotel through the end of the week."

"How am I supposed to get back to the hotel?"

Wanda sat back and smiled. "Fly, little angel, fly."

Eddie sorely wanted to turn the keys into a hummingbird just to see the look on Wanda's face, but he knew that would accomplish nothing. He dropped the keys and left Wanda Kwan's office with the manuscript under his arm.

Once outside, Eddie turned to look up at the Beacon Building. The glass pyramid shimmered surreally in the morning sun. The streets around the building were strangely quiet—a sharp contrast to the chaos of the past three days. LA had already been on edge before Black Monday, and after the moon imploded, things really went to hell. Riots, looting, arson—and that was in addition to the twenty-foot waves crashing in from the Pacific and the temblors rattling windows and setting off car alarms every few hours. Presumably the rioters were now resting up for tonight's festivities.

It had all started on Monday. *Black* Monday. That's what the humans were calling it, in their myopic and predictable manner. Why the moon? he wondered. What had the moon ever done to anyone except provide light and hope and beauty? Imploding the moon was like killing a completely harmless animal, like a penguin or something. Eddie loved penguins.

As baffled as Eddie was by the destruction of the moon, he at least knew more than the poor, frightened people hurrying past him down the street. He knew that only one thing could have caused the moon to collapse in on itself that way: an anti-bomb, so named because it *sucked* rather than *blew*. Anti-bombs were Heavenly devices that looked like ornamental glass apples. The older the anti-bomb was, the "riper" and more powerful it became. The one that had imploded the moon must have been very old indeed. So he knew the *how*, but the question remained: *Why*?

Eddie wandered aimlessly down the street, still holding the rejected manuscript in his hands. He knew that it was selfish to worry about his career as a writer when the whole world seemed to be falling to pieces, but he couldn't shake the feeling that somehow he had been cheated out of his destiny. After all, hadn't Culain—or whatever he was calling himself these days—told him that his book was the key to unleashing the End of the World? He had certainly seemed convincing at the time, but maybe Culain was just a lunatic. *Lunatic*, thought Eddie. There's a word that's going to see a resurgence. People driven mad by the moon—or lack thereof.

Culain claimed to have lived for thousands of years—claimed to be, among others, William Shakespeare and the Biblical figure Cain. Surely that was evidence of madness. But if he wasn't who he claimed to be, who was he? How did he have access to those reams and reams of Heavenly reports? How had he found Eddie—once in Ireland and once here in Los Angeles? And what did he *want*? He was apparently not an angel, but he was certainly no ordinary human. Eddie had at first assumed, in fact, that he was…well, Someone Else entirely. He rolled his eyes at the memory. Talk about a *deus ex machina*.

Whoever he was, he had taken in Eddie with his talk of the Charlie Nyx books and meta-universes and destiny. Wanda Kwan was right: no publisher on Earth would touch his manuscript. He had been a fool to think otherwise. There was nothing to do now but head back to his hotel, pack up his stuff, and…well, the rest was a little unclear. Hopefully he'd figure it out when he got to that point.

It *was* a shame, though, he thought as he stepped off the curb to cross the street. He had been rather proud of the little narrative he had put together. It had everything a good book should have: drama, humor, explosions…It was a little light on the romance, of course, but he could throw some of that crap into the sequel. He opened the manuscript to a random page and smiled at a particularly clever turn of phrase. "A tapestry of religion," he chuckled to himself.

Then he was run over by a Prius.

FOUR

"That's game," said Cain disinterestedly. He had won, 26 to 24, his deliberate, mechanical method edging out Job's reckless and unpredictable playing style. He walked toward a fragment of brick wall, making a mark with a piece of chalk that he had pulled from his pocket. "That's eight hundred fifty-six thousand, five hundred eleven for me, and zero for you. Give up?" Cain sounded tired, like he had played about 856,510 more games of Ping-Pong than he had really wanted to.

"No way," said Job cheerfully. "I'm just getting my ninety-eight thousandth wind."

"I need a break," said Cain.

Job nodded, and they both sat down, leaning against the partial wall. Not knowing what else to do, Mercury sat down between them, cold bricks pressing against his back. The three of them sat staring at the fog shrouding the buildings in the distance. Mercury tried to determine whether the fog had moved a little closer than the last time he looked. The odd thing was that it seemed to be moving in from the left and right as well. But that was impossible; that wasn't how fog worked. It had to be a trick of the light.

"Jeez, how long have you guys been playing?" asked Mercury.

Job shrugged. "Seven hundred years, off and on. I don't really keep track."

"I wonder why," muttered Cain.

"So you've never won?" said Mercury to Job. "Not once?"

Job shrugged. "I've come close a few thousand times. One game went to eight hundred and four points. I only lost because I had a cramp."

Cain snorted. "It's always something."

"Why do you keep playing?" Mercury asked Job.

"Who's to say I won't win one of these days?" Job replied, reasonably enough.

"Huh," said Mercury. Job had a point, he supposed. "So, what's the deal? Why are you guys here? Shouldn't you both be, like, dead?"

"We're immortal," said Cain. "Both of us. Cursed."

"Blessed," corrected Job. "We've been blessed with eternal life."

"How?" Mercury asked. "I thought humans had a strict age limit after the whole Methuselah debacle. A hundred and twenty years."

"Yes," agreed Job. "Except for me and Cain. We were blessed—"

"Cursed," muttered Cain.

"...to witness the whole of human history."

"But why?" asked Mercury. "By whom?"

Job cast a sideways glance at Cain. "We have a difference of opinion on that. Cain believes it's all just a big joke, the Universe screwing with us for its own amusement. Or maybe for no reason at all. He tends to think the Universe is an arbitrary, meaningless place."

Cain shrugged at what was evidently a reasonable summary of his beliefs.

"For my part," Job continued, "I think we are representatives."

"Of what?" Mercury prompted.

"Different ways of looking at the world. Faith and hope versus cynicism and despair."

Cain snorted. "More like reason and practicality versus superstition and false hope," he said.

Job smiled. "Difference of opinion."

"So," Mercury said to Job. "You're still an optimist? I mean, even after everything that happened…?" Job's suffering was legendary. There was a whole book in the Bible devoted to his travails. And who knew what had transpired since Mercury had last seen him, almost four thousand years earlier.

"I'm an optimist *because* of what happened to me," said Job.

"Really?" asked Mercury dubiously. "Do you know…?" He trailed off, not sure how much he should say. Mercury had seen some of the behind-the-scenes political wrangling that led to Job's ordeal, and he didn't know how much Job knew—or whether knowing would make him feel better or worse.

"About Lucifer abducting the archangel Michael? About how I was just a pawn in a celestial game of chess? Yeah, I found out a few hundred years ago, from one of the cherubim that used to come around here. We don't see angels anymore," he added wistfully. "They all seem to have disappeared."

"And it doesn't bother you that your whole ordeal was the result of a grudge match between Lucifer and the Heavenly authorities?" Mercury asked.

Job shrugged. "The proximate causes of my suffering are of no concern. I believe there is an overarching purpose to everything. Even suffering serves a purpose."

Cain made a *tsk*ing sound. "There's no *purpose* inherent in suffering, other than to teach you to avoid it. Suffering in itself is meaningless."

"I've heard it builds character," said Mercury.

Cain sighed. "Character is just another word for conditioning," he said. "People with 'character' are those who have been kicked around enough to know how to avoid most causes of suffering. Consider a toddler who knows not to touch a hot stove because he's been burned once before. Does he have 'character'? Or has he just learned an arbitrary fact about the unforgiving world in which he lives?"

Mercury raised an eyebrow at Cain. "You're kind of a downer, you know that?"

"Try hanging out with him for seven hundred years," said Job.

Mercury had to admit that Job's optimism given their situation—not to mention Cain's relentless cynicism—was impressive, but he wasn't sure if it was admirable or the sign of some sort of deep psychosis. Did Job have "character," or had he simply developed a coping mechanism for dealing with a harsh, capricious Universe? Cain's bleak outlook certainly wasn't an attractive option, but was Job's manic cheerfulness any better?

Cain shrugged, gazing at the fog in the distance. "I just want it to be over."

This last comment gave Mercury the chills. "Why do you guys keep looking out at the fog, like you're waiting for the three-fifteen to Queens?" The buildings on either side of them had grown less distinct, as if the fog were slowly swallowing them.

"It's not fog," said Job. "Cain calls it the Existence Horizon. It's slowly moving in on us. Once it gets here…" He trailed off, letting the words hang in the air.

"Then what?" asked Mercury anxiously. "What happens when it gets here?"

Cain shrugged. "Nothing. That's it. The end."

"The end? The end of what?" Mercury demanded.

Job answered. "The end of everything."

FIVE

Eddie regained consciousness on a sidewalk a few feet away from where he had been run over by a Prius.

"Whoa, dude," said a lanky, long-haired teenager who was crouched over him. "I can't believe you're still alive. That Prius just *laid you out*."

Eddie sat up and looked around. He dimly remembered seeing the vaguely Satanic Toyota emblem a half second before being knocked to the ground, but there were no Priuses (Prii?) to be seen. It occurred to him that maybe the hit-and-run had been intentional, but he dismissed the idea as unlikely. First of all, why would anyone want to run him down? And second, if you were going to run someone down, why would you use a Prius when there were so many oversized American cars much better suited for the task? No, embarrassing as it was to admit, Eddie had been distracted by the cleverness of his own writing and had walked into traffic. The driver must have panicked and fled.

"Need to watch where I'm going," said Eddie, stating the obvious. "Did you see…?"

The kid shook his head. "Dude took off," he said. "I didn't get a plate or anything."

But Eddie wasn't wondering about the car. He shook his head. "No, did you see a stack of papers? I was carrying a manuscript."

"Oh, man!" the kid exclaimed. "Weirdest thing. Car hits you, papers go flying. I see this dude run into the street, like he was going to do CPR or something. But no, what does he do? Grabs up all the papers! He's got this big stack of papers in his arms and just takes off. So I dragged you onto the curb. Figured you were dead."

So, Eddie thought. Someone was following me. Someone who was interested in the manuscript. They saw me get hit, probably figured I was a goner, and grabbed the manuscript. But who? Like Wanda Kwan said, no publisher on Earth would touch the thing. Oh, well. Good riddance.

To the surprise of the onlookers, Eddie got up, dusted himself off, and continued walking.

"Dude…?" said the kid behind him uncertainly.

Eddie walked a bit farther in what he thought was the direction of his hotel before coming to a conclusion that had been reached by millions of mortals before he ever came to this accursed city: walking in LA *blows*. Sidewalks started and stopped as if they were an unnecessary embellishment to the roadways, and buildings were often separated by sections of lawn, vast parking lots, or vacant lots, making Eddie feel like he was making no progress at all. Whoever laid out this city did not have pedestrians in mind. In fact, if private detective and conspiracy theorist extraordinaire Cody Lang was to be believed, this city wasn't laid out with *humans* in mind. Eddie had met Cody by accident while trying to figure out who had really written the Charlie Nyx books. Cody had been trying to answer the same question, and in the course of her investigation had unearthed a trove of data of varying relevance and reliability. Cody had come to believe that a secret organization had designed Los Angeles to serve its own mysterious, diabolical purposes. Trying to make his way back to his hotel, Eddie found that proposition surprisingly reasonable. If anybody ever walked anywhere in this city, somebody might have noticed the odd way things were laid out, but everybody in LA drove everywhere. What was it to them if it took an extra five minutes to get somewhere because of the machinations of some mysterious cabal?

Eventually he came upon a bus stop and was able to take a bus most of the way to his hotel. He took a cab the last few blocks and then made his way to his room on the sixth floor of the Wilshire. He was so tired and defeated that he nearly flopped onto the bed without doing his customary miraculous sterilization of the bedspread. Being a fastidious cherub with a preternatural sense of smell, Eddie was well aware that the bedspread was typically the filthiest part of a hotel room. Eddie had heard of people who slept on top of hotel beds rather than exposing themselves to the sheets, but to Eddie this was madness. Even at a classy joint like the Wilshire, the sheets were the only thing in the room that could be relied upon to be reasonably clean. The bedspread probably had more DNA samples in it than the Mayo Clinic.

Eddie had, of course, disinfected his bedspread before, but he didn't trust the hotel's cleaning personnel not to replace his sterile cover with one that was teeming with the germs of prostitutes and television producers. Being an angel, Eddie wasn't worried about getting sick, but the idea of bacteria crawling about the fibers of his blankets violated his angelic sense of propriety. In short, it creeped him out. So he raised his hands, preparing to transform a minute amount of interplanar energy into ultraviolet light, which would kill any microscopic organisms clinging to the fabric.

And that's when he saw it: a business card lying on the corner of the bed.

He picked it up using only his fingernails, careful not to touch the unclean bedspread. The card read:

Cody Lang,
Actress and Private Investigator

Specializing in:

- Infidelity
- Bail Bonds
- Polygraphs
- Body Double
- Thigh Model
- Crying on Command

He turned the card over. On it was written, in aggressively angular and yet unmistakably feminine handwriting:

Eddie: I've figured out EVERYTHING. Meet me at Dad's at noon.

Fantastic, thought Eddie. Now I have to deal with that ding-bat detective Cody Lang on top of everything else. Cody was easy on the eyes, he'd give her that much, but her off-the-wall theories put her just this side of the tinfoil-hat crowd. He wondered what she thought she had figured out now. Something about General Motors adding hallucinogens to the Los Angeles water supply, maybe, or supernatural artifacts hidden by ancient astronauts in the La Brea tar pits. Just trying to have a conversation with Cody was exhausting. In her mind, every aspect of reality was somehow connected in a complex web of causality that centered on Los Angeles.

On the other hand, Cody did have a knack for piecing together disparate and seemingly incongruous bits of information into a compelling narrative. It was Cody, after all, who had figured out that the supposed author of the Charlie Nyx books, Katie Midford, was actually the demoness Tiamat. She had also deduced that Eddie was himself a fallen angel.

Meet me at Dad's at noon.

It was almost eleven o'clock now. Without a car, it would be difficult to…wait, what the hell did she mean by "meet me at Dad's"? Her father was the man who claimed to be Cain. Eddie had no idea where he lived. In fact, if his story was to be believed, he didn't live *anywhere*: Cain was the perpetual itinerant, a man with no home. Even his own grave couldn't hold him.

A light went on in Eddie's mind. So that was it: "Dad's" was the gravesite behind the strip mall in Yerba Buena. That was where Eddie had met Jacob had Slater, the FBI guy. He wondered what Jacob was up to. Jacob had seemed like an awfully nice chap, from the little opportunity that Eddie had to chat with him before Jacob was abducted by demons. He hoped the demons hadn't hurt him too badly.

So. Cody wanted him to meet her at noon at the Yerba Buena mall. He sighed, concluding that he probably owed her that much. He had the front desk call him a cab and went downstairs, leaving the unclean bedspread untouched.

Eddie still wasn't quite clear on why there was a gravesite hidden behind a strip mall in a Los Angeles suburb. That is, he understood that the cemetery had been moved except for this one plot, and that the mall had since been built around it. That much he got. What he didn't get was why Colin Lang had a gravesite in the first place. Eddie wasn't sure he bought the story about Lang actually being the immortal Cain, cursed to wander the Earth for eternity, but it was fairly clear that he was not dead. Eddie had spoken to the man himself. So why did he have a gravesite? And why had the owner of the land gone to such lengths to make sure that this one plot of land was undisturbed?

The only answer was that the "gravesite" was actually a secret entrance to the tunnels that ran beneath Los Angeles. That explained how Jacob had emerged from the gravesite during Eddie's first visit here: he must have been doing something in the tunnels, probably related to an FBI investigation of some kind. Jacob himself had seemed a little confused about what the tunnels were for exactly. Eddie knew that the demoness Tiamat had once used them as an underground hideout, but he was never completely clear on who had built them, or why. He didn't think even a formidable demoness like Tiamat had the resources to pull off something like that. For all her grand schemes, Tiamat was a bit of a parasite, leeching off the efforts of the more industrious. Her stint as the figurehead "author" of the Charlie Nyx books was only the latest example. No, Tiamat couldn't have built the tunnels. But then who did?

Cody's note said that she had figured out "everything." He wondered what that meant. What the tunnels were for? Who her father really was? What Tiamat was up to? Or had Cody fallen victim to her own obsession with the "secret history of Los Angeles"?

As the cab sped away, he walked to the metal door that led to the hidden courtyard. The door was locked and covered with "tamper-proof" police tape. A notice indicated that the premises had been designated as a crime scene. Eddie wondered what sort of crime they had decided had happened here. At the very least, constructing a vast complex of tunnels under a strip mall was probably a fairly serious zoning violation.

Upon close examination, Eddie saw that the tamper-proof tape had in fact been tampered with. A very fine blade, a razor blade perhaps, had sliced through the tape to allow the door to be opened. The door remained locked, but this presented no difficulty for Eddie. There was a *click!* as the door miraculously unlocked itself and swung open. Eddie stepped inside, closing the door behind him.

He stood in a small grassy courtyard, an eerie oasis of green between the Burger Giant and the Bed Bath & Beyond. A metal box the size of a small room—an elevator, Eddie now realized—lay on its side near the remains of the gazebo that had once stood over the supposed grave. Yellow CAUTION tape hung from metal stakes ringing the scene. Where the floor of the gazebo had been, there was now a gaping hole in the ground, ringed by the concrete base of the gazebo. Engraved on the front of the base were the words:

COLIN LANG
LAID TO REST APRIL 29, 1993

PANTON IN SUUS VICIS

Stepping forward, Eddie expected to see the sheer blackness of the shaft descending hundreds of feet to the tunnels below, but he was surprised to see a layer of granite only about twenty feet down. Was he wrong about the shaft connecting to the tunnels? Or had the shaft been rigged to collapse and fill with gravel, concealing its true depth? He decided it was the latter. Whoever had built the tunnels had built them so that they could be destroyed, leaving almost no trace.

As Eddie's eyes adjusted to the dim of the pit, he realized that there was something moving in the dark. An animal of some sort, with a shiny golden pelt. A cat, maybe?

Suddenly the animal seemed to disappear. "Eddie!" called a voice from inside the pit. "You wanna give me a hand?"

"Gaaahhh!" yelled Eddie, nearly slipping and falling into the pit in a panic.

"You OK up there?" asked the voice again. It was Cody, he now realized. He had been looking at the top of her head. Now she was peering at him with a confused look on her face. "Give me a hand?" she asked again.

"Oh!" said Eddie. "Sure." He held out his hand to harness a stream of interplanar energy, causing it to reverse gravity around Cody. She floated upward until her feet were just above the lip of the pit. He gave her a little nudge and she alighted gently on the ground. For a moment Eddie stood and stared at her. The grace with which she moved, the way her blonde locks floated just above her shoulders, she looked, Eddie thought, like...well, like an angel.

I've been on this plane too long, thought Eddie. I'm thinking in human terms. Specifically, *male* human terms. Cody was wearing a sleeveless brown T-shirt and a denim skirt with knee-high brown suede boots. Two words kept popping into Eddie's consciousness: *thigh model.*

"Eddie? Do you mind?"

"Sorry!" Eddie exclaimed, suddenly embarrassed. Not only had he been staring; he had actually forgotten to fully restore Cody's gravity. She had been standing with only her toes touching the ground, her hair and...other parts floating in near-zero gravity. It was a good look for her.

He reluctantly allowed her to regain her full weight, and she settled back into a more human form. Eddie shook his head. He had heard of this happening: angels who spent too much time on the Mundane Plane gradually came to think and act like human beings. It only made sense. There was essentially no difference between human and angel biology; the advantage that angels possessed was their connection with the source of the mystical energy that flowed in invisible channels throughout every plane, known as the Eye of Providence. The Eye was a vast pyramidal structure located smack in the center of Heaven. It was where the angels came from originally and it was what sustained them over the millennia. Without the Eye, angels would gradually lose their supernatural abilities and become mortal. The Eye could sustain an angel even on a faraway plane for long periods of time, but an angel who hadn't been back to Heaven for several centuries would begin to lose his angel-ness. Eddie hadn't seen Heaven for five hundred years.

"Thanks for the help," Cody said. "You know, you could have just pulled the rope up."

Eddie noticed that there was a knotted rope that had been tied to a piece of rebar jutting out of the gazebo and let down into the pit.

"Oh," he said. "Sorry."

"Quite all right," said Cody. "A girl could get used to levitating."

Eddie nodded. "What were you doing down there?"

"Investigating," said Cody. "Unfortunately there isn't much to see down there. Seems like the tunnels were rigged to collapse and fill with gravel, concealing their true depth. The OPB left nothing to chance. They built the tunnels so that they could be destroyed, leaving almost no trace of the CCD."

Eddie nodded thoughtfully. "The OPB would want to keep the CCD on the DL."

"Oh, sorry!" Cody exclaimed. "I've got so much to tell you! Eddie, I've figured it out. All of it!"

"Yeah, that's what your note said," Eddie replied dubiously.

"It turns out I've been thinking far too small," Cody said excitedly. "Los Angeles really is the center of a grand conspiracy, but it's *so much bigger* than I thought. I was focusing on General Motors and Streetcars when I should have been focusing on the Apocalypse! I mean, it's all related, but my sense of scope was off. I couldn't see the forest for the trees."

"Uh-hmm," said Eddie.

"First of all, my dad? He really is Cain. Like, from the Bible. Once I admitted that to myself, the rest all fell into place. There's this ancient Sumerian manuscript that he's been working on translating. Well, not translating so much as retelling. The original has only survived in fragments, and they're out of order, incomplete, and sometimes contradictory. Anyway, he turned them into the Charlie Nyx books. That's right, Eddie! *Scriptor Carolingus*, the true author of the Charlie Nyx books is my father, who is Cain, not to mention Shakespeare and God knows who else. But that's not even the most amazing part!"

"No?" Eddie asked. He didn't want to rain on Cody's parade, but he had heard most of this before. Cody's father, the man claiming to be Cain, had told her all about how he had come to write the Charlie Nyx books. It was all part of Lucifer's scheme to destroy the world. With every Charlie Nyx book that was published, the world crept closer to the Apocalypse. Supposedly the manuscript that Wanda Kwan had rejected was the seventh and final book, the one that would herald the End of Days. But obviously that had not panned out.

"It comes down to you, Eddie!" Cody exclaimed. "You're the author of the seventh book!"

Eddie smiled grimly. "I know," he said. "That is, your father, Cain, he told me. But Cody, it's not true. I've already written the book. And the publisher has rejected it. In any case, none of this makes any sense. My book isn't a Charlie Nyx book. It doesn't fit in with the rest of the series. Cain is just going to have to find someone else to write the final Charlie Nyx book. As much as he wants me to fill that role for him, I'm simply not able."

Cody shook her head. "No, don't you see? There can't be a final Charlie Nyx book. At least not in the sense that people are expecting. The tunnels under Anaheim have been destroyed. And the authorities aren't going to admit it, but they know that the tunnels were real. There's no way they can keep this secret much longer. They may never be able to fully excavate the shafts under Anaheim Stadium, but they know there is something down there. Something huge. And it's too big to keep covered up, Eddie. Rumors are already circulating about the ACHOO people finding something under the site."

"ACHOO people?" asked Eddie, confused. "Can you help me out here?"

"Anaheim Command Headquarters, Onsite Operations. ACHOO."

"Bless you," replied Eddie.

Cody continued, undeterred by the interruption. "Everybody is conjecturing about what ACHOO found down there. I mean, there are anti–Charlie Nyx fanatics protesting the site because they think that Charlie Nyx, this fictional warlock, somehow created a network of tunnels underneath Anaheim!"

"OK…" said Eddie, "but I still don't see what this has to do with my book."

"Think, Eddie!" snapped Cody. "A book doesn't exist in a vacuum. Every story has an audience. And who is the audience for the Charlie Nyx books? What would be a satisfactory conclusion, from their point of view?"

"Um," replied Eddie. Where was Cody going with this?

"Man, you are dense," said Cody. "Don't you see? Everybody who was once transfixed by the plight of Charlie Nyx, teen warlock, is now obsessed with what's really under Anaheim Stadium and what happened at the Anaheim Event. If you wrote a Charlie Nyx book that just continued where the sixth book left off, without addressing the elephant in the tent, nobody would want to read it. The final book, the book that explains everything, is *your book*."

Eddie frowned. That did make a twisted sort of sense. Except for one thing.

"But my book doesn't explain anything," said Eddie. "I mean, it mentions the tunnels, but any Charlie Nyx reader expecting a satisfying conclusion is going to be disappointed."

"That's because it's not done yet."

"Not done? It's three hundred pages long already! Although I suppose I could cut out a few dozen pages of dialogue if it came down to it."

"What does that matter? The story ends when it ends."

"But it could go on forever! How do I know when I'm done?"

Cody studied Eddie somberly for a moment. "I know how it ends, Eddie. That's why I wanted to meet with you. I know my father has probably told you much of this already, but there's something he hasn't told you. Something very important. Does the word *Wormwood* mean anything to you?"

"Wormwood? You mean like in Revelation? The star that falls from the sky?"

Cody nodded. "It also appears in the Sumerian manuscript that my father was working on. Except, in the manuscript, it's not a star but a sort of evil talisman. It brings about the end of the world. It's the crux of everything. It's where all the different layers of reality intersect—the book of Revelation, the Charlie Nyx story, and *our* story. When I figured out what Wormwood was, that's when everything fell into place. When I figured out how the story ends."

"OK," Eddie said. "So what is Wormwood?"

"Wormwood is…" Cody started, but then stopped and made a sort of snorting sound, as if Eddie had done something to offend her. She looked at him with shock and horror in her eyes. Then she fell backward onto the grass. A dark stain spread across the center of her shirt.

"Cody!" Eddie cried, crouching down beside her. Cody had been shot. Judging from the fountain of blood pouring from her chest, she had been hit directly in her heart. This was beyond Eddie's ability to fix.

"Oh God," said Eddie. "Cody, you've been shot!" He glanced around, but the shooter was not visible. Of course, from his standpoint on the ground next to Cody, roofs of the nearby buildings were concealed by the brick wall of the courtyard.

The color had been flushed from Cody's face, and her body was contorted with pain. Still, she leaned toward Eddie as if trying to tell him something. "Eddie…" she gasped. "Wormwood…"

Her eyes rolled back and her head fell to the grass. Her lips were still moving. Eddie put his ear to her mouth and she whispered something that sounded like "Pull the switch." Then her body went limp. Just like that, Cody Lang was dead.

SIX
Circa 1800 BC

The story of Job is one that everybody thinks they know, at least in broad strokes: man becomes fabulously wealthy; man is held up as an example of righteousness; man is subjected to horrific torments to prove his loyalty to God; man is subjected to a lot of really unhelpful advice from his friends; man gives up trying to figure out where he went wrong; man gets all his stuff back.

The full story, however, is known only to very few. Even Job himself, playing Ping-Pong at the End of Time, remained largely ignorant of much of the backstory. It is only with the help of some recently declassified Heavenly documents that we can piece together something like the whole narrative. Observe:

After the Great Flood, there had been a lot of bickering and recriminations among the wise men of the various Fertile Crescent civilizations about who was to blame for the unprecedented calamity. There was widespread agreement that large numbers of people had been acting immorally and worshiping false gods, but that was where the agreement ended. There was no consensus on what constituted moral behavior or who the true gods were. The best the wise men could do was to come to a general agreement that everybody would be better off if people weren't such assholes all the time. Even this modest principle was undermined by the fact that the gods themselves seemed to be mostly assholes, doing a lot of assholish things like dismembering each other and scattering each other's limbs along the Nile.

One man who didn't have a lot of patience for either people or gods who acted like assholes was a young farmer in the land of Uz by the name of Job. Nobody knew where Job got his ideas exactly, but Job was convinced that life wasn't as complicated as everybody made it out to be. He believed that if you were nice to other people and you worked hard, you tended to do OK. There was no need to remember eighty-seven different deities and the specific behavior required to keep from pissing each of them off, nor was there any need to remember who had pissed you off and who you had pissed off, and which of these people were important enough to worry about having pissed them off or being pissed off at. Just be nice to people and work hard; that was Job's motto. And surprisingly enough, it worked. People liked Job. They trusted him. They liked working for him, and they liked having him work for them. With all the time and emotional energy that Job saved by not worrying about petty shit that didn't matter, he was able to get more work done and make sure he always met his commitments to other people. Job believed in just one God, who was not an asshole. He believe that his God would reward him for being nice to people and working hard. By all accounts, he was right.

Job became very wealthy. He had seven sons and three daughters, and at the peak of his wealth he owned seven thousand sheep, three thousand camels, five hundred yoke of oxen, and five hundred donkeys.[3] Pretty soon other landowners and

3 It was customary at the time to denote wealth in terms of the quantities of animals owned, which is a rather unhelpful measuring system if you think about it. Massive herds of animals are all well and good, but they don't necessarily translate to luxurious living. After all, who wouldn't trade a couple hundred yoke of oxen for indoor plumbing or, say, a house that doesn't smell like several

merchants were traveling from miles around to ask Job what his secret was. He was happy to explain his philosophy to them, but these impromptu meetings started to cut into his schedule. One of his servants suggested that he write his principles down on some clay tablets, which would then be copied and delivered to anyone who requested them, for a small fee. The result was an eighteen-pound, three-tablet book called *The Success God Wants for You!* It was an instant bestseller by the admittedly low standards of mostly preliterate Mesopotamia, outselling nearly three to one *The Seven Habits of Those Who Avoid the Wrath of Ereshkigal, Supreme Goddess of the Underworld.*

Job's success did not go unnoticed in Heaven. Members of the Seraphic Senate began to hold up Job as a model human being, proof that that the Divine Plan was back on track after the Flood. Many in Heaven believed that Job's message of working hard and being nice to people would spread across the Mundane Plane. People would cooperate against famine, poverty, and disease. War would end. Peace and prosperity would sweep the plane.

Lucifer, consolidating his power on the Infernal Plane, took notice as well. He was determined that Job's simplistic yet powerful principles would not prevail on the Mundane Plane. He would find a flaw in Job's principles and exploit it, exposing him as the simple-minded fool he was. But doing so would not be easy. Heaven, having taken an interest in Job's success, had him under constant cherubic guard. Lucifer's minions couldn't get near him.

Fortunately for Lucifer, one of his first diabolical projects after being kicked out of Heaven began to bear fruit around this time. Realizing that the interplanar hub known as the planeport was the key to all interplanar travel and communication, he expended

hundred oxen? Still, I think we can assume that Job was living pretty well, despite being surrounded by thousands of filthy farm animals.

a great deal of effort covertly corrupting a variety of planeport personnel. This allowed him to stay in the loop regarding Heavenly activities and to occasionally make a trip to the Mundane Plane to oversee his schemes without being arrested by security.

By a fortuitous coincidence, right around the time that Job reached the pinnacle of his success, Lucifer received a report from one of his spies that the archangel Michael would be making a brief stopover at the planeport on the way to the Mundane Plane. Michael rarely left Heaven, but the flooding on the Mundane Plane had gotten so bad that Michael wanted to survey the damage himself. Lucifer spotted an opportunity.

He pulled some strings to have his own agents placed on Michael's security detail. When Michael appeared, right on schedule, they incapacitated Michael's personal bodyguard—as well as an unlucky interloper by the name of Mercury—and abducted the celestial general.[4]

Of course, "Michael" was actually Michelle: her security precautions involved promoting the misconception that Michelle was a tall, brawny, white male, rather than a diminutive, dark-skinned female. It made no difference to Lucifer: the important thing was that he had captured the general of the Heavenly army, embarrassing the Senate. He knew they would do just about anything to get her back. Lucifer proposed a meeting with representatives of Heaven on neutral ground[5] to discuss the matter.

The Senate formed a special Ad Hoc Committee on Ensuring the Security of Key Military Personnel, which met Lucifer in an unremarkable conference room. Cravutius, the head of the Committee, spoke first:

"So, Lucifer. Where have you come from?"

4 Those who have read my previous report will recall Mercury's decapitation at the hands of Lucifer's planeport spies.

5 Plane 4721c, known for its delicious cheeses.

Lucifer waved his hand in a gesture of dismissal. "Oh, you know," he said nonchalantly. "From roaming throughout the earth, going back and forth on it."

The committee members grumbled to each other. Lucifer smiled. He knew that the Senate liked to think he was uncomfortably sequestered on the Infernal Plane (and, truth be told, most of the time he was), and he loved to tease them with the notion that he spent his time leisurely touring the Mundane Plane.

"You know why we're here," said Cravutius. "You need to release Michael. If you expect any sort of leniency for your crimes—"

"Leniency!" Lucifer cried. "Let's not kid ourselves. I'm well past leniency. What are you going to do, shave a few months off my ten-thousand-year sentence? No, I'll tell you how this is going to work. I'm going to give you *Michelle*, and you are going to grant me absolute power over the entire Mundane Plane."

Cravutius stifled a laugh. The committee erupted in grumbles and snarls. "See here, you insolent fool!" hissed one member.

"Silence!" barked Cravutius. "Lucifer, if you're not going to take these negotiations seriously, then I'll end these proceedings right now."

"Oh, I'm deadly serious," said Lucifer. "I've seen how you yahoos are running things down there. Wars, corruption, human sacrifice...and this damned flood! Nearly wiped out every living thing on Earth! Even your vaunted Seraphic Civilization Shepherding Program is in danger of being shut down. Tiamat has gone rogue, and now you've got that idiot Marduk running Babylon. How long do you think *that's* going to last? Gentlemen, please. This is no way to run the Universe's showcase plane. You need to put somebody competent in charge before things go completely to hell. So to speak."

He lifted a leather briefcase from beside his chair and laid it on the table in front of him. "I've taken the liberty of making several copies of my résumé for your perusal. I think you'll find that I have all the necessary qualifications." He flipped the catches on the briefcase and opened it, then pulled out a stack of papers, which he distributed to the committee members. Most of them muttered to themselves, refusing to even touch the paper, but Cravutius picked up his copy with a weary sigh and began reading:

Lucifer a.k.a. Satan a.k.a. "The Devil"
666 Lucifer Way
Diabopolis, Plane 3774d

Career Objective

I am looking for a position as the unquestioned despot of a major plane occupied by at least ten million sentient beings whom I can manipulate for my own diabolical purposes.

Key Skills

- Proficient in corrupting mortals
- Independent thinker
- Experience overseeing a rebellious throng of demonic minions
- PowerPoint

Work Experience

Director of Marketing
Heaven
Inception–Fall of Man

- Oversaw award-winning "Let There Be Light®" campaign

Demonic Overlord

Hell

Fall of Man–Present

- Spearheaded groundbreaking "Surely You Will Not Die if You Eat of the Fruit®" campaign

References available upon request

Cravutius set the paper down and glared at Lucifer. "I'm afraid we're not looking for an unquestioned despot at the moment," he said curtly.

"You should be," said Lucifer. "You need somebody to take control of things. The Mundane Plane is completely out of control."

"Out of control, is it?" said Cravutius, smiling slightly. "Actually, my impression is that things are progressing quite nicely. It's true that we've had some setbacks of late, but let me ask you this, Lucifer: are you familiar with an Uzzite named Job? There is no one on earth like him; he is blameless and upright, a man who fears God and shuns evil."

"Job!" exclaimed Lucifer, resisting the urge to cackle with glee. He knew he could provoke them into bringing up Job. "Of course Job fears God and shuns evil. He's got angels making sure he never so much as stubs a toe. You make sure all of his plans work out, so that his flocks and herds are spread throughout the land. Take away all that stuff, and I guarantee that he will curse God."

The committee broke into a buzz of urgent whispering. Lucifer stroked his chin to cover a smile. He had them right where he wanted them. If they admitted that Job's obedience was conditional, then they would be conceding that the so-called "Divine Plan" was working so well only because they were sheltering Job from the realities of the world. His success would be replicable by others only to the extent that they too were exempted from the unpredictable vicissitudes of life.

"It's a classic problem, symptomatic of poor management," Lucifer said, leaning back in his chair. "Your solution isn't scalable."

"We're getting off track," said a committee member, a red-haired seraph. "What does any of this have to do with Michael?"

"Well," said Lucifer. "I abducted *Michelle* as a form of protest against the poor management of the Mundane Plane. I don't have anything against her personally, and I'd be happy to release her if I felt that my concerns were being taken seriously."

"Go on," said Cravutius.

"If you think Job's prosperity gospel is going to succeed on a large scale, then why not put it to the test? Make sure you work out any flaws before you've got a thousand other Jobs out there using the same philosophy."

"And how do you suggest we do that?" asked the red-haired seraph.

"Remove Job's special angelic protection. Let him experience a few setbacks and see if he sticks to his principles. If you can demonstrate that Job's loyalty isn't dependent on his good fortune, I'll give you back Michelle."

There was some bickering among the committee members, but eventually they agreed. "You are not to touch a hair on Job's head, though," said Cravutius sternly.

"Wouldn't dream of it," said Lucifer innocently.

Lucifer lost no time in making Job's life miserable.

One of the main advantages that evil has in the eternal struggle between good and evil is the lack of imagination of those on the side of good. When Cravutius and his committee agreed to withhold angelic protection from Job, they had in mind that Job would occasionally lose a sheep to chlamydia or step in a pile of camel dung. What they failed to realize was that by promising not to allow Heavenly agents anywhere near Job, they were giving Lucifer free reign to fuck with Job at his leisure. And fuck with him he did.

He started by convincing the leader of a nearby tribe that Job had stolen some of their oxen. While Job's sons and daughters were feasting and drinking wine at the oldest brother's house, a messenger came to Job and said, "The oxen were plowing and the donkeys were grazing nearby, and the Sabeans attacked and made off with them. They put the servants to the sword, and I am the only one who has escaped to tell you!"

While he was still speaking, another messenger came and said, "The fire of God fell from the heavens and burned up the sheep and the servants, and I am the only one who has escaped to tell you!"[6]

While that messenger was still speaking, another messenger came and said, "The Chaldeans formed three raiding parties and swept down on your camels and made off with them. They put the servants to the sword, and I am the only one who has escaped to tell you!"

While the third man was still speaking, yet another messenger came and said, "Your sons and daughters were feasting and drinking wine at the oldest brother's house, when suddenly a mighty wind swept in from the desert and struck the four corners of the house. It collapsed on them and they are dead, and I am the only one who has escaped to tell you!"

6 Job had a hard time believing this one, but it actually happened as reported. Heaven was testing an upgrade to their Pillar of Fire project (Class 3), and Lucifer had one of his spies switch out the test coordinates (the middle of the Gobi desert) with the coordinates of Job's sheep herd.

Job waited a moment to make sure that no one else was coming. When it was clear that the entirety of the bad news had been delivered, Job got up from his chair. "Well," he said. "Despite the fact that you all keep interrupting each other, I think I have the gist of the situation. I'm pretty well fucked, is that it?"

The four luckiest servants in all of Uz nodded their heads in solemn agreement.

Job dismissed the servants, who went looking for a card game.

Lucifer, meanwhile, waited outside Job's window so he could hear Job when he cursed God.

Job tore his robe and shaved his head. Then he fell to the ground in worship and said, "Naked I came from my mother's womb, and naked I will depart. The LORD gave and the LORD has taken away; may the name of the LORD be praised."

This was not the reaction Lucifer was hoping for. A few days later he met again with the Committee.

Cravutius said to Lucifer, "Where have you come from?"

"Oh, you know," said Lucifer, concealing his disappointment. "From roaming throughout the earth, going back and forth on it."

"Asshole," muttered the red-haired seraph.

The committee charged Lucifer with excessively tormenting Job. Lucifer pointed out, however, that he had abided by the letter of their agreement. "Not only that," Lucifer went on, "but you still haven't proven that Job's love for God is unconditional."

"What?" demanded Cravutius. "You took everything from him, and still he praises God! We demand that you release the archangel Michelle at once!"

Lucifer shook his head. "What are a few sheep to a man like Job? As long as he has his health, he's perfectly content. Let me give him some nasty skin disease, and we'll see his true colors."

There was muttering among the committee members.

"Very well, then," said Cravutius. "He is in your hands, but you must spare his life."

So Lucifer afflicted Job with painful sores from the soles of his feet to the crown of his head. Job took a piece of broken pottery and scraped himself with it as he sat among the ashes.

His wife said to him, "Are you still maintaining your integrity? Curse God and die!"

"Wow, nice bedside manner," Job replied. "Sorry if my oozing sores are bringing you down."

His wife folded her arms and stuck out her lower lip at him.

"Oh, honey," said Job. "I'm sorry. I've hurt your feelings. Look, all I'm saying is this: sometimes God gives us good, and sometimes He gives us trouble. We just have to accept it. Hey, can you get this one on my lower back? It's driving me bonkers."

His wife shook her head and walked away, leaving Job to suffer alone.

SEVEN

Eddie sat in his hotel room in the dark. The lights were off and the shades were drawn.

Cody Lang was dead.

Eddie had done his best to save her, but she had slipped away after muttering her last words. "Pull the switch." Whatever *that* meant. He had set her body in the pit and caused the walls of the shaft to collapse on top of her. The daughter buried in her father's grave. He hoped the authorities would let her rest in peace.

What was he supposed to do now? Cody said he was supposed to finish his story, that he was supposed to write the final Charlie Nyx book after all. That it ended with something called Wormwood. But what the hell was that?

After Cody's heart stopped, Eddie had searched the area, trying to figure out where the bullet had come from. His best guess was that the shooter had been on the roof of one of the buildings across the street, but he found no clues of any kind. The assassin was long gone. Who would want Cody dead? Presumably someone who didn't want her talking about whatever it was she had discovered. Something about Wormwood.

There was a knock on his door. Housekeeping?

"Go away!" yelled Eddie.

Another knock.

"I said, go away!"

"It's destiny, Eddie," said an all-too-familiar voice. "Are you going to let destiny languish in the hall?"

"Go away, Culain! Or Cain, or whatever your name is!" Cain was the last person Eddie wanted to see. Eddie wondered if he knew about Cody. No, of course not. How could he? She had been dead for less than an hour. Eddie had been the last person she saw.

If I had any decency, I'd tell him his daughter is dead, thought Eddie. But I don't. Anyway, screw Cain. He's a murderer and a manipulative jerk. Let him find out on his own.

"Eddie!"

"Go away! I don't want to talk to you!"

"I'm not leaving, Eddie."

"I'll call hotel security."

"Just let me in, Eddie. I need to talk to you. I've got some information for you."

"Information about what?"

"About the story you're writing."

"I'm not writing any story. I'm done with that. Go away!"

"So you don't want to know how it ends?"

"No!"

"OK. But I'm leaving something for you. In case you get curious." He heard Cain slip something under the door. "Good-bye, Eddie," said Cain.

Eddie said nothing. He sat in the dark for another hour before his curiosity got the better of him. He turned on a lamp and walked to the door. On the carpet just inside the door lay a red plastic item the size and shape of a penknife. Eddie picked it up. It was a USB drive.

He walked to his laptop, which was resting on the small hotel desk, and plugged the drive into one of the slots in the back. The laptop had been a gift from Finch Publishing, to facilitate his writing of the final Charlie Nyx book. Eddie normally wrote all of his reports longhand, but Wanda Kwan had insisted. They had even scanned his manuscript and the boxes and boxes of background information Cain had given him, because he had refused to come to Los Angeles without them. Over the past few days, he had learned how to type passably and had become enamored of the little magic box.

The USB drive held hundreds of pages of information: everything from high-resolution scans of the Sumerian manuscript Cain had been tasked to rewrite to the six completed Charlie Nyx books to ramblings on the "secret history of Los Angeles." Cain had evidently stolen his own daughter's notes. Classy.

The Sumerian manuscript was a chaotic mishmash of unintelligible symbols and pictograms, and Cody's notes weren't much better. Her notes were composed mostly of bizarre and probably imagined correlations between disparate people and events that resembled a demented game of word association. For example:

- *Six of seven <u>Mercury</u> astronauts attended the opening of Space Mountain in Anaheim. Exception: Gus Grissom—died in mysterious launchpad fire.*

- *Gus Grissom was a MASON: Also possible relative of Karl Grissom, antichrist???*

- *Who is Mercury???*

Poor Cody, running around trying to make sense of conspiracies far above her pay grade. Eddie couldn't imagine there was any real connection between the Mercury astronauts, the Masons, and the Antichrist. And yet, somehow this chaotic method of paranoia-riddled word association had allowed her to piece together much of the convoluted scheming of Tiamat and Lucifer. Her obsession with the Los Angeles streetcar conspiracy led her to believe that diabolical entities had manipulated the development of the Los Angeles suburbs to enable the construction of a vast system of underground tunnels—a ridiculous conclusion that was nevertheless completely true. And that wasn't all. Cody believed that she had discovered the true purpose of the tunnels.

According to her notes, the tunnels were part of something called a Chrono-Collider Device, which had been built by an occult organization known as the Order of the Pillars of Babylon. The OPB—spearheaded by billionaire Horace Finch—had intended to use the CCD to unearth the most profound mysteries of the cosmos, thereby asserting their dominance over time and space. The OPB had been founded thousands of years ago in the wake of Tiamat's own failed attempts to exert control over the time-space continuum. It was unclear from Cody's notes what Tiamat's current relationship to the OPB was. Was she now its leader?

Besides the Sumerian scrawlings and Cody's ramblings, there was one other file on the drive, modestly titled "Supplemental Information." Eddie opened it and was stunned at what he found. The document was an encyclopedic accounting of virtually everything that had happened over the past three days, from Eddie's encounter with Wanda Kwan in Cork to the implosion of the moon. It was hundreds of pages long. Eddie spent the next six hours poring through the document, barely taking time to blink.

"Unbelievable," he gasped as he read of the existence of a second Chrono-Collider Device underneath Eden II, Horace Finch's vanity project in Kenya. That lunatic Finch had nearly destroyed the world with his scheme to use the CCD to trap mysterious subatomic particles called chrotons. The receptacle he was planning to use to store the chrotons was an anti-bomb—a millennia-old glass apple that Christine Temetri had found hidden in a cave. The anti-bomb would have killed everyone on Earth if he had succeeded. Fortunately, Jacob Slater had sabotaged the CCD and stolen the apple, and Mercury flew it to the moon before it went off.

Eddie got to the end of the document and cursed under his breath. "Damn it," he muttered. "Where's the ending? What happened to Mercury after the implosion?" There was nothing worse than a cliff-hanger.

But then Eddie realized the reason for the cliff-hanger: the ending hadn't happened yet. As Cain said, the levels of reality were converging on each other. Cain had told Eddie that it was Eddie's job to write the story, but as the ending approached, events were occurring almost as fast as they could be recorded. And when Eddie got to the very end, that would mean the end in real life as well. The Sumerian myth, the fictional story of Charlie Nyx, and the story of reality itself would all collapse into a sort of chronological and narrative singularity.

It wasn't completely clear to him whether his writing the story would cause the world to end, or if the impending end of the world was causing him to write it. Cain/Culain had laughed at the very notion of causality. To him, time was just a series of random events occurring in succession. And yet, he had insisted that Eddie *had* to write the story; that it was his *destiny*. Was his insistence due to a belief that Eddie's book would bring about the end of the world? Or was Cain, too, simply playing a part in a drama that had already been written? In that case, Cain's actions became a self-fulfilling prophecy: he was telling Eddie to write the story because it was Cain's destiny to tell Eddie to write the story.

But what if Eddie didn't write the story? What if he didn't feel like being part of the end of everything? After all, it was his life. Didn't he have any say in the matter? What right did that jerk Cain have to tell him what to do?

But it wasn't just Cain. He could feel that there was more to this than the ravings of a man driven mad by the inexorable succession of days. Even Cody had known it. *It comes down to you, Eddie! You're the author of the seventh book!* Eddie had gotten her killed. She died because she had tried to tell him something. Something about Wormwood.

Eddie did a search for "Wormwood" on the USB drive. It popped up in three different places: in a note in Cain's document about the Sumerian manuscript, in the sixth Charlie Nyx book, and in Cody's notes. In the Sumerian myth, Wormwood was an evil artifact that threatened to destroy the world, and in the Charlie Nyx books Wormood was an evil sorcerer, the nemesis of the hero, Charlie Nyx. But it was the reference in Cody's notes that made Eddie's blood run cold. He realized now how it was all going to come together, how the Universe itself was going to end.

"My God," Eddie gasped, regarding a crude drawing of a rectangular object in Cody's notes. "The bastards finally did it."

EIGHT

"I have to admit," said Jacob Slater, staring out the window of the 747 at the blighted moon. "It's rather Apocalyptic."

"No, it isn't," replied Christine Temetri irritably.

"I'm sorry?" said Jacob. "A third of the moon falling out of the sky? Isn't that in Revelations?"

Christine sighed. "First of all, there's no book in the Bible called Revelations. It's Revelation. Singular. The Revelation of John of Patmos. Second, I happen to know the people running the Apocalypse, and this wasn't part of the plan."

Jacob frowned uncertainly. "Did you say you know the people running the Apocalypse?"

"People, angels, whatever," said Christine wearily. "The little girl at Finch's place, Michelle? She's one of them. And that jerk Uzziel used to be, before he fell in with Tiamat. Now if you don't mind, I'm going to try to get some sleep." She closed her eyes and turned away from Jacob, who went back to staring out the window.

Jacob found his thoughts drifting to the scene in *It's a Wonderful Life* where George Bailey promises to throw a lasso around the moon and bring it down to Earth for his sweetheart. That plan was stymied by the stock market crash of October 1929—another Black Monday. Things worked out OK in the end for George, but it was hard to imagine a happy ending to this story. There would be no recovery from this Black Monday: the world had lost something that it was never going to get back.

Jacob still didn't fully comprehend what had happened in Kenya. He had prevented Horace Finch from annihilating the universe, and that Mercury fellow had somehow flown to the moon, causing a Texas-sized chunk of it to disappear into another dimension. There had been a general consensus that this was preferable to a Texas-sized chunk of Earth disappearing.

He hadn't been able to get a firm answer to the question of where the anti-bomb had come from, and he couldn't keep straight the cast of strange characters who had showed up at Finch's complex the night of his fateful experiment. Christine referred to them as angels, and he supposed that was as good a name as any, but he resisted the name on principle. It was clear that they had access to some very advanced technology, and he allowed the possibility that they were extraterrestrial—or even extradimensional—visitors. But to call them "angels" was to adopt a metaphor that was rife with potential for misunderstanding. He preferred to think of them as Beings of Indeterminate Origin.

Adding to his consternation was a vague, not fully accessible memory that before being abducted by Horace Finch, he had himself been abducted by a BIO with the unlikely name of Eddie. He remembered being carried around a parking lot on Eddie's shoulders, and he thought he recalled an intimidating blonde woman firing a gun at someone. He assumed this partially recalled episode had something to do with Horace Finch and the Chrono-Collider Device, but he couldn't imagine what.

Jacob closed the window shade and tried to get the flight attendant's attention. His Coke was empty, and he was feeling very thirsty all of a sudden. The attendants on this flight, he noted, were somewhat less attentive than those on his flight *to* Kenya. Not only that, but he and Christine had to change planes twice, whereas his flight on Finch's plane had been nonstop. He was starting to think that being kidnapped by an insane billionaire wasn't such a bad way to travel.

Jacob felt a little guilty that they had left Alistair Breem, his old physics mentor, in Kenya, but there really wasn't anything else to do. Having been abducted by Finch years earlier, he didn't have a valid passport or any means of identification, and contacting the British embassy in Nairobi hadn't been as helpful as they had hoped. Ally had been declared legally dead five years prior and was having trouble getting anyone in London to accept that he was alive and well and stranded in Africa. There wasn't anything Jacob or Christine could do, and Jacob needed to get to Washington, DC, as quickly as possible if he was going to have any chance of keeping his job. Christine had agreed to fly with Jacob as far as Washington, after which she would catch another plane to Los Angeles.

Eventually Jacob fell asleep as well and was awakened by the pilot announcing their descent into Dulles International Airport. He nudged Christine, who awoke with a start, shouting, "I told you, it's not the Apocalypse!" Jacob smiled apologetically at the passengers around them while Christine rubbed her eyes.

The plane landed without incident, and Christine and Jacob exited onto the concourse. Christine half expected Perpetiel the cherub to come buzzing down the corridor toward them. What she saw was almost as surprising.

A few yards from the gate stood a tall, bulky man with closely cropped black hair, wearing a dark suit. In his hands was a neatly printed sign that read:

SLATER/TEMETRI J

Christine pulled on Jacob's sleeve and cocked her head in the man's direction.

"Huh," said Jacob. "Somebody's expecting us."

"You think?" replied Christine irritably. "Who is it?"

"How would I know?" asked Jacob defensively.

"Aren't you in the FBI?"

"I'm a forensic blast investigator, Christine. Do you want me to defuse him?"

Christine rolled her eyes and strode toward the man. "That's us," she said.

"I know," replied the man.

"Then what's with the sign?"

"The sign was to get you over here."

"Why didn't you just walk up and introduce yourself?"

"Some people find me intimidating," the man explained. "The sign is meant to empower you. You see your name and you think, 'Hey, that's me. Somebody is here waiting for me.' "

"Frankly, it's a little intimidating seeing a stranger holding a sign with your name on it," said Christine.

The man frowned and cocked his head to look at the sign. "Even with the smiley face?"

"Who are you?" asked Christine.

"My name," said the man, "is Special Agent Roger Daltrey."

"Roger Daltrey?" asked Christine. "Like the singer?"

"The who?" asked Jacob.

Agent Daltrey glared at Jacob. "Never gets old," he said evenly. "Come with me, please. Both of you."

"Hang on," said Christine. "I don't work for the FBI. I don't have to come with you if I don't want to."

"Well," said Agent Daltrey. "I can arrest you if I need to, but I'd rather not. It cheapens the smiley face, in my opinion."

"Fine," replied Christine curtly. "Where are you taking us?"

"Best not to say right now," said Agent Daltrey. "Follow me." He spun on his heel and made for the airport exit. Christine had to admire the way he assumed that she and Jacob would follow; clearly Agent Daltrey was accustomed to people doing what he told them to do. It was only when they were outside, being herded into a waiting SUV, that she realized that they had been tailed by half a dozen plainclothes agents. No wonder Daltrey hadn't been worried about her and Jacob bolting.

An identical SUV in front of them peeled out, and half a second later the vehicle carrying Christine and Jacob did as well. She caught a glimpse of another following close behind. Two agents who had been posing as a married couple sat in the rear seat behind Jacob and Christine, and Agent Daltrey sat in the front passenger's seat. A tense-jawed black man, also wearing a dark suit, was driving.

The SUV glided through the nighttime traffic like some giant manta ray skimming the freeway for plankton. The vehicle's speedometer needle was hovering just below 95. Wherever we're going, Christine thought, we're in a hurry.

Soon they were passing the Lincoln Memorial on their right, and the unmistakable obelisk of the Washington Monument was visible ahead of them. The monument made Christine think of the Egyptians and the pyramids. She wondered if there was any truth to the myth that Washington, DC, had been laid out according to some sort of mystical Masonic plan. A few weeks ago, she wouldn't have believed it, but knowing what she did now about the engineering of Los Angeles by the secret society known as the Order of the Pillars of Babylon, she didn't know what to believe anymore. The Universe was turning out to be a pretty strange place.

The SUV turned sharply into an unmarked parking garage and was waved in by a uniformed attendant. They continued underground for a few minutes and then came to an abrupt halt, the other two vehicles sliding in alongside them. Doors flew open, and Christine and Jacob were escorted through a steel door into a dimly lit tunnel. After some ten minutes of brisk walking, the procession reached another door. Agent Daltrey held his thumb to a scanner, and a green light went on. Daltrey beckoned for them to go through, and he followed, leaving the bulk of the procession behind. At first Christine thought it strange that all these agents would come along only to be left here in the hallway, presumably just short of their destination, but then she realized that their job was finished: the whole point of this convoy was to ensure the successful delivery of her and Jacob. Somebody very important had decided that they were either very important or in a lot of danger—or possibly both.

Behind the door was a hallway lined with nondescript offices—the sort of place where government interns and other denizens clutching to the lowest rungs of the DC bureaucracy toiled late into the night drinking Starbucks coffee and pissing out press releases and legislation. After a few more minutes, with Agent Daltrey barking an occasional "Left here!" or "Keep right!" they found themselves in a somewhat better neighborhood. The offices were larger and featured floor-to-ceiling windows that were covered by shuttered blinds rather than actual walls. Clearly they were still underground, but this was the sort of underground where important people went to be protected from bombs and other unpleasant aboveground happenings, not the sort of underground where you got stuffed because there wasn't enough room for you on the surface. Daltrey led them to a door at the end of a hallway and knocked. A muffled reply came from within and he opened the door.

They shuffled inside and Daltrey directed them to sit in two black leather chairs across from a large desk. Behind the desk sat a stocky gray-haired man with thick, stubby fingers. A stern look gripped his face. He appeared to be in his early sixties. A plaque on his desk read:

D.A.D. Dirk Lubbers

"Director Lubbers," Jacob said nervously. "What are you… that is, if I may ask…"

"Shut up, Slater," growled Lubbers. "You're lucky I don't have you fired after your little disappearing act. I should have known you were holding out on me at the HeadJAC meeting." He managed to point something like a smile in Christine's direction. "You must be the reporter," he said. "Temetri."

"Yes, sir," said Christine, trying not to sound as frightened as Jacob. "I'm afraid I don't know what this is all about."

"I think you do," said Lubbers. He held up a thick, dog-eared stack of papers. On the first page, just above what appeared to be tire tracks, was written:

To Your Holiness the High Council of the Seraphim,

Greetings from your humble servant, Ederatz,
Cherub First Class,
Order of the Mundane Observation Corps

"What is that?" Christine asked.

"Well," said Lubbers, regarding the cover page intently, "obviously it's a report to the High Council of the Seraphim." After a moment, he put down the report and leaned forward, holding out his rough, stubby hand to Christine. She shook his hand uncertainly.

"Deputy Assistant Director of the FBI Dirk Lubbers," he said.

"I'm Christine Temetri," said Christine. "And this is Jacob Slater. But you know that, I guess."

Lubbers nodded. "I do. When Slater's name came up on a flight from Nairobi to Paris, it raised some alarms. When we discovered he was traveling with a reporter from Los Angeles, we looked into you as well. It seems you've had quite the adventure lately, Ms. Temetri."

Christine shrugged. "I seem to be at the epicenter of the Apocalypse for some reason."

"The Apocalypse, yes," said Lubbers thoughtfully. "Between you and me, I'm aiming to be National Security Advisor someday, and that's not going to happen if I let the world end on my watch."

Christine stifled a laugh. "And just how do you plan to stop it? It's not as easy as it sounds."

Lubbers was suddenly very serious. "By any means possible," he said. "For starters, you and Slater are going to tell me everything you know about Heaven. Specifically about any defensive systems they have in place."

Christine regarded him coldly. "Do you even believe in Heaven?"

"I didn't when I got out of bed this morning," Lubbers replied. "I've received some new intel since then." He patted the stack of papers on his desk. "Between this intercepted report, Agent Slater's suspiciously accurate assessment of the Anaheim Event, and the implosion of the moon, I've had to adjust my thinking a bit. In this job, you've got to be adaptable."

Slater said nothing. He seemed to be frozen in fear.

"Just like that?" Christine asked. "You're a believer?"

Lubbers shrugged. "I believe there's a race of beings who call themselves 'angels' living in a place they call 'Heaven.' I believe that these beings have made occasional contact with human beings. I also believe these facts go a long ways toward explaining all the superstitious bullshit that a lot of people believe."

"Hang on," said Christine. "You're presented with hard evidence of the existence of Heaven and angels and your reaction is to dismiss religion as superstitious bullshit?"

"It's pretty clear from the intel that these angels are a far cry from the godlike beings found in the Bible," replied Lubbers. "Hell, if I didn't know better, I'd think this whole report was a joke. I mean, angels doing magic tricks? Bombs that look like glass apples? An interdimensional portal disguised as a linoleum floor in an unsuspecting reporter's breakfast nook? Ridiculous."

Christine paled at the mention of the portal. She had hoped that the report left that part out.

Lubbers chuckled. "You know," he said, "I had actually pegged that last part as bullshit, but seeing the look on your face, I can tell I've hit pay dirt. So, tell me about this portal."

It was pointless to deny the portal's existence now, so Christine took another tack. "It's guarded by angels," she said, trying not to picture Ramiel and Nisroc in her kitchen, bickering over the proper way to cook SpaghettiOs. "You'd never get past them, and even if you did, you'd be stuck in the planeport. The security there is insane. Cherubim with flaming swords..." She trailed off, realizing that the cherubim with flaming swords was pretty much it for security, as far as she could remember. How would they hold up against a team of Special Forces commandos armed with assault rifles and grenade launchers? She tried to change the subject. "Why would you want to attack Heaven anyway?"

Lubbers leaned back from his desk, holding up his hands. "Nobody's talking about attacking anybody," he said. "I'm just gathering intel. I have a meeting with President Babcock in twenty minutes."

Christine's jaw dropped. "You're meeting with the *president*? Of the *United States*? About *this*?"

Lubbers smiled. "Christine, the moon was attacked by beings from another dimension. This is the sort of thing that the president likes to know about."

"Attacked?" said Christine, taken aback. "Nobody attacked the moon." She looked to Jacob for help, but he was sitting quietly with his hands in his lap, eyes staring ahead, as if he were facing a rattlesnake about to strike. She turned back to Lubbers. "What does that report say, exactly?"

"About the attack on the moon?" replied Lubbers. "Nothing. This report seems to only cover events up to about six weeks ago. It's pretty obvious, though, that the device used on the moon was of the same type as the one used in Anaheim—although a lot bigger, of course. Clearly somebody intentionally detonated one of these 'anti-bombs' on the moon. That's something the president needs to know."

"No, wait," said Christine desperately. "It wasn't like that. The bomb was going to go off; there was no stopping it. Mercury had the idea of flying to the moon—"

"Mercury!" exclaimed Lubbers. "Yes, where is this Mercury? He figures prominently in the report. He seems like the sort who could be swayed to see our point of view."

"He's…" Christine started. "I don't think anybody really knows where he is. He sort of disappeared."

"Figures. I'd have gone underground too if I were in as much trouble as he is. Sounds like everybody in Heaven and Hell wants to see him strung up. For his sake, I hope we find him first."

Christine was momentarily puzzled by this statement, but then she remembered that the report Lubbers was reading didn't cover Mercury's turning himself in to Uzziel. As far as Lubbers knew, Mercury was still wanted by Heaven for his role in undermining the Apocalypse.

"All right, I've got to go," said Lubbers. "Anything you want to add before I talk to Babcock?"

Christine didn't think it would do any good to tell Lubbers anything else. She got the impression that anything she said would be used to build a case against the angels.

Lubbers put on his jacket and walked to the door. When he opened it, Christine saw that Agent Daltrey was standing at attention in the hall.

"Agent Daltrey will take you and Slater to your hotel."

"Our hotel? What hotel?"

"Someplace safe. And nearby. You're not leaving Washington for a while."

NINE
Circa 1800 BC

It was shortly after Job was afflicted with festering sores that Mercury entered the story. Tiamat's reign in Babylon had just ended, and Mercury had been recalled from his assigned duty of surveilling her.

Mercury sat across a large walnut desk from his nominal boss, Uzziel, director of the Apocalypse Bureau, trying to appear nonchalant while Uzziel shuffled through a stack of papers in front of him.

"Got a new assignment for you," said Uzziel, not looking up from the papers. "This one's a favor for Cravutius. Some special committee he's set up. Have you heard of Job, the Uzzite?"

"I don't get down to Uz much," replied Mercury.

"This guy's reputation has spread far past Uz," said Uzziel. "He's like a living legend. He's the richest…well, *was* the richest man in the East. You've never heard of him?"

Mercury shrugged. He had been pretty busy dealing with Tiamat and the ziggurats.

Uzziel set the papers down and leaned back in his chair, eyeing Mercury. "The details are classified, but the assignment should be pretty straightforward. You just have to keep an eye on Job and report back to me if he does anything, well, questionable."

"Define questionable," said Mercury. "Are we expecting him to invent leg warmers or something?"

"Oh, nothing like that," said Uzziel. "Mostly I need to know if he's cursed God."

"Cursed God? Why would anyone do that? Seems like asking for trouble."

"Job's hit a spot of bad luck recently," replied Uzziel. "Like I said, I can't get into the details, but it's important for us to know whether he curses God or not."

"Whatever," said Mercury. "I'll take the Megiddo portal. Should be in Uz in a couple of hours. I'm assuming I'll be able to find the legendary Job easily enough?"

"Yeah, that shouldn't be a problem," said Uzziel. "He will be the guy sitting in a pile of ashes scraping his sores with pot shards."

"Scraping his...Hang on a minute," said Mercury. "Did Job do something to piss off Heaven? Why is he sitting in ashes, scraping sores? I thought you said he was rich."

"Classified," said Uzziel. "Even I don't know all the details. Your job is just to watch him and let me know if he curses God."

"So I get to sit out in the sun in a pile of ashes with some guy who is scraping his sores with a pot shard? This is the top-secret assignment you were telling me about?"

"I can put you on flood cleanup if you'd prefer."

"Ugh," said Mercury. "How long do I have to do this?"

"I'm not a hundred percent clear on that. I'm assuming I'll be informed when you're no longer needed. Of course, if Job curses God, that's pretty much game over. Once he curses God, there's not much point in watching him anymore, as I understand it."

"Uh-huh," said Mercury. "So as soon as he curses God, my job is done?"

"Don't get any ideas, Mercury," said Uzziel, scowling. "Your job is to observe. You need to stay at least fifty paces from Job at all times. You are not to interfere in any way. If I hear that you're coaching Job to curse God just to get out of this assignment..."

"Fine, fine," said Mercury. "No interference, got it."

He found Job as promised, sitting in a pile of ashes scraping his sores. Mercury took a seat under a nearby palm tree just over fifty paces away, where he could observe Job. Job took no notice of him. Mercury hoped that when Job cursed God he did it loud enough for him to hear it. It would suck if Job cursed God and he missed it.

After about twenty minutes of waiting in the hot sun, with the palm tree providing only nominal shade, Mercury was exceedingly uncomfortable and bored. His only entertainment was in the form of a little boy who would periodically leave his hiding place behind some rocks to run over and poke Job with a stick. He would then run screaming back to his hiding place as if Job were a monster that he had just awoken. Job seemed to take no notice. After three hours, even this started to lose its novelty.

"Hey, kid," whispered Mercury to the boy as he crept out of his hiding place for the fiftieth time.

"What?" said the boy, stopping to look at Mercury.

"You want a mango?"

"What's a mango?"

Mercury held up a ripe, round, yellowish fruit. The boy's eyes widened, and he stepped forward to take the mango from Mercury.

Mercury pulled the fruit back. "First, I need you to do something for me. Get me some cloth. At least three feet square. Something lightweight. Silk would be best, but a light cotton will do. Also, some string. Got it?"

The boy nodded and ran off toward Job's house. The place had been overrun by thieves and vandals, who had absconded with the silver and gold and left the less valuable items lying strewn throughout the rubble. Mercury figured the kid wouldn't have much trouble finding what he needed. Sure enough, a few minutes later he returned with a stained silk tablecloth and a spool of string.

"Excellent!" said Mercury. "Now just one more thing. I need your poking stick. And three more just like it. Straight, like that one."

The boy nodded and ran off again, returning shortly with three perfectly straight sticks, each around four feet long.

"Perfect!" exclaimed Mercury, handing the mango to the boy. The boy sat down next to Mercury and began to eat with gusto, mango juice running down his chin.

"What's your name?" asked Mercury.

"Elihu," said the boy between bites of mango.

"Nice to meet you, Elihu. I'm Mercury."

Mercury pulled a knife from his pocket and began whittling at the sticks. When he had gotten them to the desired length, he cut notches in them so that two of them fit together in a right triangle, with the other two sticks arranged perpendicularly to each other inside the triangle. Then he wrapped string around the joints and tied them off. He stretched the silk across the frame, secured it with string, and then tied the remaining length of string to three points on the bottom of the frame. When he was finished, it looked like this:

"What's that?" asked the boy, his face sticky with the remnants of mango.

"You've never seen a kite before?"

The boy shook his head.

"Hours of entertainment," Mercury said. "We just have to get it airborne."

"How do we do that?" asked the boy.

"Here," said Mercury, handing the kite and the spool of string to the boy. "Hold it like this, above your head. Got it? Then run and let go of it. When it starts getting some air, let some string out. Just a little at a time. Keep the string taut so it doesn't crash."

The boy took off running. He let the kite go, and it fluttered around a few inches above his head, barely retaining its modest altitude.

"Keep running!" Mercury shouted. "You'll get it!"

Unfortunately, the slight breeze that was blowing while Mercury was building the kite had died down to nothing, and he didn't have the heart to tell the kid that he didn't have a chance of getting the kite more than five feet into the sky. Still, at least it would keep him occupied for a while.

Job still sat silently, occasionally coughing or scraping one of his sores.

Mercury dozed off, awakening hours later with a start. "What's that?" he exclaimed, thinking that he had heard Job say something. But it was just the boy.

"Wheeeee!" yelled the boy, running circles around Job, the kite still fluttering just inches above his head.

Mercury took a deep breath and leaned back against the tree. He tried to remember if he had ever had a worse assignment than this. Even working for that scheming megalomaniac Tiamat had been leagues ahead of sitting in the sun all day waiting for some diseased fool to curse God.

"Seriously," he said to no one in particular. "What have I done to deserve this? No one deserves this sort of treatment."

Job swatted absently with a pot shard at a fly that was buzzing around his head.

"Wheeeee!" yelled the boy again. Seeing that Mercury was awake, he ran over to him. "You got any more of those mangoes?"

Mercury handed the boy a second mango, which he devoured furiously in a matter of seconds. He then returned to his tireless running with the kite.

An hour or so later, Mercury thought he heard something behind him and turned to see three men approaching. He stood to meet them.

"Greetings," said one of the men. "I am Eliphaz. These are my friends Bildad and Zophar. We have come to comfort our friend Job. Is he around?"

Mercury's brow furrowed. "You didn't notice the guy sitting over there in the ashes, scraping his sores with pot shards?"

The men's eyes went wide. "Holy shit," said Eliphaz. "*That's* Job? I didn't even recognize him. He looks *awful*."

"Well, yeah," said Mercury. "I mean, I didn't know him pre–oozing sores, but I'd have to agree, he's not the picture of health."

"Has he said anything?" asked Zophar.

"Like cursed God, you mean? I don't think so. He might have muttered some anti-God sentiments under his breath, but nothing I was able to pick up on. I hope you guys can talk some sense into him."

"What do you mean, talk some sense into him?"

"Er," said Mercury, "I meant, I hope you guys can give him some small measure of comfort. He's been through so much. A lesser man probably would have cursed God by now, you know? Really loudly too, so that there would be no question about it."

The men muttered confusedly among themselves and left Mercury so they could go sit in the ashes by Job.

Mercury's hopes for a quick resolution of his situation were not met. Eliphas, Bildad, and Zophar sat in silence for a full week, commiserating with Job. At last Job spoke, but not loudly enough for Mercury to make out what he was saying.

"Hey, kid!" Mercury whispered to the boy, who was, incredibly, still trying to get the kite airborne. The boy ran over to Mercury.

"Tell me what he's saying. Quick!"

The boy ran over and perched behind Job. After a moment he ran back to Mercury. "He says, 'May the day of my birth perish, and the night that said, "A boy is conceived!" ' "

"OK," said Mercury. "He's still talking. Tell me the rest."

The boy ran over to listen and then returned again to Mercury. "He says, 'That day—may it turn to darkness; may God above not care about it.' "

"Got it," said Mercury. "Go!"

The boy ran over again to listen and returned. "He says, 'May no light shine on it. May gloom and utter darkness claim it once more; may a cloud settle over it; may blackness overwhelm it.' "

"Utter darkness," said Mercury, nodding. "OK, go!"

The boy returned again. "He says, 'That night—may thick darkness seize it; may it not be included among the days of the year nor be entered in any of the months.' "

"Jeez, more about the day, huh? OK, go get the rest."

"He says, 'May that night be barren; may no shout of joy be heard in it. May those who curse days curse that day, those who are ready to rouse Leviathan.' "

"Rousing Leviathan, got it. OK, go."

The boy returned again. "You got any more mangoes?"

"He's asking for mangoes?"

"No, I want more mangoes."

"Fine, here. What's he saying?"

"He says, 'May its morning stars become dark; may it wait for daylight in vain and not see the first rays of dawn.' "

"Seriously? He's still talking about the day he was born? Tell you what: wake me up when he either curses God or gets to the point in the story where he soils his first nappy." Mercury leaned back against the tree for another snooze. It didn't look like his torment was going to end anytime soon.

TEN

Christine and Jacob found themselves once again in the back of a black SUV. Agent Daltrey was driving while another agent, a tight-faced, thickly built woman named Ruiz, rode shotgun. The vehicle was barely moving, hemmed in by traffic. Christine was exhausted, and the glare of headlights was giving her a headache.

"How much farther?" she asked.

"Just a few blocks," said Agent Ruiz. "Traffic is bad tonight. Riots."

"Riots?" asked Christine. "What are they rioting about?"

Ruiz glanced back at her. "Whaddaya got?"

Jacob was gazing out his window, apparently enraptured by the city lights. Christine turned to look out hers. She saw throngs of pedestrians on the street, but they seemed peaceful enough.

Ruiz spoke again, without looking back. "Charlie Nyx fanatics, antiwar protesters, and end-of-the-world fanatics, not to mention a grab bag of assorted lunatics. You're going to want to stay off the streets. Not that you have any choice in the matter."

The FBI agents were escorting Christine and Jacob to a nearby hotel, where they would evidently be staying indefinitely. It was made quite clear to them that the FBI would be more than happy to save money by letting them sleep in underground holding cells if they objected to their accommodations. A second SUV was following them, carrying agents who would stand guard outside their hotel rooms.

Anger rose in her throat as she thought of Director Lubbers's arrogance and presumptuousness. What gave him the right to hold her and Jacob against their will? If they knew what we've done, they'd throw us a parade. Not that she particularly wanted a parade, of course. In fact, a hot shower and a hotel bed sounded pretty damn good when she thought about it. This thought was augmented by the occasional whiff of overripe sweat emanating from Jacob in the seat next to her. In his present condition, with his hair mussed and his clothes torn and stained, he bore an uncanny resemblance to Pig Pen from the *Peanuts* comic strip. He stared out the window as if wondering, Pig Pen–like, where all the dirt kept coming from.

Jacob still hadn't snapped out of the trancelike state he had fallen into during their interrogation. Christine felt a tinge of pity for him. He hadn't had as much time as Christine to adjust to how strange a place the Universe really was, and now he was being asked to account for his behavior by his employer, which happened to be one of the more hard-nosed and humorless extensions of the federal government. Jacob seemed like the type to chafe at contact with his superiors in even the best of circumstances, and these circumstances were far from the best. He now seemed to have shut down completely. Every so often he would lean his head back and make a strange sound in his throat, but he hadn't spoken since they had left the underground facility.

What did Lubbers want with them? He had asked about the angels' "defensive systems." Was he just taking precautions, or was he actually planning some sort of attack?

An attack on Heaven, she thought. The idea was insane. Even if you could somehow get through the planeport's security and get to Heaven, you'd be facing the full might of the Heavenly army commanded by Michelle herself. How many angels was that? Hundreds? Thousands? She had no idea, but she imagined that each of them was easily a match for an entire platoon of Special Forces commandoes. She had witnessed Mercury restarting Karl Grissom's heart simply by laying his hand on him. How much harder could it be to *stop* a heart? Or a hundred hearts, for that matter? You'd have to be a madman to send human soldiers up against angels.

And what could Lubbers hope to accomplish with such an invasion, even if, against all odds, it somehow succeeded? Sure, the angels could be manipulative troublemakers on occasion, but their overall effect seemed to be benign. Well, there was the whole Apocalypse thing, of course, but Heaven had lost control over that plan weeks ago. At this point, they were mostly doing damage control. In fact, the last she knew, Michelle was mobilizing her troops to help with earthquake relief efforts. This memory made her a bit uncomfortable. If Lubbers were to launch an attack, now would be a good time: the Heavenly army was scattered all over the globe, with probably only a small remnant left behind to guard Heaven.

She tried to see things from Lubbers's perspective. The implosion of the moon was unsettling, to say the least. There would be political pressure to figure out what had happened and to keep it from happening again. But Heaven wasn't responsible for what happened to the moon. Nor were they responsible for the Anaheim Event, for that matter. Those events were both the doing of a few rogue angels, primarily Lucifer, Tiamat, and Mercury's ex-boss, Uzziel. Assuming the account that Lubbers had read about the Anaheim event was accurate, then he knew that Heaven was not to blame. And Christine herself had told him what had happened with the moon. Why would he plot an invasion of Heaven when he *knew* Heaven was not responsible for these tragedies?

In any case, a military action against a foreign power would have to go through President Babcock, who was a right-wing Bible thumper. Harry Giddings, Christine's late fundamentalist boss, had been a major contributor to Babcock's campaign. Babcock had ultimately lost the contest for the Republican nomination to the more moderate Alexis Friedman, but she had added him to the ticket as a sop to the Religious Right. The idea of Babcock launching an attack on Heaven was ludicrous. One of the charges of the Left had been that Babcock intended to make the United States into a theocracy; that if given the option, he'd hand the keys over to Jesus Himself. Babcock launching an assault on Heaven would be like Fidel Castro attacking Moscow.

Still, Christine's grilling by Lubbers about the "defensive systems" of Heaven had unnerved her. Clearly he was planning *something.* She wondered how much information was in that report. Who had written it? How had it fallen into the hands of the FBI? And most importantly, how much havoc would it allow Lubbers to wreak? One thing was certain: no good could come from it. Both Heaven and the United States government had done just fine over the past two hundred years without the latter having a backdoor into the former. Christine needed to warn the Heavenly authorities so they could shut the portal down.

Christine's musings were cut short when the SUV came to an abrupt halt. On a whim, she tried opening her door. As she expected, pulling the latch had no effect. The door was rigged to be locked by the driver in cases where he might be transporting people who might be tempted to escape from the vehicle.

"Shit," growled Daltrey.

Christine looked out the windshield to see the source of his frustration: several cars up, a minivan had stalled in the middle of the street, and a gaggle of youths had climbed on top of it. They were jumping and dancing on top of the vehicle, and a crowd had followed them into the street, either to egg them on or to persuade them to get off the car. As a result, traffic was now completely stopped in both directions.

Daltrey checked the rearview mirror and then turned to look behind him. "Shit," he growled again. "We're boxed in." His hands alternately tightened and released his grip on the steering wheel as he assessed the situation.

Ruiz had her cell phone to her ear and was speaking quietly in a near monotone to someone about their situation. After a moment, she put the phone down on her lap. "They say to hold tight," she informed Daltrey. "DC Metro is en route. ETA twenty minutes."

"Twenty minutes," grumbled Daltrey, his knuckles going white. "This crowd will hit the flashpoint in ten. It'll be like something out of Hieronymus Bosch by the time DC Metro gets here."

Ruiz scowled at him, presumably because she recognized what his tone portended and not because of her distaste for sixteenth-century moralistic painters. "Chill," she said with a hint of motherly concern. "You'll only make things worse if you go out there."

In the minute or so that they had been waiting, the crowd had already gotten larger, and now a squirrelly-looking young man in a tank top and baggy shorts was approaching the minivan with an aluminum baseball bat.

"Things are getting worse on their own," said Daltrey. "Wait here." Daltrey pushed open his door and stepped outside.

"Damn it, Daltrey..." began Ruiz. The force drained from her words as she realized the futility of trying to prevent Daltrey from intervening.

Daltrey slammed the door and strode boldly through the crowd, his right palm hovering an inch above his sidearm. With his left hand, he pointed directly at the teen with the baseball bat and shouted something at him. Christine couldn't make out what he was saying over the sound of the engine and the cacophony of the crowd.

The throng shrank back from Daltrey's impressive form, and the kid with the baseball bat froze like a spooked animal. Several people who were about to step onto the street from the sidewalk took a step back. Daltrey seemed on the verge of calming the maelstrom through sheer force of will.

Then something strange happened.

Something small, maybe the size of a baseball, flew from somewhere on the right side of the street toward Daltrey, striking him square in the temple. The object splattered against Daltrey's skull, falling in juicy chunks from the side of his head. It took Christine a second to realize that it was an apple. Not the imploding sort of apple, fortunately, just a regular apple. Still, not something you want to get hit in the head with. Daltrey went down.

He fell to his knees, stunned, his right hand pressed against his temple. The kid with the bat snapped out of his daze and took a step toward Daltrey. The crowd went wild.

"Son of a bitch!" exclaimed Ruiz. "Don't move!" she growled in the general direction of the back seat and exited the vehicle. She motioned to the agents in the SUV behind them, and several men came running forward to assist her. "FBI!" shouted Ruiz, drawing her pistol. "Drop the bat! Now!"

Jacob sat stock-still, watching the scene unfold as if it were a particularly unremarkable episode of *Law & Order*.

"Let's go!" Christine hissed at him. He frowned and looked at her as if she had suggested changing the channel to *Glee*.

"Come on, Jacob," she said urgently. "This is our chance!"

Jacob turned again toward the scene ahead of them. Ruiz had the bat-wielding teen on his knees, and the other agents were ordering people out of the streets. They seemed to have the situation nearly under control.

"My job—" Jacob started.

"Your job is done," snapped Christine. "You don't work for the FBI anymore. You're their prisoner, got it? They have no idea what—or who—they're messing with, and they're going to hold on to us as long as they think we're of use to them. And after that...God knows what they'll do with us." She was being a bit overdramatic, she knew, but she had no intention of being sequestered by the FBI indefinitely. Besides, if Lubbers was serious about launching a preemptive attack on Heaven, somebody needed to warn the Heavenly authorities. She needed to escape, and she had started to feel a little like an older sister to Jacob. She didn't like the idea of him having to face endless interrogation by the FBI alone.

"I'm leaving," said Christine, trying to sound decisive. "You're not going to get another chance. Come with me or spend the rest of your life in FBI custody." She scrambled between the front seats and pushed the driver's-side door open just far enough to crawl out of the SUV. The SUV was angled so that it would be difficult for Ruiz and the others to see her if she kept close to the vehicle. Too frightened to check whether Jacob was following her, she crawled to the rear of the SUV and then stood up, walking briskly toward the sidewalk. She half expected to hear Ruiz's gruff voice shouting at her to stop, but she heard only the random cacophony of the crowd.

She made it to the sidewalk and pushed her way through the crowd, trying to put as many people between her and the scene as possible. The unruly crowd frightened her, but her even greater fear of being apprehended by the FBI propelled her forward. Just when she thought she had escaped, she tripped and fell headlong into a heavyset man who smelled of stale beer and sweat, knocking a Subway meatball sub out of his hand.

"The fuck, woman?" demanded the man.

"I'm sorry," said Christine. "I just need to get—"

"You gonna be sorry," said the man, puffing up his chest and glaring down at Christine.

"Step back, sir," said a voice behind Christine. It was nervous but firm. Jacob. He must have been following Christine the whole time. He was now standing beside her.

The big man laughed. He towered at least a foot over Jacob. "I'ma give you options, little man," he said to Jacob. "You know what options are?"

"I do," said Jacob, calmly.

"Options is like an either/or situation," explained the man. "For example, I'ma give your woman the option of *either* getting me another sammich, *or* the option of sucking my—"

Something happened at that point that caused the man to pause. Christine couldn't be sure of what it was at first. There had been a flash of movement and suddenly the man stopped talking. He fell to his knees, unable to catch his breath.

"You know what the solar plexus is, asshole?" Jacob asked, his voice still calm. He was rubbing his left hand with his right.

Christine realized that she was standing with her mouth open, staring at Jacob. Had he *punched* the man? She had never seen someone move so fast.

"Come on," she heard herself saying. "We need to get out of here."

Jacob nodded.

They left the man wheezing on the concrete and took off down the street.

ELEVEN
Circa 1800 BC

If Elihu was to be believed, Job spent another good twenty minutes cursing the day of his birth, but he never did curse God. Mercury decided it was time to change tacks. He had Elihu summon Job's three friends for a huddle.

"Look, guys, I admire your loyalty to Job and all," he said, "but I don't think any of us wants to spend the rest of our lives sitting in ashes with some poor sap scraping his sores and cursing the day he was born. We need an exit strategy. It's time to brainstorm. Come on, guys, don't be afraid to toss out ideas."

"Who *are* you?" asked Bildad. "What are you *doing* here?"

"I'm just a guy who wants to see Job's ordeal end," said Mercury. "Now, who's got an idea of how we can make that happen?"

"Well," said Eliphaz, "in my experience, suffering is caused by wrongdoing. God doesn't just punish people for no reason. And God is also merciful. So if we can get Job to admit what he did wrong, maybe God will forgive him and end his suffering."

"OK, good," said Mercury, rubbing his chin. He had actually been hoping one of them might suggest euthanasia, but this seeking-forgiveness-for-wrongdoing idea had some potential too. "All right, we need to present a unified front. You guys should each come at him from a slightly different point of view, but the gist has to be that Job has committed some sin for which he needs to beg forgiveness."

The three friends nodded in agreement. They came up with three bang-up speeches, which they would deliver one after another. Job wouldn't have a chance. He'd be begging God's forgiveness just to get the three of them to shut up. Hopefully God would respond, maybe by striking Job by lightning or something, and this ordeal would finally end.

One by one, the three friends delivered their speeches imploring Job to admit his wrongdoing, but Job would not be swayed. He challenged each of them to point out where he had gone wrong, yet none of them could do so.

Job began weeping and mumbling to himself.

"Quick," said Mercury to Elihu. "What's he saying? Is he cursing God?"

Elihu ran over and listened for a bit. He returned, shaking his head. "Doesn't sound like it. He's pretty pissed off at those three guys, though. He called them 'worthless physicians' and told them to shut up."

"Oh boy," said Mercury. This was not going at all the way he had hoped. Rather than getting Job to either give up or change his attitude, they had only caused him to dig in and stick with his stubborn refusal to either admit guilt or cast blame. Mercury didn't know what it was going to take to end this stalemate, but it seemed pretty clear that unless he did something drastic, they were going to be stuck out here in the ashes for a long time.

"OK, change of plans," Mercury said to Elihu. "You need to talk to him."

"Me?" asked Elihu. "I'm only nine years old!"

"No worries," said Mercury thoughtfully. "Just tell Job that you don't have to be old to possess wisdom."

"Why don't you do it?" Elihu asked.

"Oh, I can't interfere," said Mercury. "I've got to stay fifty paces from Job at all times. If you can pull this off, there will be a lot of mangoes in it for you."

Elihu's eyes lit up. "All right, what do I say?"

Mercury sighed. "Hell if I know. Anything to end this torment. Clearly we're not getting anywhere trying to get him to confess his sins, so I think we're back to trying to get him to curse God."

Elihu frowned. "Curse God? You mean Marduk?"

Mercury snorted. "No, not Marduk, you dope. I curse Marduk sixteen times a day before lunch. Mucking Farduk. That hammer-brained jackaninny can suck a pig's knuckle. No, Elihu, I'm talking about *the* God."

Elihu's brow furrowed.

"Jeez, you people. Monotheism is not that complicated. Don't you live around here somewhere? Didn't you ever listen to anything Job said? There's just the one God. The rest of us are, you know, middle management."

"So there's one big God who's in charge of the whole *universe*?" asked Elihu.

"Yep."

"Wow," said Elihu, staring open-mouthed at the sky, trying to take in this new information. "Like, in charge of the sun and the moon and the earth and the oceans and the deserts?"

"Uh-huh."

"And all the people of the world, and all the animals and plants?"

"Correct."

"And night and day and the seasons?"

"Right."

"And the rain and clouds and wind and sickness and health and life and death?"

"Everything, Elihu. Ev-er-ree-thing. Everything. He's in charge of *everything*."

"And, uh, you want Job to curse him?"

"That's the plan."

Elihu was silent for some time, considering this notion. Finally he said, "That sounds like a bad idea."

"Look, Elihu," replied Mercury irritably. "If you've got a better idea, I'd love to hear it. Maybe you should go back to poking him with a stick. That damn kite is never going to fly, you know. You can run around like a moron all you want, but it's not going anywhere without wind."

Elihu began to cry.

"Oh, jeez," muttered Mercury. "Hey, I'm sorry. I shouldn't have yelled at you. I'm just frustrated. I used to be in charge of some pretty important ziggurats, and now I'm stuck here indefinitely, watching this blithering lump of self-righteousness bitch and moan about the day of his birth."

Elihu nodded, wiping the tears from his face. He probably didn't understand half of what Mercury was saying, but he seemed to get the gist of it.

"Seriously," Mercury continued. "This guy has no freaking clue. I mean, I'm an angel. An *angel*, Elihu. I could torch this whole estate by calling down a pillar of fire if I wanted to. And even I have no idea why Job's been singled out for this sort of treatment." He was telling Elihu far more than he was authorized to, but he needed to vent to someone. Besides, the kid was nine. It's not like anybody was going to believe anything he said.

Mercury continued, "Even my boss, Uzziel, director of the Apocalypse Bureau—I'm willing to bet you ten thousand mangoes that even he doesn't have a clue what's going on with Job. 'Classified,' he says. You know what that means. It means he doesn't have a *freaking clue*!"

Mercury was now pacing back and forth under the palm tree, shaking his fists in agitation. "And Cravutius? One of the top seraphim. You think *he* knows anything? Of course not! I mean, sure, maybe he's got a few more details than Uzziel, but does he really know anything? Does he know, in the grand scheme of things, why any of this is happening? Hell, even these supposed 'Eternals,' if they exist, probably don't even know the full story. You see what I'm saying? This guy sits here in a pile of ashes trying to make sense of the Universe, and he has absolutely no idea just how far out of his league he is. He wants to know why God is picking on him. I mean, hello? Assuming that God exists, Job should be thrilled that God takes any notice of him at all. You know what I mean, Elihu?"

Mercury looked around, but Elihu was not to be found. Mercury had been talking to himself. "Brilliant," he muttered. He looked over at Job and found that Elihu was addressing him and the other men.

"What the hell…?" Mercury murmured. He strained to hear what Elihu was saying, but a breeze had picked up and was muffling his speech. A storm was gathering in the west.

After some time, Elihu ran off, trailing the kite in the air behind him. A gust of wind caught the kite, and the boy let out a bit of string, letting it climb higher.

Meanwhile, Job's hands were raised and he was crying out to the heavens. It began to rain.

"Wait!" yelled Mercury after Elihu. "What did you tell him?"

Elihu smiled and yelled something back.

"What?" yelled Mercury.

"It works!" hollered Elihu.

"What works?"

"The kite!" hollered Elihu. "There was nothing wrong with it! It just needs wind to fly!"

"That's fantastic," said Mercury. "But what did you..." But Elihu was too far away to hear him.

Rain was now coming down hard. Lightning flashed in the distance. Job's three friends were trying desperately to get him to leave his ash heap, but he was oblivious to them, raising his hands to the heavens and shouting incomprehensibly. Finally, the three men left without him to seek shelter.

Mercury, confused and now soaking wet and shivering in the cold, tried to make sense of the situation. What had Elihu said to Job? And what the hell was Job doing? Had he finally lost his mind completely? And what was up with the weather?

"Hey!" he yelled to Job, forgetting his oath of noninterference. Job, taking no notice, continued to yell and wave his hands in the air.

Mercury walked a few steps closer. "Hey!" he yelled. "What are you doing? Are you cursing—"

As he spoke, there was a blinding flash and a tremendous boom. The earth shook and Mercury fell to the ground. Looking behind him, he saw that the tree he had been sitting under had splintered into thousands of pieces. A fire blazed on the remains of the stump, sizzling and hissing violently in the downpour. Still Job took no notice.

"OK, then!" Mercury exclaimed. "I'm going to go ahead and figure that you've cursed God and that it's not really safe to hang around you anymore. Good luck!" And he left Job alone to howl in the rain.

TWELVE

It took Christine and Jacob a good ten minutes to break free of the unruly crowd. Once they were alone on the street, however, they became painfully aware of how exposed they were. Daltrey and Ruiz had probably put out an APB on them as soon as they had noticed their captives were missing. The area was swarming with police; it was only a matter of time before they were spotted. To make matters worse, Jacob and Christine were both bleary-eyed and exhausted. Adrenaline and hyperawareness had given way to the barely conscious placing of one foot in front of the other to keep moving. They were in no shape to run or even to spot danger in time to run from it. They were, in short, sitting ducks.

"We need to find a place to rest," said Christine. "Someplace out of sight."

Jacob nodded. "There are some hotels up ahead. I think the Ritz-Carlton is up here somewhere."

"Do you have any money?" Christine asked.

Jacob shook his head grimly. Daltrey had taken his wallet, as well as Christine's purse and both of their cell phones. Christine felt in her pocket, pulling out a few crumpled bills and some change.

"Seven dollars and thirty-six cents," she said. "Too bad the Ritz-Carlton isn't a Motel 6. And it's not 1962."

"Maybe they'll let us rest in the lobby for a bit," Jacob suggested.

They trudged down the street in the direction of the Ritz.

Christine was jolted out of her reverie by the strident hiccup of a siren behind her, the sound that a squad car makes when the polyester-clad misanthrope behind the wheel wants to remind pedestrians who's boss. Christine and Jacob were suddenly bathed in harsh white light. Glancing over her shoulder, Christine judged that the car was maybe fifty feet away.

"This way!" whispered Jacob, tugging on Christine's sleeve. He took off down an alley between a 7-Eleven and a Taco Bell. The police car halted at the curb in front of the alley, its spotlight throwing long shadows ahead of them. Behind them they heard the squawking of police radio but no footsteps. The cop wasn't chasing them.

That didn't mean much, of course. These days, cops don't do much chasing, either by car or on foot. Chasing is strenuous and dangerous work. Everybody knows that car chases are dangerous, of course, but people often unfairly discount the pitfalls of an old-fashioned foot chase. You could trip over something, or get shot at, or get hit in the face with a two-by-four. Your car could get broken into or stolen while you're out pursuing justice the old-fashioned way. And that's not even to mention the ever-present threat of pulling a hamstring. Even the most robust agent of the law was at risk for a pulled hamstring when breaking into a sprint after sitting behind the wheel of a squad car for six hours. Much is made of the long arm of the law, but its Achilles' heel is insufficiently limber hamstrings.

What modern police forces lack in tendonal pliancy, though, they make up for in numbers and good use of controlled bursts of radiation. The officer who declined to chase Christine and Jacob, for instance, was instead transmitting a burst of radiation that was the analog equivalent of the phrase *Two fugitives heading north on foot in an alley off K Street, between Twenty-First and Twenty-Second. Caucasian female and an African American male. May be armed. Request backup.*

This message was received by another police car, and as a result, by the time Christine and Jacob emerged from the alley onto L Street, that police car was lying in wait for them at the end of the street. "You two, stop right there!" called an amplified voice.

"This way!" Jacob urged again, leading Christine into the middle of the street. Tires screeched and horns blared. Christine was too frazzled and worn down to fully appreciate the danger of their situation, her awareness lost in a myriad of glaring lights and loud noises. It was all she could do to keep Jacob in sight and follow numbly after him. He darted down another alley, and Christine followed. Twenty seconds later they emerged in the parking lot of a Best Western. Yet another police car was pulling into the lot, maybe a hundred yards away. It stopped just inside, shining its spotlight around the lot. Christine and Jacob ducked behind a nearby minivan.

They were fenced in. The only ways out were past the police car at the exit or back through the alley they had just come through. Very soon, more police cars would arrive. The police would form a perimeter and execute a thorough search of the area. There was no escape.

"Hey," said Jacob, pointing to something in the distance. "Isn't that Harry Giddings's organization?"

Christine looked where he was pointing. Behind the hotel, a bus pulled up that bore the unmistakable *CH* of her late boss's grassroots evangelical organization known as the Covenant Holders.

"Damn it," moaned Christine.

"What?" asked Jacob. "I thought you worked for Harry. Maybe these folks can help us."

"Ugh," said Christine ambivalently. When Harry was alive, Christine hated relying on his largesse, and she had always vaguely looked down on the Covenant Holders, thinking of them as mindless sheep. The last thing she wanted was to beg them for help. She imagined Harry looking down on her from Heaven and laughing.

"I don't think we have much choice," said Jacob. "It looks like they're about to pull out. If we can get on that bus, we might be able to slip out of here before the trap closes."

Too exhausted to fight, Christine mumbled assent, and they made their way across the parking lot, sprinting from car to car while the spotlight was pointed in another direction. Finally they reached the bus and made their way as nonchalantly as possible through the assembled Covenant Holders loading up their luggage and sipping at Styrofoam cups of coffee in the wee morning hours.

No begging turned out to be necessary. Christine and Jacob presented themselves as tourists from Los Angeles who had been mugged, and the Covenant Holders practically tripped over each other offering them aid. Several of them even made the point of mentioning what an "attractive couple" they were—which Christine belatedly realized was a reference to Jacob being black. It was like they expected to get extra righteousness points for overlooking the fact that they were a "mixed couple." Christine was too tired to make an issue of it.

The group had traveled from Los Angeles to Washington to meet with President Babcock about the Anaheim Event. Many of them had lost friends and family members in the mysterious implosion of Anaheim Stadium, and they had been invited to the White House for a special ceremony. Now they were packing up for their trip home. They seemed oddly upbeat, considering the somber purpose of their trip.

"We've got plenty of room, if you want to ride back with us," said a young man named Gary, who was evidently a youth pastor at a church in Glendale. Christine and Jacob anxiously agreed. Jacob had no particular reason to go to Los Angeles, but he certainly couldn't stay in DC.

The bus pulled out not five minutes later, passing several more police cars on the way in. Christine smiled as she watched police officers erecting a cordon behind them. "Somebody must be looking out for us," she said, turning to Jacob across the aisle.

Jacob grunted noncommittally.

"You OK?" asked Christine.

"Fine," said Jacob. But he seemed to be slipping back into his pre-escape trance.

"Seriously," Christine went on, trying to prod him out of his funk. "It's a miracle we got out of there. I mean, what are the odds…"

"One in one," Jacob muttered.

"What?"

"The odds of what has already happened having happened are always one in one. One hundred percent."

"That's dumb," replied Christine.

Jacob shrugged.

"You're saying that we were bound to escape, no matter what we did?"

"I'm saying that what happened happened and that it's pointless to talk about probability in that context."

"So you never look back on something that just happened and think, 'Wow, that was really strange. I didn't expect that to happen'?"

"Of course some events are unexpected," Jacob answered tiredly. "And if you compare similar situations, there are going to be outliers. That is, in some cases, events are going to occur that appear out of the norm. But the fact is that every situation is unique, and that unusual events are expected to occur occasionally, as part of a long-term distribution pattern. You just happen to notice the unusual events, because they are unusual."

"Unusual," repeated Christine. "You mean like someone flying into outer space and imploding the moon with a glass apple?"

"That was an atypical scenario," said Jacob, in what Christine thought was a solid candidate for Biggest Understatement of All Time. "I will grant you that there were some natural forces at work there that I don't fully comprehend."

"What makes you think they were *natural* forces?" Christine asked. "What qualifies as *super*natural in your book?"

"I don't think there's any such thing as supernatural forces," answered Jacob. "More precisely, I don't think *supernatural* is a useful term. When you say something is supernatural, what you're really saying is that it's *un*natural, which is a negative definition. It's basically saying that there is a class of phenomena that we understand, which we call *natural* phenomena, and then there's a class of stuff that we don't understand, which we call *supernatural.*

So when you say something is supernatural, all you're really saying is that you don't understand it. And that's not a property of the phenomenon; it's a property of the observer of the phenomenon. In other words, a television set would be supernatural to a Neanderthal, because television falls outside of the Neanderthal's understanding of what is natural. But you and I know there is nothing supernatural about television. A smart Neanderthal would classify television as something that he doesn't understand, not as something that is intrinsically inexplicable—that is, not something that's supernatural." Jacob's eyes drooped as he talked. His speech had become almost robotic; he seemed to be lulling himself to sleep with his own postulating.

"So you think Mercury flew to the moon with some kind of invisible jetpack? Some sort of technological innovation that the angels haven't shared with humans?"

"I'm sure it's not that simple," said Jacob, yawning widely. "But yes, I think there is some sort of natural explanation. As Arthur C. Clarke said, 'Any sufficiently advanced technology is indistinguishable from magic.' Maybe these so-called angels are more technologically advanced than we are. Or maybe their technology has simply advanced in a different direction than ours."

"*So-called* angels?" asked Christine. "You don't think those were angels in Kenya? You don't believe that Mercury and Michelle and the lot are angels?"

Jacob shrugged. "I don't know what they are. But *angel* is a word with supernatural connotations. Using a word like that indicates that you've given up trying to understand them. That they are somehow beyond the realm of human understanding, which I don't buy. I'm going to get some sleep."

With that, he curled up on the seat and closed his eyes.

"You know what I think?" asked Christine. "I think that refusing to use a word says just as much about someone's biases as using the word."

Jacob didn't respond. Within a minute, he was snoring.

Christine sighed and lay down in her own seat, using her wadded-up shirt as a pillow. She felt too wound up to sleep but was powerless against the comforting hum of the diesel engine reverberating through the bus.

THIRTEEN

"So what did Elihu say to you?" Mercury asked.

"Basically," said Job, "he told me that I was looking at things all wrong. It's kind of an obvious point in retrospect, but he helped me understand that everything isn't about me."

"Huh?" asked Mercury dimly.

"I was looking at it like, 'Why is this happening to me? What did I do wrong? How do I fix it?' But that's a dead-end way of thinking. I mean, self-reflection is all well and good, but ultimately you have to accept that there are going to be some things that you're never going to understand. If you insist that things make sense from your own finite, selfish perspective, you're never going to be happy. I accepted that there is a God who is running things, and that everything that was happening to me happened for a reason, even if I wasn't privy to what that reason was."

"Mystical mumbo jumbo," murmured Cain. Mercury and Job ignored him.

"So you never did curse God?" Mercury asked.

Job shook his head. "Haven't you read the Bible? There's a whole book about me."

"Yeah, but you know how people exaggerate. Like how Goliath wasn't really nine feet tall."

"Nine and a half," said Cain.

Job nodded.

Mercury looked from Job to Cain and back again. "Goliath was *not* nine and a half feet tall."

"Were you there?" asked Job.

"No, but...the tallest man on record was less than nine feet tall. The human frame simply can't support—"

"Crippling back problems," said Job. "He wasn't really a bad guy, but what are you going to do when you're the world's tallest man and you have the bad luck to be born a Philistine? They made him their champion. He had no choice. He was miserable. Could barely walk in that armor, much less fight anyone. I understand he leaned into that pebble. Poor guy."

"Forget I said anything," said Mercury.

"They fudged the ending of my story a bit," said Job. "I guess Heaven felt pretty bad about screwing me over, so they gave me eternal life. Well, technically they gave me ten thousand years, I guess. They sent an angel to explain it, but I wasn't really paying attention."

"How long has it been?" asked Mercury.

"Hmm," replied Job. "Must be getting close."

"How can you not know?" asked Mercury.

"I don't count the days," said Job. "That's Cain's gig. I focus on living."

"Don't look at me," said Cain. "I don't know what year he was born. We didn't meet until he was already a few hundred years old. My best guess is that it's been around nine thousand, nine hundred years, give or take a century."

Nearly ten thousand years! thought Mercury. Most angels weren't that old. Hell, Mercury wasn't that old. Well, technically he was probably older, but only if you counted however many centuries had elapsed between the implosion of the moon and his reincorporation here. The number of years that Mercury had actually experienced was around seven thousand, his inception date being roughly 5000 BC. What would it be like to experience ten thousand years trapped on the Mundane Plane? Even the angels, who had the freedom to travel many different planes, tended to get bored after a few thousand years. Job's life—and Cain's too—must have been nearly unbearable.

Yet Job didn't seem like he was suffering. He seemed, despite the fact that he lived amid the rubble of human civilization, perfectly content. Cain, on the other hand, seemed constantly ill at ease. He frequently looked into the distance, apparently trying to gauge how far away the fog was.

Mercury suddenly stood and climbed onto a nearby pile of rubble to get a better vantage point. He turned slowly, taking in a 360-degree view. There was no doubt about it anymore: the fog was creeping closer in all directions. Buildings that had been fully visible a few minutes earlier were now shrouded in mist.

"What is up with this fog?" Mercury asked. "It's…not normal."

Cain laughed. "No," he said. "It most certainly is not."

"This whole situation is weird," said Mercury. "I mean, the two of you, playing Ping-Pong in the rubble while Ernie and the gang huddle underground, poking at the fire. Is this really what the world has come to?"

"This is the way the world ends," said Cain. "Not with a bang, but with a whimper."

"Boy, I bet you're a riot at parties," said Mercury to Cain. Cain shrugged.

"I'm more optimistic," said Job. "I believe that there is a reason for everything. Even this."

Cain snorted. "You and your *reasons*," Cain scoffed. "There's always some grand plan, some *deus ex machina* that's going to make everything turn out OK. How much longer are you going to keep up the show, Job? You can see the fog as well as I can, always creeping closer. Are you really going to insist on spouting platitudes with your last breath?"

Job sighed heavily. "Not platitudes, my friend. It's called *faith*. And yes, I still believe, despite overwhelming evidence to the contrary, that somehow everything is going to work out for the best."

Cain spat at the ground. "You see what I have to deal with?" he asked Mercury. "The perpetual Pollyanna of the Apocalypse."

"Dismiss me if you like," said Job. "But you know what I've been through. You know I've suffered every bit as much as you."

"Have you now?" asked Cain.

"If you've suffered more," retorted Job, "it's only because you chose a life of suffering. Your curse is in your head."

"In my head!" Cain growled. "So I imagined being cursed to wander the Earth for all eternity, did I?"

Job sighed again. "Why don't you tell Mercury your story, and he can judge for himself."

Mercury was at that moment more interested in the insidious fog that was threatening to envelope them, but he bit his tongue, afraid to anger Cain further.

"You know my story," Cain began. "The first part of it, anyway." He recited, like a bored Sunday school student:

And Adam knew Eve his wife; and she conceived, and bare Cain, and said, I have gotten a man from the LORD. And she again bare his brother Abel. And Abel was a keeper of sheep, but Cain was a tiller of the ground. And in process of time it came to pass, that Cain brought of the fruit of the ground an offering unto the LORD. And Abel, he also brought of the firstlings of his flock and of the fat thereof. And the LORD had respect unto Abel and to his offering: But unto Cain and to his offering he had not respect. And Cain was very wroth, and his countenance fell. And the LORD said unto Cain, Why art thou wroth? And why is thy countenance fallen? If thou doest well, shalt thou not be accepted? And if thou doest not well, sin lieth at the door. And unto thee shall be his desire, and thou shalt rule over him. And Cain talked with Abel his brother: and it came to pass, when they were in the field, that Cain rose up against Abel his brother, and slew him. And the LORD said unto Cain, Where is Abel thy brother? And he said, I know not: Am I my brother's keeper? And he said, What hast thou done? The voice of thy brother's blood crieth unto me from the ground. And now art thou cursed from the earth, which hath opened her mouth to receive thy brother's blood from thy hand; When thou tillest the ground, it shall not henceforth yield unto thee her strength; a fugitive and a vagabond shalt thou be in the earth. And Cain said unto the LORD, My punishment is greater than I can bear. Behold, thou hast driven me out this day from the face of the earth; and from thy face shall I be hid; and I shall be a fugitive and a vagabond in the earth; and it shall come to pass, that every one that findeth me shall slay me. And the LORD said unto him, therefore whosoever slayeth Cain, vengeance shall be

> taken on him sevenfold. And the LORD set a mark upon Cain, lest any finding him should kill him.

When he had finished, they sat in silence for a moment. "Wow," Mercury said at last. "So it happened just like that? I mean, no offense, but I always kind of thought that story was allegorical. You know, like Plato's 'Myth of the Cave.' "

"The myth of what?" asked Job.

"The Myth of the Cave," said Mercury. "It's an allegory about knowledge. These people live in a cave and try to make sense of the world by looking at shadows on the wall."

"I don't get it," said Job. "Why don't they just go outside?"

"I think they're chained up or something," said Mercury. "Honestly, it never made much sense to me. I asked Socrates to explain it once, but he wasn't very helpful. You could never get a straight answer out of that guy. He seemed to think I was being too literal about it. He said sometimes you just have to take a bizarre situation as the writer presents it and not worry too much about how ridiculous it is."

Job nodded. "There's something to that, I think."

Cain continued as if he hadn't heard them. "I've been around since the beginning of the world. I lived through all of it. The rise of civilization, the birth of Christianity, the rise and fall of the Roman Empire, the Middle Ages, the Renaissance, the Reformation, French Revolution, World Wars One, Two, Three, Four, and Five, and finally the gradual decline of all human civilization over the last few thousand years."

"I don't get it," said Mercury. "I mean, what's the point of making you go through all of that?"

"The *point*?" growled Cain. "There is no point! It just goes on and on, for no reason. 'Life is a tale told by an idiot, full of sound and fury, signifying nothing.' There's your point!"

"Like I said," interjected Job, "he's a tad bitter. Personally, I like to think that God is trying to teach me something."

Cain snorted again.

"Like what?" asked Mercury.

"Well, before I lost everything, I thought I had everything figured out," said Job. "I was a good man. I followed all the rules, and I was rewarded for it. But ultimately I was a rather shallow person. I was like a dog who obeyed his master's commands because he had learned that's how you get the treat. I was good because being good worked for me. I learned through my suffering that the sort of mechanical religion I was pushing ultimately isn't any different than the nihilism of someone like my friend Cain here. Believing in something because it benefits you isn't any better than believing in nothing at all. They both lead to the same place. No offense," he added, glancing at Cain.

Cain shrugged. "I used to believe in something too, you know. I was a scientist. I thought I had figured out the secrets underlying reality. The problem is that once you've figured them out, the mysteries of the universe are just more data. And there are always more mysteries to figure out."

"But isn't that the point?" Mercury asked. "I mean, aren't you supposed to find meaning and purpose in the figuring out?"

"Sure," agreed Cain. "That works for about five hundred years. But here's the thing: science is a closed system. There's no bridge between science and what you call *meaning* or *purpose*. You can fool yourself into thinking that you're creating your own meaning by exploring the nature of the Universe, but when you spend all day dismissing hypotheses because of insufficient supporting data, eventually you have to accept that meaning and purpose are themselves unsupported hypotheses."

Mercury, puzzled, looked to Job for help. Job just shrugged.

"Think of it this way," Cain went on. "When I was Bacon, I tried to—"

"Hang on," said Mercury. "When you were *bacon*?"

"He was Francis Bacon for a while," explained Job. "Father of empiricism."

"Oh, OK," said Mercury, as if that made perfect sense.

"As I was saying," Cain went on impatiently, "when I was Bacon, I tried to maintain my belief in both God and science. I mean, belief in God struck me as absurd, but I tried to convince myself that was all part of faith. The more absurd a belief was, in the light of the known facts, the more faith it required to believe in it."

"I have to stop you again," said Mercury. "Didn't God Himself mark you for murdering Abel? I mean, in the story, it sounds like you and God were pretty tight. At least until, you know."

"Please," said Cain dismissively. "The story may not be allegorical, but the author took a few liberties. I never actually *saw* God. I never had any actual evidence of His existence. Despite this, I maintained my belief in Him while spending my days engaged in scientific pursuits. But eventually I realized that I was essentially maintaining two competing belief systems. Realizing I had taken my Bacon identity as far as it could go, I faked my own death—again—and spent some time reflecting. I actually tried to give up science for a while and became a Presbyterian minister in Scotland. But my empirical bent eventually reasserted itself, and I took up philosophy again. You may have read some of my stuff. I wrote under the name David Hume."

"Wow, you were Hume too?" marveled Job. "I suppose I should have guessed."

Cain nodded wearily. "As Hume, I did my best to rid myself of superstitions and other notions not supported by direct evidence. The problem is, that doesn't leave you with much. Ultimately you just have to accept certain things as true. For example, I can't prove scientifically that there's any correlation between my senses and what actually exists. I can't prove that because I see fog in the distance, there is actually fog in the distance. Any proof I give will rest on additional observations, and observations rely on the senses. So ultimately I just have to say, screw it, if I see something, it's probably real. And frankly that's pretty arbitrary. It's like a blind and deaf man saying, 'I don't believe in automobiles, except for this bus, because this bus just ran me over.' And then he gets hit by a motorcycle, and he says, 'Well, OK, I guess I accept the existence of the motorcycle too.' It may make the blind and deaf man feel better to know that he's not accepting the existence of automobiles on somebody else's assurances, but that doesn't mean he's acting rationally. And then there's the whole *is-ought* problem."

"The which?" asked Mercury.

"The is-ought problem," repeated Cain. "Science only tells you what *is*. It can't tell you what *ought* to be. It can't help you make moral judgments. It's like those people who used to say homosexuality was a sin because animals don't engage in homosexuality. This is the way it *is*, they'd say, so this is the way it *ought to be*. Of course, that's nonsense. On top of which, anybody who's ever raised cattle can tell you that animals can get pretty damn kinky when the opportunity arises. Er, what was I talking about?"

"Is and ought," Job prompted.

"Right," said Cain. "Ideas of meaning and purpose, unfortunately, belong to the realm of *ought*. You can't get to meaning or purpose simply by observing things. Those are value concepts. I mean, you can observe a chair that's missing a leg and say, 'That's a bad chair,' but only because you know what a chair's purpose is. If you were an eighteen-foot-tall knee-less Martian who had no experience with human beings, and you found a three-legged chair floating in deep space, you'd have no reason to call it a bad chair."

Mercury and Job exchanged confused glances.

"The point is," Cain went on impatiently, "at the end of the day, I can say, 'I've discovered the principle of electromagnetism, and therefore my life has meaning,' but that's just another unproven proposition. I might just as well say, 'I ate scrambled eggs for breakfast, and therefore an intelligent, loving Creator exists.' You can't prove that your life has meaning because of science any more than you can prove that God exists because of what you had for breakfast."

"But why does everything have to be proved?" asked Job. "Can't you just enjoy the process of discovery and call it good enough?"

"Of course," said Cain. "But if I'm going to arbitrarily find joy in scientific discovery, without any rational basis for that joy, then I can't very well condemn someone for believing in God because it makes him happy. For that matter, I can't condemn someone for believing in unicorns or leprechauns. If personal enjoyment is the standard, then all I can do is argue that when it comes down to it, science is more fulfilling than unicorns. And frankly, I don't know that it is. It might be really enjoyable to believe in unicorns. I just don't know."

"Unicorns are overrated," said Mercury. "Gamey."

There was a moment of awkward silence.

Job got to his feet and walked back to the Ping-Pong table. As if following an unspoken agreement, Cain followed. The two began another game.

After some time, Mercury broke the silence. "So where does that leave you?" he asked Cain. "I mean, with your outlook on life."

"Well," said Cain. "I was an existentialist for a while. I don't really like to talk about it. Fucking existentialists. I guess these days I'm a nihilist, like Job says."

"That doesn't sound like much fun."

Cain shrugged, gazing at the fog in the distance. "I just want it to be over."

Mercury shuddered. "What happens when it gets here? The 'Existence Horizon'? "

"Nothing," said Cain.

"We don't know for sure," said Job. "Ha!" This last exclamation was in response to Cain's failure to return Job's wickedly fast serve.

"You're still down thirteen to eleven," grumbled Cain. "Don't get cocky. Nothing's going to happen."

"When you say nothing is going to happen," asked Mercury pensively, "do you mean that nothing is going to happen, or that, you know, *nothing* is going to happen?"

"I mean that reality will cease to exist," Cain answered, while deftly returning Job's volley. "Time itself will cease to exist, and with it the past, present, and future will be annihilated. Nothing will ever have existed."

"Oh," replied Mercury. "So the bad kind of nothing, then."

"Neither good nor bad," replied Cain. "Nothing just *is*."

"You mean it isn't," said Mercury.

"Ha!" Cain yelled as Job dove for a shot and missed. "Fourteen, eleven. My serve."

"So you're saying that this little area of Manhattan is all that's left of the world? How is that possible? What about the Sun? Does the Sun still exist?" Mercury peered at the gray sky, trying to pinpoint where the light was coming from.

"The Sun still exists, more or less," said Job. "It's been growing less distinct for a while. We haven't actually seen it for a couple hundred years. What's left is sort of a vague idea of the Sun."

"Don't even try to make sense of the physics," Cain warned. "You'll drive yourself batty. The laws of physics have broken down, along with everything else. Don't worry, though. It will all be over with soon."

"Are there other people around?" asked Mercury. "Or are we it?"

"I think we're pretty much it," said Job. "Us and the guys downstairs. Ernie and his gang."

"Yeah, what's up with them?" asked Mercury. "Is there something special about that fire they're huddled around? This is going to sound nuts, but it seemed like they were somehow observing human history through the fire. And not just observing it, meddling with it."

"It's possible," said Job. "Cause and effect are breaking down too. Can a group of hobos huddling around a fire retroactively change history? Sure, why not? It's always seemed a little arbitrary to me that causality can flow in only one direction."

Mercury held his head in his hands. This whole situation was completely absurd.

"Think of it this way," said Cain. "For most practical purposes, we live in a deterministic universe. By this I mean that if you could somehow know the exact state of a system at its starting point, then you could predict the exact state of the system at its ending point."

Mercury stared at Cain uncomprehendingly, his hands still on his head.

"Take this Ping-Pong ball. If I drop the ball, it's going to fall to the concrete and bounce in some seemingly unpredictable way until it finally comes to rest somewhere, probably a few feet away from where I dropped it. I say *seemingly unpredictable* because if you actually knew the exact position of the ball when I let go of it, the structure and composition of the ball, the texture and slant of the concrete, et cetera, you could predict exactly, within a thousandth of a millimeter, where the ball would end up. Got it?"

Mercury nodded.

"Now reverse the whole process. Let's say you know the exact position of the ball after it comes to a rest. Can you predict where the ball started out? That is, where it was when I let go of it?"

Mercury frowned. "It doesn't seem like it."

"Right!" said Cain. "Because you'd be missing some data. When the ball hit the ground, it displaced a minute amount of concrete, and it also converted a minute amount of kinetic energy to heat. Now let's say that you have access to that information as well: you know exactly how much concrete was displaced and where it went, and you know exactly how much heat was radiated and where it ended up. Now could you tell me where the ball started out?"

"I suppose so," said Mercury. "Theoretically."

"Right again!" exclaimed Cain. "So you see?"

Mercury shook his head.

"You can predict the future using information from the past, and you can predict the past using information from the future!" said Cain. "In other words, we think of the initial state of the system determining the end state of the system, but you could just as well say that the end state of the system determines the initial state. Which is just another way of saying that *the future causes the past*. And now that all of reality has been condensed into this one small area, everything that we do will theoretically have massive repercussions on the past. Hell, my scoring of that last point against Job may have caused the extinction of the dinosaurs for all we know. So could Ernie and his friends be meddling with human history by poking at a fire with a stick? Absolutely! And all of this, of course, underscores the absolute absurdity of the human condition. You could sneeze and kill half the population of Europe."

Mercury wasn't sure he followed all of this, but one thing was certain: he was *not* going to sneeze.

The fog continued to creep closer. Wispy gray tendrils were caressing a corroded street sign just down the road.

"But…I don't understand," Mercury said. "Was Manhattan built on top of a haunted leper colony or something? Where did this fog, or whatever it is, come from?"

Job shook his head. "I think that's the wrong question. The question is, where did everything else come from? Why does anything exist at all?"

"Look," said Mercury. "All I'm saying is that where I'm from, there's no Creeping Fog of Nonexistence threatening to wipe out reality. So my question is, where did it come from? What changed?"

"The fog has always been there," answered Cain. "It's been trying to annihilate us since our Universe came into being in a freak accident six billion years ago. It's picked up steam in the past few thousand years, so to speak."

"But why?" Mercury asked. "Why is it advancing so quickly now? What changed?"

Job and Cain exchanged glances.

"It isn't exactly clear," said Job. "Something seems to have happened in the early part of the twenty-first century. We've heard plenty of rumors—more like myths—about what happened. They all seem to center on something called Wormwood."

"Wormwood?" asked Mercury. "What's that?"

"Like I said," Job replied, "it isn't clear. In most accounts, it's some sort of artifact, a crucible of great evil. The evil is awoken by an angel, who doesn't seem to have a name. He's simply referred to as a 'lost angel' who somehow gains control over the Wormwood. Usually Lucifer is said to be involved."

"Lucifer," snorted Cain quietly.

"What about him?" asked Job. "Is there something you haven't told me about Lucifer's involvement with Wormwood?"

"I've been waiting for the right time," said Cain. "I guess now is as good as any. It's true that Lucifer was involved, but he was only a tool of destiny. As was your mysterious 'lost angel.' The fact is, though," Cain answered, savoring each syllable, "Wormwood was *my* doing. It couldn't have happened without me."

"What couldn't have happened?" asked Mercury.

Cain grinned wickedly. "The destruction of Heaven itself."

FOURTEEN

Christine awoke hours later, feeling groggy but somewhat rested. Sunlight streamed through the bus windows. The bus had stopped at a fast-food place somewhere in Virginia. Jacob was still sleeping soundly, so Christine bought a couple of breakfast sandwiches and two cups of coffee with the little money she had. One of the Covenant Holders, a roundish woman named Debbie, struck up a conversation with her.

"So neat to see the nation's capital," she said, beaming at Christine. "So much history."

Christine nodded politely.

"This is my first time here," she added. "Washington, DC, I mean."

Christine smiled.

"My husband, Phil, was a huge history buff. He would have loved to see Washington."

Christine nodded and smiled. Debbie smiled back. An awkward silence crept up on them. Christine realized that she had missed her cue.

"Your husband!" she said, a little too loudly. "Is he…?"

"Phil went to be with his Lord. He was one of the elect."

"The elect?"

Debbie nodded, smiling beatifically. "He was in the stadium. He was one of the one hundred and forty-four thousand who were called home ahead of the Rapture."

Christine's mouth went dry. This woman's husband had been killed just six weeks earlier, along with tens of thousands of other people, and here she was, standing in a Burger Giant in Virginia, chatting with Christine about how "neat" it was to see the capital.

"Do they…" she started. "Is that an exact number? A hundred and forty-four thousand? I haven't been watching the news lately."

Debbie nodded. "That's the number in Revelation," she said. " 'Then I looked, and there before me was the Lamb, standing on Mount Zion, and with him a hundred and forty-four thousand who had his name and his Father's name written on their foreheads.' I'm so happy that Phil was one of the chosen. I hope he remembers me when I get to Heaven."

Christine was baffled by this turn of the conversation. The last she had heard, the total dead and missing from the Anaheim Event had been estimated at around a hundred and fifty thousand. About a third of these had been attendees of the Covenant Holders conference; the rest were people who happened to be in the vicinity of the stadium at the time—including a hundred or so assorted atheists, feminists, and pro-homosexual activists who had been loitering around the entrance, harassing the attendees as they entered. Had God called them all home? She supposed the atheists and fundamentalists meeting each other in Heaven would both have a fair amount of explaining to do.

"So the Rapture…is that happening soon?" Christine asked.

"No one knows the day or the hour," said Debbie. "But the signs are all around us. The hundred and forty-four thousand being called home, a third of the moon falling out of the sky, war in the Middle East...The End will be here soon, praise God."

Christine forced a smile. "Praise God," she echoed faintly.

When she returned to the bus, Jacob was awake, staring out the bus window. As she approached, his head jerked back and he made that strange noise in his throat again. He was wearing a T-shirt that one of their fellow pilgrims had given him. It read "Darwin is dead. Jesus is ALIVE!" Jacob had scowled when he saw it but suspended his principles so that he could remove the stained and reeking polo shirt he had been wearing for two days. Christine had changed in the restaurant bathroom, peeling off her dirty blouse and sticky bra to put on a sweatshirt that had Matthew 12:30 printed on the front of it, inadvertently causing her breasts to threaten, "Whoever is not with me is against me." Jacob blushed and looked away as she approached.

"Got you some breakfast," she said, sitting down next to him.

"Oh," said Jacob. "Thanks. I don't drink coffee, though. The caffeine..."

"Sorry," said Christine, who was secretly thrilled to have doubled her coffee supply for the morning. She handed him the sandwich.

"These people kind of creep me out," he whispered to her.

Christine laughed. "You and me both."

They ate in silence. "So," Christine said when they had finished, "what was that back there? With that jerk in DC? What did you do to him?"

Jacob smiled meekly. He tapped the center of his chest. "A well-aimed blow to the solar plexus will incapacitate the receiver for a good sixty seconds or so. I've had some basic hand-to-hand combat training."

Christine frowned. "That looked like more than basic combat training," she said. "You moved so fast I didn't even know what happened."

Jacob appeared to blush again, although it was difficult to tell with his dark complexion. His head jerked back and he made the noise in his throat again. It was something between a grunt and a cough.

"Shit," Jacob muttered to himself.

"What is it?" Christine asked. "Something wrong?"

"I don't have my medication," Jacob replied. "My tics are getting worse."

"Ticks? You have ticks?"

"*Tics*," said Jacob. "No *k* at the end. Involuntary muscle movements. It's part of my condition."

"Your condition?"

Jacob sighed. Clearly this was not something he wanted to talk about, but given their situation, he seemed resigned to having to explain it to Christine.

"Condition," said Jacob, with a touch of bitterness. "Syndrome. Syndromes. Call it what you want. They have names, but the names aren't very helpful. People substitute names for understanding something. Give it a name, put it in a box, don't have to think about it anymore. Unless you're the one in the box."

"OK," said Christine hesitantly. "So help me understand."

"One name they use is Tourette's Syndrome," Jacob said. "I also have Asperger's. And clinical depression. I take medication for all of it."

"You have Tourette's?" asked Christine. "Isn't that where you can't stop swearing?" She felt a little queasy as she imagined Jacob letting loose a torrent of profanity while trapped on a bus with two dozen religious zealots.

"That's coprolalia," Jacob said. "It affects fewer than ten percent of people with Tourette's. Tourette's is characterized by tics—sudden, repetitive movements. They can be either motor tics or phonic tics. I have both." As he said this, his head jerked backward, and he made the throat noise again. "I take medication for it, but I've been off it for a few days, so the tics are getting worse."

"Does it hurt?" Christine asked.

Jacob shrugged. "It's like a cough. Something that you have to do. Sometimes you can hold it in for a while, but eventually it comes out. Of course, when you cough, people don't give you weird looks and hold their children closer. It does have one positive side effect, though."

"Really?" asked Christine. "What's that?"

"Do you have a coin?" asked Jacob. "Anything, a penny, quarter, whatever."

She nodded, pulling a dime from her pocket. "That's a sizeable percentage of my savings, so don't waste it," she warned him.

Jacob laughed. "Hold it on your palm."

Christine held out her right hand, with the dime resting in the center of her palm. "Now what?"

"Close your hand."

Christine closed her hand.

"Now open it."

She did. The coin was gone.

Jacob smiled, holding the coin between his thumb and forefinger.

"Holy..." Christine gasped. "How the hell did you do that?"

Jacob laughed again. "Why'd you close your hand so slowly?"

"I didn't...OK, let's do it again."

He gave Christine the dime and she once again placed it on her palm. "Tell me when to close," she said.

"Close," he said. She snapped her hand shut. This time, she noticed Jacob moving, almost imperceptibly. He held the dime in his fingers.

"No one can move that fast," said Christine, as if she suspected Jacob of being possessed by demons.

"When I'm off my meds, I perceive time differently," explained Jacob. "Everything moves very slowly around me."

"You're like The Flash," said Christine in awe.

Jacob smiled weakly. "Kind of," he agreed. "If The Flash had uncontrollable muscle spasms and crippling social anxiety."

The bus got back on the road. Evidently they were going to travel straight through to LA, with several people taking turns driving. They drove all day, stopping every few hours for a meal or a restroom break. At the first stop, Christine and Jacob's newfound born-again friends took up a collection for them, which came to an embarrassing $316.41. Whatever faults these people had, they were certainly generous.

Sometime after dinner, Christine began to see signs for Oklahoma City. Christine had been to Oklahoma City only once before, when she was very young. Her family had been on vacation in Texas when the Murrah Federal Building was destroyed in a terrorist attack, and her father had thought that seeing the site of the bombing would be a good lesson in current events. There hadn't been much to see: just a pile of rubble surrounded by police barriers. Her father had tried to explain to her that the pile of rocks was all that was left of a government building after a very troubled man had exploded a truck bomb. Christine didn't get it. She wanted to know what the building had looked like. Had it looked like the Alamo? No, she was told, it had just been a regular old square building. She felt like they were putting her on. Why would they drive six hours out of their way to see a building that hadn't been anything special even *before* it had been blown up?

A few years later, when she realized the point of their detour, it still struck her as a bit odd. What had been the point of dragging a child to see the site of a horrific catastrophe that she couldn't possibly comprehend? She hadn't really understood it until very recently, when she had made her own pilgrimage to the site of the Anaheim Event. It was a way of coming to terms with the gaping nothingness that constantly loomed at the edges of human civilization. It took only one lunatic with a rented truck and a few thousand pounds of fertilizer and fuel oil to reduce to rubble a building that had taken hundreds of people years to build. And it took only one little glass apple to suck Anaheim Stadium right out of existence. She shuddered at the thought and looked up at the pathetic moon. Things could very easily have gone much worse—*would* have gone much worse if it weren't for Mercury's quick thinking and nerve.

Mercury.

Where the hell is he? she thought. The archangel Michelle had said that Mercury might be stranded on some remote plane with no way back to the known Universe. But something in the back of Christine's mind told her that wasn't right. No, she thought. This isn't over yet. The world is in too much danger, and I can't do this by myself. Somehow, he's got to come back.

Christine turned to look at Jacob, who was sleeping soundly, curled up in a fetal pose in the seat across the aisle. Occasionally his left hand would jerk wildly, as if he were shooing away an invisible insect. *Ticks*, thought Christine, smiling at the pun. The hand-jerking was almost cute, making Jacob resemble a dog that was dreaming of running. Certainly less annoying than the weird vocalizations and head-jerking he did when he was awake.

Her smile faded when she realized the pettiness of these thoughts. If she found the tics annoying, how much worse must it be for Jacob? The tics weren't something he *did*; they were something that *happened to him*. What would it be like to be unable to control your own body? To feel a near-constant compulsion to act in ways that appeared to observers as bizarre affectations, probably hinting at some severe underlying mental illness? Ironically, Jacob was probably the sanest person she had met since all of this stuff with the Apocalypse had begun. The extent of his neurosis was a debilitating social awkwardness—a condition that she could only assume was not helped by his uncontrollable muscle spasms. As amazing as Jacob's inhuman reaction speed was, she couldn't imagine Jacob wanting to be the way he was. In fact, he had specifically chosen otherwise, taking medication to suppress his symptoms. Presumably, the medication also suppressed what Christine had come to think of as Jacob's "ninja powers."

Despite Jacob's quirks, Christine was glad he had come along, and not just because she feared what the FBI would do to him. Having him near made her feel less alone.

Somehow her debriefing with Director Lubbers had spooked her more than her encounters with demons like Tiamat and Lucifer. There was something profoundly unnerving about the way Lubbers talked about Heaven as if it were just another security threat to be dealt with. She couldn't deny being a bit disillusioned with her own experience of Heaven, but somehow she still believed that underneath all the bureaucracy and infighting, there was something mystical and sublime—that Heaven was more than it appeared to be, that it was the source of some sort of ineffable power that gave people reason to hope, even in the most dire circumstances.

Lubbers had evidently come to the opposite conclusion: that Heaven was just another foreign dictatorship with an arsenal of dangerous weapons and interests at odds with those of the United States. As such, the logical course of action was to act quickly to neutralize the threat. In a demented sort of way, it made perfect sense—and that's precisely what terrified her.

FIFTEEN

Some 3,800 years after the Job debacle, Lucifer sat in a wheeled leather office chair in the center of the living room of his unassuming pink stucco house at 666 Lucifer Way, nestled among the plastic trees of the Hidden Oakes subdivision of Plane 3774d, also known as the Infernal Plane. The room was dominated by a semicircular bank of plasma screens that could be configured to display input from 1,024 different cameras placed in strategic locations scattered about the Mundane Plane. Currently, though, they were set to act as a single monitor displaying one gigantic image. For one hour a day, Lucifer took a break from his surveillance to indulge a guilty pleasure: drinking a tall, icy glass of Schweppes ginger ale and watching *The O'Reilly Factor*.

Bill's guest was an antiwar activist by the name of Medeia Sayed. Medeia was denouncing President Babcock's speech. "This is the exact sort of intentional ambiguity that got us into Iraq," she was saying. "Everybody knows this president wants to go to war with Syria, and now he's got an excuse. There is absolutely no reason to think the Syrians had anything to do with the destruction of the moon, but Babcock wants us to think—"

"Shut up, Medeia, you stupid whore!" howled Lucifer. He liked hurling epithets at Bill's guests. It helped him relax.

"Who do you think blew up the moon?" Bill asked pointedly.

"Yeah, Medeia, who the fuck blew up the moon, you ignorant bitch!" Lucifer added. He took a sip of ginger ale.

"I couldn't begin to speculate who was responsible for that," said Medeia.

"Well, you realize the president of the United States doesn't have that option, right?" asked Bill. "He can't just throw up his hands and say, 'Gosh, I don't know who did this, so I guess I'd better just ignore it.' "

"Zing!" yelled Lucifer.

"I'm not saying that he should ignore—"

"Yes you are, Medeia!" shouted Bill and Lucifer simultaneously. "You simpering diseased cunt!" added Lucifer.

"What I'm saying, Bill, is that as far as we know, the attack on the moon is completely unrelated to the ongoing troubles in the Middle East, and that it would be premature to—"

"You're premature!" screamed Lucifer, shaking so hard he nearly spilled his ginger ale. "You're the premature, syphilis-ridden retarded orphan daughter of Joseph Stalin and a goat!"

He downed the rest of his ginger ale. "Karl!" he yelled into the kitchen. "You're missing *O'Reilly*! And I need another ginger ale!"

After an initial rough period, Lucifer and Karl the Antichrist were getting along surprisingly well. They enjoyed many of the same reality programs, particularly *Jersey Shore*. Karl had been teaching Lucifer *Battlecraft* cheats, and Lucifer had been helping Karl on his epic rock opera, *Shakkara the Dragonslayer*. He had convinced Karl that any rock opera worth its salt had lots of satanic messages encoded in it. Karl hadn't seen the point of making the satanic messages hidden, and Lucifer had explained that they were meant to be subliminal.

"Sublibitable?" asked Karl.

"*Subliminal*," said Lucifer. "The messages can't be perceived by the conscious mind. They slip into your subconscious and make you think evil thoughts, like *sex* or *Coca-Cola*. Of course, your brain has to be trained to decode the messages."

"Trained? How do you do that?"

Lucifer explained that the training program had been dismantled in the early nineties as the subliminal marketing campaign hadn't led to the levels of Satanism and Coca-Cola consumption he had been aiming for. "For a while, though, we were running several million middle-schoolers through the training program every year. We'd show them a couple hundred advertisements with the pretext of warning them about the dangers of subliminal advertising. Liquor ads, cigarette ads, car commercials… hell, half of the ads they showed weren't even part of the program. It didn't matter. They had kids seeing satanic messages in *Scooby Doo* cartoons. There was a whole generation of teenage boys who couldn't see three ice cubes in a glass without getting an erection."

Karl didn't see the point of including backward messages in *Shakkara the Dragonslayer* when the target audience hadn't been trained to receive them. Lucifer tried to explain that these days it was more about the principle, but Karl wouldn't assent until Lucifer agreed that half of the messages would be about Karl.

Karl returned from the kitchen bearing two cans of ginger ale and a plate of pizza rolls. "What'd I miss?"

Lucifer took one of the ginger ales. "Bill is going to town on some libtard peacenik buttaface," said Lucifer.

"…just days after Israeli troops surrounded Damascus. And then, less than twenty-four hours after the Israeli prime minister hints that tactical nuclear weapons might be used, someone bombs the moon, making a pretty effective demonstration of the relatively limited capabilities of Israel's nuclear arsenal. Are you saying that's a coincidence?"

"Look, Bill," Medeia replied. "Obviously the Anaheim Event and Black Monday were both terrible tragedies, and America will not rest until it has found those responsible for these events and held them accountable…"

Lucifer sat open-mouthed, ready to deliver another barrage of obscenities, but the words didn't come. He found himself enthralled by what this Leftist loony had just said.

America will not rest until it has found those responsible for these events and held them accountable.

Yes, thought Lucifer. If there was one thing that America was good at, it was finding bad guys and punishing them. Evil was, to the American way of thinking, something that could be identified, rooted out, and destroyed. Lesser peoples seemed to think of evil as a sort of pervasive miasma that could occasionally be avoided, but Americans knew that evil was a discrete thing that existed out there somewhere, waiting to be hunted down and vanquished by those with the means and the courage to do so. Sometimes, of course, they needed a little shove in the right direction, like the time that Lucifer had one of his minions whisper in Dick Cheney's ear about weapons of mass destruction in Iraq.

"You're stupid, you stupid bitch!" Karl yelled at the TV.

"Shut up, Karl," snapped Lucifer.

No longer listening to the talking heads, Lucifer muted the channel. He had been in a bit of a funk lately, what with that asshole Mercury once again screwing up his attempt to destroy the world. Truth be told, he was also a little angry with himself for letting the opportunity slip through his fingers. He could have let the anti-bomb detonate on Earth rather than helping Mercury dispose of it on the moon, but that would have resulted in Lucifer's eternal incarceration in Heaven. He would have made his point, sure, but that was a steep price to pay.

In the end, Lucifer had made a leap of faith. He had trusted what he felt to be true about the Charlie Nyx books: that somehow the completion of the series would result in the end of the world. He couldn't explain how he knew it; he just knew it. All he had to do was ensure that the series was completed and the world would end, putting to an end all of Heaven's vain plotting, and revealing Creation itself to be one big, pointless joke. Blind faith had caused him to walk away from a sure thing, and now he doubted the wisdom of that choice.

Cain, the agent he had tasked with writing the books, had once again disappeared. The last time they had met, Cain had pleaded that he had hit a roadblock, but that he had an idea for how to write the final book. Lucifer hadn't really understand it; Cain had been talking about levels of reality and metanarratives and other stuff that sounded like high-falutin' literary bullshit to Lucifer. "Just write the damned book," he had told Cain. That was nearly three weeks ago, and Lucifer hadn't heard from him since.

"Should have imploded the whole planet when I had the chance," he grumbled. But Medeia Sayed, that mewling ass-kitten, had given him an idea. Perhaps he didn't have to sit here and wait for the End to come. Perhaps he could still do something to help things along.

"Azrael!" he barked to the minion lurking in his foyer. "Alert our people at the planeport. I need to make a trip to Washington, DC."

SIXTEEN

Mercury and Job were unable to get Cain to tell them any more about Wormwood. Mentioning the name seemed to have triggered something in him. Cain simply sat on the curb staring at the fog rolling in, laughed, and muttered incomprehensibly to himself. Mercury began to reconsider his conclusion that Cain was the saner of the two.

"So what happens if I just step into the fog?" Mercury asked.

"Hard to say," replied Job. "Maybe nothing."

Mercury sighed. "Again, what kind of nothing are we talking about? Do you mean nothing happens, like it's just regular fog? Or *nothing* happens, where I get erased from history and all that?"

"I honestly don't know," said Job. "Cain tried it, and nothing happened. Which is to say, he simply reemerged from the fog, as if he had walked in a circle and ended up where he started. Presumably the same thing would happen to me, although I haven't tried it. I remain hopeful that there is something else beyond the fog, but that may just be my own bias."

"Why don't you try it?" asked Mercury.

Job shrugged. "I have no great desire to end this life. Whatever is coming will come soon enough. In any case, as I said, I suspect the same thing would happen to me as happened to Cain. He and I seem to be in this until the end."

"But you have thought about it," Mercury insisted. "You must have some idea what's out there."

Job nodded. "What's out there," said Job, his gaze lost in the fog, "is only what you take with you."

"Really?" asked Mercury, peering into the fog in awe.

"What am I, Yoda?" asked Job. "I told you, I don't know what's out there. Maybe nothing. Maybe everything. My best guess is that what's out there depends on what you bring with you. Your hopes and fears will determine your reality, as they always have."

Cain momentarily broke from his deranged giggling to snort in disgust. "*Your hopes and fears!*" he repeated in a gushing mockery of Job's optimistic tone.

Job sighed and shook his head. "For his sake, I kind of hope he's right," said Job. "If we get swallowed by the fog and it turns out that it's just the beginning of some entirely new reality—or worse, a continuation of the old one—he's going to lose it completely. Look at him. He can't take much more."

But Mercury was still staring into the fog. "I'm going to do it," he said.

"Do what?" Job asked.

"Go into the fog. The waiting is killing me. And who knows, maybe it's not too late."

"Too late for what?"

"I don't know. To fix this somehow. Keep reality from disintegrating completely."

Job smiled. "I sure hope you're right. So when are you going to do this?"

"I was thinking now-ish."

"Well, don't let me stop you."

"Tell me it's going to be OK."

"It's going to be OK."

"All right then," said Mercury. "Here goes nothing." And with that, he walked into the fog.

After a few steps, he was completely enveloped by the gray haze. He felt nothing: no dampness in the air, no thickness in his lungs. Whatever the fog was, it wasn't water vapor. Striding boldly forward into the blinding cloud, he began to think that Job and Cain had been putting him on. Clearly there was something a little weird about the fog, the way it moved in from all sides and the way it felt—or didn't feel—on his skin, but—

Suddenly his right hand felt like it was waking up. Pinpricks of something unpleasant but not exactly painful shot through his hand. He tried to pull his hand back, but it was immobilized, as if encased in amber. The sensation then crept into his left toes and swept across the right side of his face. Then the right foot, the left hand, his ears, his lips. Soon his whole body was paralyzed, enveloped by some nauseating hybrid of numbness and agony.

Hopes and fears! thought Mercury frantically. What are my hopes and fears?

The only thing that popped into his mind was the face of Christine Temetri. I hope nothing bad happened to Christine, he thought. I hope she's OK.

The fog was inside him, tearing him apart—limb from limb, cell from cell, atom from atom. Somehow, amid all of this, he remained conscious of what was happening—of his very physical essence exploding and expanding in every direction, until it filled all of reality in every dimension. Mercury screamed, and his scream was the sound of a universe dying.

And then—

Falling. The sensation of air blowing past. Condensation collecting on his skin. And then a blinding light in an azure sky dotted with clouds. The sun!

Orienting himself, he spun to see a vast expanse of darker blue below him. Ocean? He gradually slowed his descent until he was hovering maybe a mile above the water. There was plenty of interplanar energy here, wherever he was. Closing his eyes, he felt the tendrils of energy around him, emanating in different strengths from the east, south, north, west…Yes, this was definitely Earth, and not the far-future Earth he had just left, either. The strength and configuration of the streams matched that of Earth just after the reconfiguration caused by the LA earthquake. The LA convergence was a long way from here, though—several thousand miles to the west. About the same distance to the southeast he could feel the Kenyan convergence, where Horace Finch had constructed his chrono-collider device. That put Mercury somewhere above the Atlantic, just off the coast of southern Europe.

Sure enough, peering into the distance he spotted the familiar outline of the Azores. He had spent some time in these islands not long ago, when he had been on the run from the Heavenly authorities. They were a good place for an angel to get lost because they were so far from the routes that angels typically traveled on the Mundane Plane.

Now what?

Somehow he had to stop whatever had happened to unleash the fog, whatever had made the world such a miserable, hopeless place. He had to warn Heaven about Wormwood.

He took off toward the Megiddo portal. It would take him about four hours to get there. He could always request a temporary portal from the Azores, but Heaven had really been cracking down on unbudgeted expenditures and he wasn't exactly sure where he stood with the Heavenly bureaucracy at this point. Presumably he'd earned some goodwill by saving Earth from annihilation, but there was also a chance that he'd be held accountable for unauthorized travel outside the stratosphere. In fact, with Uzziel out of the Bureau, he wasn't even sure whom to call about authorizing a portal. No, it was better for him to just show up in Heaven in person and tell whoever would listen what Cain had said about Wormwood.

With a tailwind coming in from the Atlantic, Mercury made it to the Megiddo portal in just over three hours. Slipping out of Mundane Reality, he appeared in the planeport and made his way toward the portal that would take him to Heaven. He hadn't even made it halfway when he ran into a familiar figure.

"Hey, Perp," Mercury called, waving at the infantile winged cherub buzzing down the concourse. Perp was the only cherub Mercury knew who still sported the classical winged baby look, in defiance of angelic fashion trends of the last four hundred years. This was, surprisingly, not the most jarring of his personal attributes; Perp was also well known for his tendency to pepper his speech with impertinent and banal maxims of dubious quality.

"Mercury!" Perp hissed, altering his course to make a beeline toward Mercury. "What the hell do you think you're doing? To keep potatoes from budding in the bag, put an apple in with them."

"Long story," said Mercury, ignoring Perp's tuber truism. "After I imploded the moon, I got sucked into some far-future version of Earth where Job and Cain—you know, from the Bible—were playing Ping-Pong and—"

"By Heaven's Gates," said Perp, staring aghast at Mercury, "you've completely lost it."

"Look, I know it sounds crazy, but there was this fog that was going to erase everything, and Cain said the fog was because of Heaven being destroyed by something called Wormwood, so I—"

"Shhhh," said Perp. "We're going to get you the help you need. But first, come with me. If you have bubblegum stuck to your shirt, put it in the freezer and then scrape it off with a knife. Come on now, quickly!" Perp spun around and darted off toward a door that read PERMITTED PERSONNEL ONLY.

"Look, Perp," said Mercury. "I don't really have time to explain everything to you. I need to get to Heaven and tell them—"

"Heaven!" exclaimed Perp. "Goodness, no! The last place you need to be right now is Heaven. Come with me. Hurry! Security could spot you at any moment!"

Mercury sighed and trudged after Perp. Hopefully Wormwood, whatever it was, could wait for another five minutes.

Perp opened the door with a key that hung from a key ring that he pulled from the cloths wrapping his loins and ushered Mercury inside. It was some sort of utility closet. Cleaning supplies and tools hung from the walls. The room was dimly lit by a small fluorescent panel in the ceiling.

"You know I like you," said Merc, "but if you take your diaper off, I'm screaming."

Perp didn't seem to hear him. "What in blazes do you think you're doing?" he demanded. "Do you have any idea how much trouble you're in?"

Mercury frowned. "You mean for imploding the moon? Perp, come on. I don't think that's even technically illegal. And in any case, there were extenuating circumstances. Michelle was there, she can back me up. It was the only way to save the Earth."

Perp stared at him, open-mouthed. "Mercury, what are you talking about? This isn't about the moon. It's about going AWOL and screwing up the Apocalypse. You're in a lot of trouble. When designing an outdoor pen for a tortoise, you should provide a pen that is at least ten times the length and five times the width of the tortoise."

Mercury shook his head. "No, I worked that out with Uzziel when I turned myself in. The Apocalypse thing, not the tortoise thing. He's going to have to sort out his own tortoise husbandry issues. They gave me leniency because I turned in Gamaliel."

"You turned in Gamaliel?"

"Well, no. But Uzziel seemed to think I did. He called it a 'token of goodwill.' I wasn't about to contradict him."

"Mercury, Gamaliel is still on the loose. He's still out there somewhere, doing Tiamat's dirty work. They've got about a hundred angels scouring the Mundane Plane for him."

"Well, sure, he's out there *now*. Because Uzziel let him go. Uzziel's in league with Tiamat. I thought you were supposed to be in the know, Perp. Next thing you're going to tell me you haven't heard about the moon."

"Mercury, listen to me," said Perp. "Don't pull the choke in a motor boat if the motor was running within the past forty minutes. You never turned in Gamaliel. I don't know anything about Uzziel working with Tiamat. And your obsession with the moon is frankly scaring me. What on Earth happened to you?"

A queasy feeling arose in Mercury's stomach. Something wasn't right here. Perp always knew everything before anyone else. If he didn't know about it, it hadn't happened.

"Perp, what day is it?" Mercury asked.

"It's Saturday. October twenty-seventh. Two thousand twelve *Anno Domini*."

All the air rushed out of Mercury's lungs. He leaned against the wall of the closet to steady himself.

"What is it, Merc? What's wrong?"

"I came back before I left," Mercury said numbly. "The moon hasn't been destroyed yet."

"I'm not sure I like the way you said 'yet' at the end there," replied Perp.

"And I haven't turned myself in yet. I'm still wanted by Heaven. And Gamaliel is still out there."

"OK, so now we're both up to speed on what hasn't happened yet," remarked Perp. "I feel like we've made real progress today."

"I've got to turn myself in," said Mercury.

"What?" exclaimed Perp. "No!"

"I have to warn them about Wormwood. It's the only way."

"What the hell is Wormwood?"

"Not sure, exactly. But apparently it's the cause of a lot of bad shit. I have to warn them."

Perp frowned. "OK, first? They aren't going to listen to you. You have no credibility at this point. Second, even if they did listen, what are they going to do about it? You don't seem to know anything other than the fact that some 'bad shit' is going to happen. And third, you keep forgetting that you're in a lot of trouble. If you turn yourself in, you're going to spend the next couple hundred years in lockup."

Mercury rubbed his chin thoughtfully. Perp had a point. Turning himself in now would be futile. It also occurred to him that if it was only Saturday, that meant that Christine hadn't yet found the anti-bomb inside Mount Mbutuokoti. And that meant that there was still a chance to intercept the anti-bomb before it fell into the hands of Horace Finch. This time around, Mercury would have time to get the anti-bomb somewhere safe before it detonated. There was still time to save the moon.

"I've got to get out of here," Mercury said. "Back to Kenya."

Perp shook his head furiously. "You'll never make it out of the planeport," he said. "It was a miracle that I intercepted you before security ID'd you. The odds that you'll make it back to the Megiddo portal are practically nil."

"I've got to try," said Mercury.

"And if you fail? If they catch you?"

Mercury considered this for a moment. If he got caught, then he wouldn't be able to intercept the anti-bomb *or* stop Wormwood. And he'd get thrown in prison.

"You know what?" said Mercury. "You're right. Change of plans. I need to turn myself in."

"Good, now you're starting to...wait, what? Didn't we already decide that was a bad idea?"

"I mean, not me. I'm going to turn in the other Mercury."

"The other...?"

"I need a pen and a sheet of paper."

Perp produced both from his swaddling clothes. Mercury regarded the implements suspiciously for a moment, then shrugged. It was best not to think about Perp's storage system. He put the paper on the floor and pulled the archangel Michelle's card from his pocket. On the back was written:

The rain comes from above.

- M.

Mercury smiled grimly as he remembered getting this message from Michelle in answer to his quest for answers about the Great Flood. He never did find out what the cryptic message was supposed to mean. He set the card next to the paper and started writing, doing his best to mimic Michelle's graceful but no-nonsense script.

"What are you doing?" Perp asked.

"Writing a note to myself."

"Of course," replied Perp dryly.

Mercury knew exactly what to write. He shivered as he experienced an eerie sense of déjà vu. When he was done, the note read:

Christine needs your help.
Turn yourself in.
- M.

He could have written something different, he supposed, but he didn't want to take any chances.

"Why don't you sign your own name?" asked Perp.

"Please," replied Mercury. "I'm not exactly trustworthy, am I? I need myself to think the note is from Michelle. Then I'll turn myself in, and I can get out of here."

Perp's face was twisted in confusion. "You're lying to yourself?"

"I'm letting myself believe an untruth," said Mercury. "If I fall for it, it's my own fault for being gullible."

Perp was speechless.

"OK," Mercury said, folding the note and handing it to Perp. "I need you to deliver this to me. I'll be at a bar called La Traviata on Santa Maria Island, in the Azores. Just give the note to the bartender and tell him to give it to me when I arrive. Make sure I don't see you."

"I don't..." Perp started. "You're going to be in a bar in the Azores?"

"Yes. In about five hours. I'm at a bullfight in Pamplona right now. I'd like to go back and tell myself not to bet on the matador with the eye patch, but sometimes you've got to let yourself make your own mistakes. Otherwise, how am I ever going to learn?"

Perp seemed to have reached some sort of mental overload threshold. Realizing he was never going to fully understand what Mercury was talking about, he focused on the instructions he had been given. "OK, so I give this to the bartender and tell him to give the note to you when you show up. Does he know your name?"

"Nope," said Mercury. "Haven't met him yet. Nice guy, Jorge. We talked about football together. American football, that is. Not a lot of Denver Broncos fans in the Azores. Just tell him that a tall guy with silver hair will be coming in."

Perp nodded slowly. "And you're sure you aren't completely insane?"

Mercury considered this for a moment. "Can't be one hundred percent sure," he admitted. "But if you do this for me, I promise to sit here in this broom closet until you come back."

"No turning yourself in?"

"None."

"And then what?"

"You come back and help me get back to the Mundane Plane. I have to get to Kenya to stop a crazy billionaire from making me destroy the moon."

"All right, then," said Perp. "You realize this is going to take a while. I can't get authorization for a temporary portal. I'll have to use the Megiddo portal and fly to the Azores and back."

"I know," said Mercury. "We've got plenty of time. I'll just hang out here until you get back."

Perp opened the door and walked onto the concourse.

"If you see me, just play dumb," Mercury said.

"Not a problem," said Perp. "Zigzag to outrun a crocodile."

"And you have to promise never to tell me that I did this. I'll never forgive me for pulling such a dirty trick on myself."

Perp sighed and closed the door behind him.

SEVENTEEN

Lucifer sat in a waiting room reading a six-month-old copy of *Reader's Digest* and listening to the somnambulant strains of Jack Johnson leeching out of speakers recessed in the acoustic ceiling tiles. He had been reading selections from "Humor in Uniform" to a dour-looking gentleman sitting across from him, deliberately misstating the punch lines to ratchet up the severity of the man's torment.

"And then the corporal says, 'I'll wait as long as you need me to, but that's not the general's briefcase.' Ha! Ha! Get it? That's not the…Wait, there's another line after that. Oh, then the sergeant says, 'Then why are his pants in it?' I suppose that's the punch line there. 'Why are his pants in it.' I'm not sure I get that one. Ah, 'Life in These United States'!"

The dour man flapped his newspaper loudly, holding it up like a ward against Lucifer's insipid commentary.

"Anyhoo!" Lucifer exclaimed, making the man jump a little. "What are you in for, chief?"

"Excuse me?" said the man, lowering his paper to glare at Lucifer.

"Oh, that's what I say when I'm stuck in a waiting room," said Lucifer. "Sort of an icebreaker. 'What are you in for, chief?' As if we were in prison together."

"Hm," grunted the man, returning to his paper.

"We're not, of course," added Lucifer.

"What?" asked the man irritably.

"Not in prison," clarified Lucifer. "We can leave whenever we want."

"Hm," grunted the man.

"Why, you could leave right now if you wanted to," Lucifer went on.

The man made no response.

"If I'm bothering you, I mean. You could *leave right now*."

The man muttered something under his breath.

"What's that?" asked Lucifer.

"I could leave right now," the man repeated.

"Yes!" Lucifer agreed. "You could! Leave right now!"

The man folded up his newspaper and walked out the door without a sound.

Lucifer chuckled to himself. "Still got it," he said. He loved pulling this Jedi mind trick shit.

The receptionist, a dumpy old broad with dishwater-colored hair, announced, "Mr. Thomason. Director Lubbers is ready for you."

Lucifer stood and approached the woman. "Mr. Thomason had to leave for an emergency meeting. I'll be taking his place."

"And you are?"

"My name is Rezon. R-E-Z-O-N. Lawrence Rezon. You can call me Larry."

"Well, Mr. Rezon," she replied, "you're not on Mr. Lubbers's schedule. I'm afraid I can't—"

"Don't be afraid!" Lucifer exclaimed. "There's no need to be afraid of anything. Rules, procedures, et cetera. These things are just guidelines, correct?"

The receptionist nodded dumbly.

"We shouldn't substitute the tyranny of the bureaucracy for good old-fashioned common sense. If Director Lubbers is expecting Mr. Thomason, and if Mr. Thomason has selected me to act in his stead, then it stands to reason that Director Lubbers should be allowed to see me. Correct?"

"Correct," the receptionist mumbled.

"Listen to reason!" exclaimed Lucifer.

"Reason," the receptionist repeated.

"Yes?" Lucifer asked.

"Um, I'm sorry?"

"You called my name. Mr. Rezon. R-E-Z-O-N. I'm here to see Director Lubbers?"

"Oh," replied the receptionist, confused. "Oh, um, I suppose you can go in, then."

"Thank you, my dear," said Lucifer, bowing slightly at the woman. She blushed and looked away.

He strolled down the hall to a door that read:

DEPUTY ASSISTANT DIRECTOR DIRK LUBBERS

He opened the door to find Deputy Assistant Director Lubbers scowling at a stack of papers on his desk. He looked up with a start as Lucifer entered.

"Who the hell…?" he began.

"Director Lubbers," cooed Lucifer. "It's an honor to meet you. My name is Mr. Rezon. R-E-Z-O-N. Lawrence Rezon. You can call me Larry."

"I'm ten seconds from calling a security escort to haul your ass out on the street, *Larry*," growled Lubbers, his right hand reaching for something under his desk. "How'd you get in here?"

"No need for that," said Lucifer. "I'm here because we have mutual interests."

"Speak plainly," said Lubbers, waving a .38 caliber revolver. "I don't have time for this shit."

"Fine," said Lucifer. "I happen to know that you've just lost your best leads into Black Monday and the Anaheim Event. You let two very troublesome individuals, Christine Temetri and Jacob Slater, slip through your fingers. I also know that this puts you in a precarious position, career-wise. Fortunately for you, I'm in a position to help."

"How's that?" asked Lubbers dubiously.

"I have information," Lucifer said coolly, "regarding a certain extradimensional portal in Southern California."

Lubbers glared at Lucifer for a moment and then put the pistol away. "Close the door," he said. Lucifer shut the door and took a seat.

Lubbers studied him thoughtfully. "Who are you, Mr. Rezon? How do you know about this portal?"

Lucifer's eyes lit up as he saw the cover sheet of the papers Lubbers had been reading. The first line read: "To Your Holiness the High Council of the Seraphim." So, somehow Lubbers had gotten a hold of one of the MOC's reports. Clearly Lubbers was smarter than Lucifer had given him credit for. He wondered how much Lubbers already knew about Heaven.

"Who I am is immaterial," replied Lucifer. "The important thing is that I know how dangerous these supposed 'angels' are. You see, I'm one of them. Used to be, anyway."

"You expect me to believe—"

"I expect you to use your head, Director Lubbers. You know as well as I do that there are no such things as angels. Angels are mythical creatures, the stuff of fairy tales, correct?"

Lubbers nodded.

"However," Lucifer went on, "alternate dimensions are quite real. Your scientists have long suspected as much. And some of those dimensions are populated by intelligent beings. In some cases, beings who possess technology and military capabilities that dwarf those of even the great United States of America. For example, destructive devices in the form of glass apples that make your most powerful nuclear warheads look like children's toys. But I know their weaknesses. I can hand them over to you."

Lubbers appraised Lucifer skeptically. It certainly did sound like he knew what he was talking about.

"You find this troubling, yes?" Lucifer asked.

"Find what troubling?"

"The idea that there's somebody out there who is more powerful than you."

Lubbers snorted. "Of course I find it troubling!" he spat. "We're the big kid on the block. Our whole foreign policy—hell, our whole worldview—is based on the idea that nobody can tell us what to do. And now we find out that we're at the mercy of an alien race from another dimension? Alien beings who have no compunction about blowing up entire cities or even planets? Hell yes, I'm troubled."

"Ah," said Lucifer, smiling beatifically. "But surely you don't mean *nobody* can tell you what to do?"

Lubbers frowned. "I'm not following you."

"Nor should you be," said Lucifer. "But I was under the impression that…well, isn't America a *Christian* nation?"

Lubbers scowled. "I don't know about all that. My job is to protect the American people from all enemies, foreign and domestic."

"Indeed," said Lucifer. "But you must understand something. Although I am a traitor to my race, I am not without principles. It is, in fact, my principles that prompted me to rebel against my superiors. What happened in Anaheim is an absolute atrocity, and I am very eager to help you prevent something like that from happening again. But before I can enter into any sort of agreement with you, I need to know that you are on the right side. The side of good."

"Of course we're on the side of good!" barked Lubbers. "We're the United States of America, goddammit. We're a beacon of freedom and justice!"

"So you would say that the United States is a Christian nation?"

"Sure, I guess."

"Please do."

"Do what?"

"Say it."

"Jesus Christ," grumbled Lubbers. "What are you, some sort of zealot?"

Lucifer leaned back in his chair and smiled. "Far from it," he said. "Just someone who wants to make sure he's picked the right man for the job. The United States government is a vast entity, Director Lubbers. I could have gone to the secretary of defense or Homeland Security. I could have approached the president directly, if I had wanted to. I'm a very persuasive man with a lot of connections. But I chose you, because I believed you are the right man for the job. Was I mistaken?"

Lubbers regarded the man for a moment. Damned if this guy doesn't know just what buttons to push, he thought. "What's in this for you?" he asked.

Lucifer shrugged. "In a narrow sense, nothing. It would be far easier for me to sit back and see how things play out. But I have a soft spot for underdogs. I'd really like to see what humanity is capable of without the interference of our race. It's time for humanity to seize its destiny, to free itself from the shackles of belief in gods and angels. Do you agree?"

"Absolutely," said Lubbers.

"Then would you say it for me?"

"Fine," said Lubbers. What difference did it make? "The United States is a Christian nation."

"Wonderful," said Lucifer, barely able to control his glee. He felt like doing a little jig—like he did that time Pontius Pilate asked him for a towel.

"Now," said Lubbers, "tell me how to kick some angel ass."

"I have a plan to do just that," replied Lucifer. "However, I'm afraid that the resources of the FBI are not going to be sufficient for the task. We're going to need some serious firepower."

"Like what? Artillery? Tanks? I can pull some strings, get whatever it takes to do the job."

Lucifer shook his head. "Artillery, tanks, fighter jets...these are all worthless. Worse than worthless; they would use them against you. No, what we need is something far more dangerous and far more subtle. As far as I know, President Babcock is the only one with the power to deliver the weapon you would need to defeat my people."

Lubbers smiled. "Well, let's go talk to him then."

"What?" Lucifer asked, seemingly impressed. "You can get a meeting with the president of the United States, just like that?"

"They put me in charge of the Anaheim Event, and since this moon thing is obviously related to what happened in Anaheim, it sort of fell in my lap too. Since Black Monday I've had a direct line to the president himself. Hell, I've actually been dodging his calls, because I haven't had much to report. But I'd say this is worth a meeting, wouldn't you, Mr. Rezon?"

Lucifer smiled. "Whatever you say, chief."

EIGHTEEN

Having flown three hours from Pamplona to the remote Pacific island of Santa Maria, Mercury alighted on a rocky beach and stood for a moment, straightening his hair and admiring the view. The orange sun was just sinking behind the palm trees, making for a very pleasant vista. The Azores were about as far off the beaten path for angels as you could get. As long as he kept his head down and avoided performing unnecessary miracles, there was virtually no chance of any of Heaven's agents ever finding him—and since Mercury was currently wanted for insubordination and interference with the orderly procession of the Apocalypse, that was a good thing. He needed to lay low for a while, and there were worse places to spend a few centuries than the Azores.

Mercury strolled up the beach and had soon located a friendly-looking old bar with a weathered sign that read LA TRAVIATA. He smiled. A cold beer sounded pretty good.

The place was nearly deserted. A small, balding man stood behind the bar watching an old color television that hung from the ceiling across the room. On the screen was a football game: the Miami Dolphins versus the Denver Broncos.

"Football fan," said Mercury, approaching the bar.

"*Sim*," said the man with a scow. "*Meu Broncos estão perdendo*."

"Lions fan myself," said Mercury.

"*Sinto muito*," replied the man. "You must have a lot of... *como se diz*...character. You do not look old enough to remember when the Lions were good."

"Almost nobody is," replied Mercury. "*Uma cerveja por favor*."

"Sure," said the man, filling a mug with amber liquid from a tap. "I'm Jorge."

"Mercury. Nice to meet you, Jorge."

"*Ai!*" exclaimed Jorge suddenly, slapping himself on his forehead. "*Mercúrio. Cabelo prateado*. I forget. This is for you." He held out a wrinkled piece of paper that had been folded in half.

Mercury eyed the paper suspiciously. "I think you're confused, Jorge. No one knows I'm here. I mean, *no one*. In Heaven or on Earth."

Jorge shrugged and set the paper on the bar. "Little chubby man, look like *bebê*, says I give it to man with *cabelo prateado*. Silver hair."

Mercury's heart skipped a beat. Little chubby man who looked like a baby? There weren't a lot of people who fit that description. How could Perp possibly know he'd be here?

He grabbed the note and opened it. It read:

Christine needs your help.
Turn yourself in.
- *M.*

"Son of a bitch," Mercury grumbled, shaking his head. A note from the archangel Michelle? He pulled the card from his pocket and compared the handwriting. They certainly were similar. It was hard to tell if the same hand had written them both, but certainly he could trust Perp not to give him misleading information. And in any case, whoever left this note obviously knew he was here. If it was a trap, he'd already be in custody.

And if it was a trap, why play on his sympathy for Christine? How many people even knew about his relationship with Christine? A relationship that amounted to, what, saving the world together a couple of times. It's not like they were particularly close. As far as he knew, Christine thought of him as an arrogant jerk. After all, he *was* an arrogant jerk, and Christine was certainly as good a judge of character as most of the humans he had encountered. What would make anyone think he'd stick his neck out because of some vague threat to Christine? And why would Christine need his help anyway? Last he knew, she was safely back in Los Angeles. None of this made any sense.

At least this message was less ambiguous than the last one he had gotten from Michelle, some four thousand years earlier. *The rain comes from above.* He still hadn't figured out what that was supposed to mean. This note at least had a clear message. *Christine needs your help. Turn yourself in.*

"Bad news?" asked Jorge.

Mercury shrugged. "I'm not sure. It says a friend of mine needs help. But if I go help her, I could get in a lot of trouble. And frankly I'm not sure how I can help her anyway."

"Ah," Jorge replied, smiling. "A woman friend. Sounds like you are in trouble either way, *amigo*."

"Yeah, it's not like that," said Mercury hurriedly. "I mean, she's…That is, I'm…Well, let's just say we're from two different worlds."

"*A fruta proibida é a mais apetecida*," said Jorge, nodding.

"Sorry," replied Mercury. "My Portuguese mostly revolves around beer."

"An old saying," said Jorge. "The forbidden fruit is most desired."

Mercury sighed. "Boy, you said it, brother." He downed the rest of his beer, placed a generous tip on the bar, and walked outside. The western sky was on fire with the dying light.

Christine needs help. Turn yourself in.

Did he really need any more information than that? What difference would it make? The message came from someone he trusted. It didn't matter if he didn't understand how giving himself up would help her. If Christine needed his help, that was all there was to it. So much for hiding out until the heat had died down.

Mercury leaped into the air, heading toward the Megiddo portal to throw himself on the mercy of Heaven.

NINETEEN

Travis Babcock was not a bad man. He was friendly, good-natured, and generally fair in his dealings with other people. He would have made an above-average manager of a local hardware store. Unfortunately, the overlap of the skill sets required for managing a hardware store and managing an unruly bureaucracy tasked with the health, safety, and education of three hundred million people is smaller than one might expect.

His brother, Joshua Babcock, would have made a great president, somewhere in the upper Roosevelt range. Joshua was brilliant and hardworking, and possessed an encyclopedic knowledge of history and economics. Unfortunately for the country, Joshua was born with a rare condition that prevented his body from producing saliva and was, therefore, unofficially disqualified for public office. He worked unhappily in Chico, California, as a marginally competent and perpetually cotton-mouthed hardware store manager.

Travis executed his office with dignity and an arsenal of facial expressions that concealed the fact that he rarely felt like he had any idea what he was doing. He reassured himself that this was how all presidents felt; the trick, he figured, was to act confident and stick to his principles, which were composed of a not entirely coherent mishmash of notions picked up from Sunday school lessons and *Schoolhouse Rock*.[7] As long as he stuck to his principles, he figured, history couldn't judge him too harshly.

Travis was at present concealing his confusion and self-doubt with his generic Look of Genuine Concern, which he was directing at Deputy Assistant Director Dirk Lubbers and a man named Lawrence Rezon, who claimed to have inside knowledge about the Anaheim Event and Black Monday. Travis wasn't sure what to make of Rezon. He had insisted on meeting alone with Lubbers and Travis, claiming that he wasn't sure who else in the government he could trust. Rezon claimed to be a member of an alien race from another dimension, the same race that he claimed had perpetrated the destruction of Anaheim Stadium and the moon. This idea was a bit difficult for Travis to swallow, but Lubbers seemed to think his story checked out, and Lubbers was the most hardheaded, practical man Travis knew. It was certainly worth listening to what this man had to say. Plus it allowed him to postpone a meeting with Lia Sokhov, the secretary of agriculture, who wouldn't shut up about some strain of mutant corn that was causing problems in Africa. Like Travis didn't have bigger problems to worry about.

"Our civilization has grown complacent," Rezon was saying. "Overconfident. Our success has led to hubris. And that will be our downfall."

"And you don't feel any guilt about betraying your fellow… what are we calling them?" said Travis, frowning. He squinted at a two-page document lying on the desk in front of him. Rezon and Lubbers sat across from him in the Oval Office.

7 On more than one occasion while president he had resorted to humming the "I'm Just a Bill" song to remember the sequence of the legislative process.

Lubbers had provided the president with a report that was basically a very abbreviated and sanitized version of Eddie's account. No references to "Heaven" or "angels" in the official report.

"Beings of Indeterminate Origin," said Lubbers. "BIOs." It was the term Jacob Slater had used in his debriefing, and Lubbers had adopted it for his report.

"Does that work for you, Mr. Rezon?" asked Travis.

Rezon shrugged. "BIOs is fine," he said. "In answer to your question, I don't believe guilt is a useful sentiment. What has happened has happened. I do not regret turning against my superiors. I believe they have acted in an arrogant and condescending way toward your race, and these latest atrocities have confirmed my desire to see humanity free of their influence."

"Why did they destroy the moon?" asked Travis. "And Anaheim Stadium? Are they trying to send us some kind of message? Because I gotta tell ya, they've got our attention but I don't know what the hell they are trying to say."

Rezon shook his head. "My best guess is that they felt threatened by Harry Giddings and his Covenant Holders organization. You have to understand that my people—the BIOs—have cast themselves in the role of angels. Before that, they were considered gods. They feel marginalized by the genuine faith of people like Harry."

Travis nodded. Harry Giddings had been a good friend and a fervent supporter of Travis's campaign. He liked the idea of Harry as a saint who had been martyred by heretics who felt threatened by the Truth. What right did these alien creatures, these BIOs, have to call themselves *angels*? That bordered on blasphemy.

"As for the moon," Rezon went on, "your guess is as good as mine. I would assume that it was some sort of display of power, to show you that you're out of your league. But honestly I'm only guessing. The BIOs are, as a rule, strange and capricious beings, with little understanding or tolerance of human morality or conventions. You could go mad trying to puzzle out their motivations. Fortunately, I have spent a great deal of time on Earth and have come to understand and appreciate humanity. My love for your race has made me a pariah among my own people."

Travis Babcock nodded in appreciation of Rezon's sacrifice on humanity's behalf.

"What do you mean that their overconfidence will result in their downfall?" asked Lubbers, anxious to get back to the nuts and bolts of how they were going to turn the tables on these interloping assholes. Having grown restless with the abstract discussion, he had gotten up and was standing across the room, examining a series of black-and-white photographs hanging on the Oval Office wall. Directly in front of him was a photo of Nixon shaking hands with Elvis Presley. *Strange bedfellows*, thought Lubbers.

"Ah," replied Rezon. "You are familiar with the Biblical story of Goliath?"

"Of course," replied the president. "Goliath was a giant, the champion of the Philistines. David killed him with a stone from his sling."

"Exactly," said Rezon. He recited: " 'A champion named Goliath, who was from Gath, came out of the Philistine camp. His height was six cubits and a span. He had a bronze helmet on his head and wore a coat of scale armor of bronze weighing five thousand shekels. On his legs he wore bronze greaves, and a bronze javelin was slung on his back. His spear shaft was like a weaver's rod, and its iron point weighed six hundred shekels. His shield bearer went ahead of him.' Do you know how much a shekel is?" asked Rezon.

The two men were silent.

"It's about point four ounces," Rezon explained. "That means his coat of armor alone weighed *a hundred and twenty-five pounds*. The head of his spear weighed *fifteen pounds*. That's heavier than most bowling balls. The point is, this was a big man. David was probably around fifteen when he challenged Goliath. He had no armor and no weapons other than a slingshot. So how did he beat Goliath?"

"God was on his side," said President Babcock.

"Yes!" exclaimed Rezon. "Also? Goliath wasn't prepared to defend against a kid with a slingshot. He was so used to fighting the biggest, scariest, most well-armed men around that he forgot that a well-aimed shot with a stone the size of a marble could crack his skull open. And that's how we're going to beat Heav… that is, those big, heavy BIOs."

"So…what?" asked Lubbers, turning away from the photos to regard Lucifer. "We send a SEAL team armed with slingshots through this portal in Glendale?"

"Ye of little faith," said Lucifer, smiling at the president. The president smiled back. Lubbers frowned. He had been worried that Babcock might not be receptive to Rezon's case, but now he seemed to be in danger of being *too* receptive. If Babcock got any more receptive, Rezon would be taking up residence in the Lincoln Bedroom.

"I'm a practical man, Rezon," said Lubbers. "Don't talk to me in metaphors."

"May I ask you a personal question, Director Lubbers?" asked Lucifer.

Lubbers frowned. "If it's relevant to the discussion at hand," he replied cautiously.

Lucifer gazed hard at him. "Have you accepted Jesus Christ into your heart?"

Lubbers swallowed hard. "I have not," he said.

"Hmm," replied Lucifer, stroking his chin.

Goddammit, thought Lubbers. I'm going to get locked out of the decision-making process just because I'm not a Jesus freak. What a crock of shit. I work my ass off for thirty years, claw my way up to deputy assistant director of the FBI, and now I'm going to get shut out because I won't spout some fairy tale religious bullshit.

In point of fact, Deputy Assistant Director Dirk Lubbers was in no danger of being cast aside by Lucifer, who had learned centuries earlier that one of the most effective ways to keep someone from questioning their loyalties to a group was to imply that they didn't belong in the group in the first place. Human beings didn't like feeling out of control, particularly control freaks like Lubbers. Lubbers would fight tooth and nail to get into any club that was trying to keep him out, even if that club was run by the devil himself. Had Lucifer let up on him, Lubbers might have realized how insane Lucifer's proposition was, but instead he was entirely focused on not being the odd man out. Not only that but—truth be told—Lucifer hadn't had this much fun since the Crusades. Toying with a hardheaded atheist like Lubbers was sheer bliss. Getting atheists to renounce their principles and accept Christianity was almost as much fun as provoking good Christian souls to apostasy.

"Is that going to be a problem?" asked the president. His question was directed at Lucifer, but he was sitting back in his chair, observing Lubbers coolly.

"Oh, not for me," clarified Lucifer. "I try to be tolerant of others' religious beliefs—or lack thereof. But I believe that I am on a holy mission, directed by God himself. If I may be so bold, I believe that each of us here has an important role to play. President Babcock is obviously the ultimate authority, the one God has chosen to oversee the operation. I am to act as his humble counselor. That leaves you, Director Lubbers, to be the hands and feet. To make a theological analogy, you are Son to our Father and Holy Spirit. This is a lot to ask of a skeptic."

"I'll be fine," Lubbers said through gritted teeth. They weren't getting rid of him that easily. After all, he was the one who had brought Rezon to the president. This whole thing was *his idea.*

"Dirk," said Travis earnestly, leaning over his desk, "would you like to commit your life to Jesus Christ right now?"

Oh, for fuck's sake, thought Lubbers. No! No, I don't want to fucking commit my life to Jesus Christ. All I want to do is fucking kill the motherfuckers who blew up the moon! What in fucking fuck does this namby-pamby Jesus bullshit have to do with anything?

"Yes," Lubbers said, as evenly as he could. "Yes, I would."

"You would like to what?" asked Lucifer.

"I would like..." said Lubbers. Fucking fuckety fuck! "...to dedicate my life to Jesus Christ."

"Mr. President, would you pray for our brother Dirk?"

Babcock nodded. "I would be honored."

Lubbers reluctantly sat down, trying to hide the revulsion that was boiling up from his gut. Lucifer held out his hands and the three of them joined together in a circle. The president led the prayer, thanking Jesus for accepting a degenerate sinner like Lubbers into the Kingdom, with Lucifer interjecting the occasional *Amen!* or *Preach it, brother!*

Lubbers, for his part, was having none of it. He was acting a part, pure and simple. If accepting Jesus into your heart was the price for admission to this club, then he would pretend to do that. While Babcock prayed, he was going over budget numbers in his head, stopping to mutter "Amen" whenever the president paused. At some point, though, he started to worry that they weren't buying his act, that they could tell he was just going through the motions. *I need to accept somebody into my heart,* thought Lubbers. *Not Jesus, but somebody. Otherwise they're going to know.*

The first image that popped into Lubbers's head was that of Nixon shaking hands with Elvis. Nixon was out of the question, of course. He'd rather have Jesus in his heart than Nixon. So, Elvis then.

"Elvis," Lubbers mouthed. "Come into my heart." And as soon as he said it, a profound feeling of peace came over him.

"Wow," Lubbers said, opening his eyes. Travis and Lucifer were staring expectantly at him. Evidently the prayer was over.

"How do you feel?" asked President Babcock.

Lubbers smiled crookedly at him. "Man," he said, "I feel great. Whattaya say we take care of business?"

TWENTY

Mercury watched from a crack in the utility room closet as his double was escorted through the planeport by security. "Poor bastard," he muttered. "I hope they're not too hard on me."

The only thing that had saved him the first time around was the mysterious appearance of the battered and unconscious Gamaliel in the planeport. He still wasn't sure who had actually captured Gamaliel and brought him to the planeport, but he hadn't complained about them giving him credit for it. Hopefully whoever had caught him last time would catch him again this time around. Otherwise, past-Mercury was going to be in a lot of trouble, with no "tokens of goodwill" to help balance the scales. They'd lock him up for a couple hundred years at least. Uzziel would never assign him to retrieve the missing Attaché Case of Famine, which meant that he would never be captured by Tiamat's agents and brought to Finch's facility in Kenya, which meant that he would never fly the anti-bomb to the moon and be transported to the post-Apocalyptic future, which meant that he would not now be here in a utility closet, watching himself be marched down the concourse by cherubim with flaming swords.

He shook his head. That sort of thinking could drive a cherub crazy. He couldn't worry about what would or wouldn't happen to the other Mercury and how that would affect him in the present. Or the future, or whatever it was. The important thing was that he was now a step ahead of Tiamat and Finch: he knew what they were up to, and now that the other Mercury was in custody, he could slip back down to the Mundane Plane and intercept the glass apple before Christine ever found it. He'd deliver the antibomb to the authorities and then tell them about Wormwood, saving the Earth *and* Heaven. Not bad for a day's work.

But not quite yet. He had to wait for Perp to get back to help him get out of the planeport safely. At this point, while he wasn't technically wanted anymore, security still might stop him, thinking he'd escaped. Then they'd have two Mercurys in custody, which would be extremely difficult to explain—especially to the other Mercury.

After another three hours, he began to worry. What was taking Perp so long? Presumably, he'd have taken the Megiddo portal, which meant that he should have returned a good hour before the other Mercury turned himself in. The flight from the Megiddo portal to the Azores and back from the Middle East would take about eight hours. That was about a four-hour flight each way. But it had been almost eleven hours now since Perp had left.

Finally, the door opened, and an exhausted-looking Perp fluttered inside and closed the door behind him.

"Demon dogs, Perp!" exclaimed Mercury. "What the hell took you so long? I thought I was going to have to come out of the closet on my own. Er, you know what I mean."

"You know," replied Perp irritably, "I do have a job to do around here. When I disappear for half the day, things get backed up. Put this on." He had somehow pulled a tan fedora from his swaddling clothes.

"A fedora?" asked Mercury distastefully. "What am I, hipster cherub now?"

"It's to hide your hair. I got you a security escort back to the Megiddo portal. If anybody asks, your name is Todd. Microwave a smelly sponge to kill bacteria."

Mercury donned the fedora. He grinned broadly and held out his hand to Perp. "Hey there, guy," he oozed. "I'm Todd, the hipster cherub."

"Cut it out," Perp growled. "Just keep your head down."

"Can do, chief!" said Mercury, adjusting the hat.

"I don't know why I put up with this crap," grumbled Perp, peering out the cracked door. "OK, let's go."

He led Mercury back out onto the concourse toward a pair of waiting security guards.

"What kind of music does Todd like?" asked Mercury. "He strikes me as a Maroon 5 fan."

"Shut up, Mercury," hissed Perp. "I mean it."

Mercury trailed after him in silence. When they reached the guards, Perp said, "This is the VIA I was telling you about."

The guards nodded sternly at him and regarded Mercury.

"I'm Todd!" exclaimed Mercury. "I wear this hat because it's ironic."

"Let's go," said one of the guards. "Stay close."

Mercury touched the brim of his hat and nodded toward Perp. "Thanks, Perp," he said, and they trudged off down the concourse toward the Megiddo portal.

"Good luck," said Perp. "A vinegar and salt solution can help relieve pain associated with a bladder infection." He added, in a whisper, "I hope you're not batshit crazy."

The guards got Mercury safely to the portal. He thanked them for their service and then blinked out of existence, reappearing on a rocky outcropping in the Jezreel Valley. Megiddo. This was supposed to have been the location of the final battle between good and evil. Man, had that plan ever gone off track.

Mercury ditched the ridiculous hat and took off again, this time due south toward Kenya. The sun was already rising in the east, which meant that in only a few hours, Christine and Horace Finch would reach Mount Mbutuokoti, where the glass apple was hidden. Mercury needed to get to it first. Perp had taken longer than expected, but he should still have time to get to the apple before they crested the top of the mountain. He could get in and out without them ever seeing him.

Soaring high above the clouds, Mercury pushed top speed at around three hundred miles per hour all the way to sub-Saharan Africa. Once he was above Kenya, he sank below the cloud layer and looked for the distinctive shape of Mount Mbutuokoti. He had never been there but knew roughly where it was, and Christine had described it as a near-perfect cone, rising some two thousand feet above the plain.

As expected, it wasn't difficult to spot. Mbutuokoti stuck out incongruously from the flat plain surrounding it. As Mercury descended toward the plateau at its peak, his heart jumped. A few hundred feet directly below him, a group of people were ascending the rocky slope of the mountain. There were maybe a dozen tall, dark-skinned, nearly naked men and two light-skinned people wearing Western clothing. One of them was short, squat, and male, the other a thin female with brown hair. Christine.

If they thought to look up, they'd see him soaring above them, but they were intent on keeping their footing on the treacherous terrain. Mercury flew silently over their heads, landing softly on the plateau. He had only a few minutes to find the glass apple before the group reached the summit. Unfortunately, all he knew was that Christine found the apple in a cave accessible from one of the fissures in the mountain. There were dozens of fissures big enough for Christine to have climbed into—and some of them would be too tight for someone of Mercury's size. Best to just start with the largest ones and work his way down through the smaller ones.

As he approached one of the fissures, something hard struck him on the back of the head, knocking him to his knees and almost causing him to fall into the crevice. Stars danced in front of his eyes and pain shot through his skull. What the hell?

Dazed, he turned in the direction from which the projectile had come. Standing maybe thirty feet away, with a fist-sized rock in his hand, was a tall, muscular angel with an evil grin on his face. Gamaliel.

"Hey, Merc," said Gamaliel. "Catch!"

Gamaliel wound up like a major league baseball pitcher and hurled the rock at Mercury. Mercury rolled so the rock glanced more or less harmlessly off his left shoulder.

"Gamaliel. What the hell are you doing here?" Mercury stammered.

"I have interests in the area," said Gamaliel, bending to pick up another rock. "I patrol the region, looking for suspicious characters. Heads up!" He pitched another rock at Mercury. Mercury flattened himself against the ground, and the rock sailed over his head.

"I'll let you know if I see anybody suspicious," said Mercury, pulling himself to his feet.

"Hey, you're quick!" said Gamaliel, picking up another rock. There seemed to be an endless supply at his feet. "Not quick enough though!" He hurled the rock.

This time Mercury couldn't get out of the way. He held his hands in front of his face, and the rock smacked into his right wrist. He heard a bone break. Grunting in pain, Mercury grabbed his wrist and turned his back to Gamaliel. He stumbled away, trying to get some distance between himself and Gamaliel's throwing arm.

"Coward," Mercury growled. "Sneaking up on a guy..."

A rock smacked him in the back, thumping the wind out of his lungs and nearly knocking him over. Gamaliel wasn't going to give him a chance to catch his breath. He had caught Mercury off guard, and he wasn't going to give up the advantage. He'd keep pummeling Mercury until he was a bloody remnant of a cherub.[8] Mercury stumbled a few more steps and was struck again, this time in the right shoulder. He fell to his knees. Another rock knocked him forward onto his palms. He winced as pain shot through his right arm. Angel bones heal quickly, but not *that* quickly.

"Damn it, Gamaliel," Mercury muttered. "I can't believe you're going to make me do this." He fell flat on his stomach, unmoving.

Gamaliel stepped closer. "Give up, Merc? I can keep this up all day, you know."

Mercury said nothing.

Gamaliel wound up and hurled another rock, hitting Mercury squarely in the small of his back. The pain was nearly unbearable. Mercury couldn't be certain, but he suspected Gamaliel had broken his spine. Still he didn't make a sound.

8 It may strike the reader as odd that an angel would use such a primitive method of attack. In fact, angels often resort to using crude projectile weapons (such as handguns or rocks) because it tends to be quicker and easier than harnessing interplanar energy. *Mano a mano* fights between two angels armed with only their own miraculous angelic powers tend to go on for days, ending only when one of them becomes too bored to continue. An angel armed with a steady supply of rocks can keep the defender too off balance to get a handle on the energy streams, eventually pelting him into submission.

Gamaliel stepped closer. Now he was only a few feet away. "Give up?"

Mercury didn't move.

Gamaliel stepped up to Mercury and kicked him hard in the side. Mercury winced but didn't make a sound.

"Come on, Merc," Gamaliel chided, kneeling down next to him. "I was just getting—"

Mercury turned to face Gamaliel, bringing his left hand up from underneath him. His fist was full of sand.

The sand hit Gamaliel squarely in the eyes. "Gaaaahhh!" he yelled, stumbling backward. "You bastard!"

"I didn't want to have to do it, you asshole," grumbled Mercury. "It's like the oldest action movie cliché ever. Throw sand in the bad guy's face when he comes in close to gloat. Don't think I feel good about it, because I don't!"

As he spoke, he managed to get to his feet. His spine was bruised but not broken. He staggered toward the edge of the plateau, which was now only about fifty feet away. If he could get to the edge, he might have a chance to get away and regroup.

Gamaliel was stumbling toward him, trying to rub the sand out of his eyes. The two angels moved in a sort of slow-motion parody of a chase sequence, getting ever closer to the edge of the plateau.

As he neared the edge, Mercury heard voices from the far side of the plateau. Men speaking in a strange tribal tongue. Then what sounded like a goat bleating, followed by a woman's voice. He couldn't make out what she was saying, but he would know that voice anywhere. Christine. The expedition had reached the summit.

Mercury reached the brink of the plateau. Looking back, he saw that Gamaliel had picked up another rock—this one nearly the size of his head. He hoisted the rock over his shoulder as he blinked the sand out of his eyes. Mercury leaped off the edge.

The rock face fell away at a sharp angle, allowing Mercury to use minimal energy to keep himself aloft, skimming just a few feet above the slope. Glancing back, he saw Gamaliel hurling the rock. Fortunately, it was too large for Gamaliel to throw with much force; it arced through the air toward Mercury, and he dodged it without much difficulty.

Gamaliel cursed and took off after Mercury. He knew that he had to catch him before Mercury had recovered from his pummeling. Once Mercury was back to full health, Gamaliel would have a hard time beating him.

Mercury soared down the slope until he reached the plain below, touched down briefly, and then shot into the air again. His back and wrist still ached, but he could fly at close to full speed for as long as he needed to in order to keep Gamaliel at bay. As he rose above the plain, something whizzed past his ear. Another rock? He turned to see Gamaliel coming toward him from below. He had something small and bluish-white in his right palm. It seemed to be growing as Mercury watched.

Mercury changed course just in time to dodge the projectile, which turned out to be a baseball-sized ball of ice. Gamaliel was pulling moisture out of the air and freezing it into hailstones! Mercury had experimented with controlling the weather for a while but had never had much luck with it. He'd be no match for Gamaliel in an ice-ball fight.

Rather than engage Gamaliel, he darted back and forth at random, trying to keep distance between them while dodging the onslaught of hailstones. Occasionally he would fly close enough to the plateau to catch a glimpse of Christine and the men, who seemed to be engaged in some sort of ritual involving a goat.

After a few minutes of evading Gamaliel's volleys, the aches in his wrist and back had nearly subsided. If he was going to have any chance of retrieving the anti-bomb, he was going to have to go on the offensive.

Changing tacks abruptly, he soared directly toward Gamaliel. Gamaliel hurled an ice ball as he approached, but Mercury managed to deflect it with his right arm. Before Gamaliel could form another, Mercury's shoulder slammed into his stomach.

Gamaliel brought both of his fists down hard on Mercury's back. Mercury cried out in pain but held tight to Gamaliel's midsection, squeezing until he heard ribs crack. Gamaliel howled.

The two angels tumbled through the sky above the Kenyan plain, locked tightly together, neither able to seize an advantage. Dark clouds had begun to gather as a result of Gamaliel's unnatural hailstorm, natural forces doing their best to change their behavior to accommodate the supernatural occurrences. The clouds seemed to darken further in response to the celestial struggle. Thunder rumbled in the distance and a spattering of rain began to fall. This was the downside to screwing with the weather: if you gave weather ideas, it tended to run with them. A few miraculous hailstones were about to snowball into a full-on thunderstorm.

Out of the corner of his eye, Mercury caught a glimpse of something glowing bright yellow on the top of Mbutuokoti. A fire?

Suddenly Mercury realized how he was going to end the stalemate. Christine had said that the tribesmen had been burning a goat carcass when the mountaintop had been struck by lightning. He remembered Christine's vivid description of a flaming goat head flying through the air and landing inches in front of her.

Mercury broke free of Gamaliel's grasp and darted in the direction of the mountain. Gamaliel cursed and followed him. Mercury soared over the flaming pyre, stopping when he was even with the far edge of the plateau. He spun around to face Gamaliel, who was clearly puzzled at Mercury's tactics. By stopping in midair, it seemed as if Mercury was deliberately skewing the odds in Gamaliel's favor. But Gamaliel was a cherub of action, and he wasted little time deliberating on Mercury's mistake. He paused some two hundred feet directly above the pyre, a ball of ice growing rapidly in his palm. Lightning flashed in the distance, followed quickly by a loud clap of thunder.

Gamaliel wound up and hurled another fastball.

TWENTY-ONE

President Babcock had wanted to call several of his advisors and cabinet members into the Oval Office to discuss their next steps against the BIOs, but Lucifer was cool on the idea. He claimed that he had reason to believe that the federal government was riddled with BIO spies.

"How do you know?" asked Lubbers.

"Simple," said Lucifer. "Some of the spies are double agents, working for me. In fact, I am here because of certain information I have learned from these spies."

"You have spies in our government?" demanded Babcock, suddenly angry. "Who? What information?"

"You misunderstand me," said Lucifer. "And frankly, you're missing the point. The spies don't *belong* to me. The BIOs have spent decades, if not centuries, infiltrating your government. Some of them are human, some of them are BIOs. We are fortunate that some of these spies sympathize with my cause and have been feeding me information. But I only know a handful of them. I have no way of knowing what other members of your government are BIO spies. And truth be told, some of the agents who have revealed themselves to me could very well be triple agents, providing information about me to their bosses, or intentionally providing me with faulty intelligence. Espionage, as you know, can be exasperatingly complicated. So you understand my reluctance to reveal my plan to your advisors."

"Sure," said Babcock. "But I can personally vouch for several of them. Gabe Horton, my chief of staff, for example. I've known him since high school."

"Understand, Mr. President," said Lucifer, "that we BIOs are, for all practical purposes, immortal. Many of us are several thousand years old. Do not underestimate the patience or foresight of your enemy. It's quite possible that my superiors anticipated that you would one day be in a position of importance and placed Gabe Horton next to you as second trombonist in your high school marching band back in 1985."

Babcock was stunned for a moment at Lucifer's recall. "That's absurd," he said at last.

"Is it?" asked Lucifer. "Tell me, did you know in 1985 that you were going to run for President?"

Travis was silent. The fact was that he *did* know. He had felt that he was destined for greatness since first watching *Star Wars* in 1977. Maybe it wasn't such a stretch to think that these mysterious BIOs had somehow seen incipient greatness in him, like Darth Vader feeling the presence of Luke Skywalker. Now that he thought about it, he did remember being a little suspicious about Gabe when his family had first arrived from Delaware. What kind of kid willingly played trombone in a high school marching band? And who had ever heard of anyone being from *Delaware*? If he couldn't trust Gabe, he realized, he couldn't trust anyone.

"In any case," Lucifer went on, "I am not as worried about betrayal as I am about being misunderstood. Not many people are capable of understanding the true scope of the threat you are facing. My people—the BIOs—will not take kindly to having their authority questioned. Your politicians will understandably want to act cautiously, but there is no room for half measures. If you attack the giant, you must kill the giant. You are in a war for your survival. You did not start the war, but you must finish it."

"I understand," said Travis.

"I knew you would," replied Lucifer. "Because you are a man of action. And more importantly, a man of faith. You see, I believe it is no accident that you are president at this time. I believe that I was led to seek you out, to provide you the tools you require to vanquish the greatest threat your race has ever known. Gentlemen, will you pray with me?"

There was a moment of uncomfortable silence.

"Pray?" Lubbers said, unable to fully conceal his disdain. He had hoped they were done with that crap now that he had accepted the King into his heart.

Travis nodded. "Absolutely," he said. "I think that's a wonderful idea."

Lubbers bit his tongue. Better to just go along with this nonsense than to make an issue of it. Whatever it took to get Rezon to give them the information they needed.

Lucifer held out his hands to Travis and Lubbers. The three of them joined hands and closed their eyes. Lucifer turned his face skyward.

"FATHER IN HEAVEN," Lucifer began, theatrically. "We come before Thee, a triumvirate of supplicants seeking Thy favor and guidance, in this great egg-shaped room cradled in the uterus of this White House, an edifice built in the style of the temples of the wise pagans of old, who might very well have been saved by Thy grace were it not for their poor timing and penchant for buggery."

"Amen," muttered Travis.

"Father," Lucifer continued, "this nation—a nation founded by Thy divine providence and dedicated to the principles of democracy and free market capitalism espoused in Thy holy scriptures, a nation saved by the blood of Thy Son and sustained by the blood of patriots—is under siege. Yea! Under siege by the very powers and principalities of which Thou warned us about in Thy word. But we believe that Thou in Thy excellent wisdom will reward the remnant who has remained true to Thy word and grant unto us salvation, for it is written:

" 'From millions of men…one man must step forward who with apodictic force will form granite principles from the wavering idea-world of the broad masses and take up the struggle for their sole correctness, until from the shifting waves of a fire thought-world there will arise a brazen cliff of solid unity in faith and will.'

"Father," implored Lucifer, "we ask that Thou wouldst allow President Travis Babcock to be that man."

"Amen," muttered Travis again, not realizing that Lucifer was quoting from *Mein Kampf.*

Lucifer went on, "We know, Lord, that Thou art a merciful God, delighting in forgiveness and peace. But we also know that Thou art a just God, pummeling Thy enemies into submission with Thy powerful fists. We beseech thee, O Heavenly Despot, to allow the fighting men and women of the US military to be the iron gauntlets sheathing those fists, and to bless our mission to blast these blaspheming motherfuckers to Kingdom Come. In JESUS'S NAME, AMEN!"

"Amen!" exclaimed Travis.

Lucifer opened his eyes, and the men released each other's hands. Lubbers was all shook up. If it weren't for the calming presence of Elvis in his heart, he might have lost his head.

"That was some prayer," Travis said after a moment. He was clearly in awe. Anyone who could pray like that couldn't be a bad guy—although Travis thought he could have done without *motherfuckers*.

"I believe very strongly in the cause," explained Lucifer. "It makes me emotional."

Travis nodded. Lucifer's sincerity could not be doubted. It was comforting to know that even this stranger from another dimension recognized the truth of the Christian faith and American ideals. If Travis could be sure of anything, it was this: God was on their side.

TWENTY-TWO

The fastest pitch ever recorded in the history of Major League Baseball was thrown by Cincinnati Reds southpaw Aroldis Chapman on Saturday, September 24, 2010. The ball traveled at 105 miles per hour for roughly half a second before smacking into the catcher's mitt. The batter, Tony Gwynn, Jr., said that he never saw the ball until it was behind him. A pitch that fast can kill a man. If you drove a car that fast on the interstate, you'd likely be thrown in jail for the reckless endangerment of your fellow motorists.

The least vigorous angel in all of creation[9] is stronger and faster than any Olympic athlete. A baseball team made up of the nine clumsiest angels in existence, playing in clown shoes while wearing burlap sacks filled with angry wasps tied around their heads, could beat any All-Star team in history like they stole something, as the saying goes.

Gamaliel was not a particularly unathletic angel. Gamaliel was, in fact, the quarterback of the cherubic football team, the starting pitcher for the cherubic baseball team, and—during the off-season—a surprisingly competent scrapbooker. On a good day, he could throw a baseball over two hundred miles per hour

9 Generally believed to be a listless cherubic paper-pusher named Ederatz.

into the strike zone of a legless dwarf, if the situation called for it. And Gamaliel was having a good day.

The ball of ice spun off his fingers so fast that merely the friction of the air caused it to release a fine spray of water as the surface vaporized. It shot from his hand like a bullet aimed squarely for Mercury's heart. Mercury didn't even have time to duck.

Whoopf!

Mercury's sternum cracked, and the air gushed from his lungs. The shock sent him tumbling backward. For a few seconds, his heart stopped. He lost consciousness and began to plummet to the mountainside below. Lightning flashed again, closer this time. The thunderclap was deafening.

When he had fallen fifty feet or so, he regained his senses. Gasping for breath and clutching his chest in agony, he rose again to meet Gamaliel in the air.

Gamaliel fired one more. This time the ice ball struck Mercury in the shoulder, nearly tearing his left arm off. He screamed. The pain was intolerable. Still he did not yield.

"I'll never understand you, Mercury," said Gamaliel, a tinge of pity in his voice. "You flit about without any sense of duty until you get some misguided idea of purpose in your head, and then you just won't give it up, like a bird trying to get out of a closed window. What are you even doing here? Why don't you stop bothering the grownups and go play on an island somewhere?"

Mercury was making a small noise in his throat. After a moment, Gamaliel realized he was laughing.

"What's so funny, Merc?" demanded Gamaliel, readying another hailstone.

Mercury smiled. "You said *doody*," he chuckled.

"Goddamn you, Mercury!" Gamaliel howled in rage. "I'm going to shut that idiotic mouth of yours for—"

Unfortunately, Mercury never learned what it was that Gamaliel was going to shut his mouth for, due to an unlucky imbalance of electric charge between the mass of Mount Mbutuokoti and the clouds above it. Given that Gamaliel was the proximate cause of this imbalance, he really had only himself to blame. Anyone who is going to play with weather needs to know a little basic meteorology—or at the very least fulminology. Fulminology is the study of lightning.

It's often erroneously reported that the American inventor, philosopher, and kite aficionado Benjamin Franklin discovered electricity. This is not true. Electricity was a known phenomenon before Franklin was born. What Franklin discovered was that lightning was a kind of electricity, no different in theory from the shock you get when walking across your carpet and then touch the cast-iron door of your wood-burning stove. In fact, he realized, you don't actually have to touch the stove to get the shock. If the built-up charge is strong enough, it will arc through the air from the stove to your finger—or, more accurately, from your finger to the stove. Franklin decided, rather arbitrarily, that the stove was "positively" charged and that your finger was "negatively" charged. Nature abhors this imbalance between positive and negative and will even things out as soon as it possibly can, by spewing negatively charged ions (electrons, which were too small for Franklin to see, even with bifocal lenses) into the stove. The greater the imbalance, the greater distance the arc can span. When there's a massive imbalance of charges between the earth and the sky, caused, for example, by the sudden formation of a thick mass of water vapor, you get a *really* big arc. Observe:

Somewhere in the neighborhood of two hundred quintillion pent-up electrons leaped from the clouds to the zenith of Mbutuokoti, easing the imbalance between earth and sky and shedding a trifling amount of energy along the way in the form of light, sound, and the disruption of the molecular structure of one overconfident angel and one very unlucky goat. The goat, mercifully, was already dead. The angel, being immortal, was not. If the goat's spirit were watching from some sort of goat heaven, it might be somewhat heartened to see that the twelve men who had recently cut its throat were now also dead, their central nervous systems having been shut down by an electrical charge a trillion times bigger than their conduits were designed for.

The angel's central nervous system, being essentially identical to that of a human being, also shut down. The only qualitative difference between angelic biology and that of humans is that when the human machine shuts down, the ghost that occupied it is evicted permanently. Where it goes exactly is anybody's guess. Where the angelic spirit goes, on the other hand, is well known: nowhere. The spirit of the angel simply hangs around in a noncorporeal and unconscious state, doing its best to repair the machine until it's in fit shape to be inhabited again. Thus did Gamaliel's charred and effectively dead but still entirely reparable body fall to the plateau atop Mount Mbutuokoti, where it was virtually indistinguishable from the dozen men lying splayed like paper dolls around the remnants of their altar.

Mercury might have cheered at the sight of Gamaliel's demise except that, for one thing, it was really gross. For another, he was still in a ridiculous amount of pain. And on top of that, it now seemed that Christine, running down the side of a mountain during a thunderstorm with a doomsday device in her pocket, was determined to kill herself and quite possibly destroy the world in the process.

While the two angels had been fighting in the sky above, Christine had retrieved the glass apple from the cave and was now fleeing from a volcanic eruption that seemed to have been triggered by the lightning strike, followed closely by that malignant bastard Horace Finch. The pressure inside the volcano must have been building for weeks, and the lightning had weakened the rock just enough to allow the lava to break through. Dumb luck, thought Mercury. Or synchronicity.

It was clear that Christine wasn't going to make it. Even if she somehow managed to keep her footing on the wet, slippery rock slope and avoid falling to her death (and undoubtedly triggering the anti-bomb in the process), it would take a miracle to keep her from being struck by one of the globs of molten rock spewing from the mountaintop. Fortunately for her, a miracle was something that Mercury could provide.

With his left arm still hanging by strands of muscle and sinew and his rib cage shattered, what he really wanted to do was land on the plain out of range of the volcano and lie down for a day and a half or so. But there was no time for that. Gritting his teeth against the pain, he forced himself to focus on the invisible channels of supernatural energy that riddled the Mundane Plane. Grabbing ahold of the energy, he formed an invisible umbrella of warped gravity just above Christine, causing any lava clumps that would have hit her to change their trajectory just enough to land a few feet away from her. Unfortunately, Finch was following so close that the umbrella protected him as well.

The farther down the mountain they got, the better their chances of survival were, but from Mercury's vantage point far above the mountainside their progress was excruciatingly slow. They were no more than a quarter of the way to the plain. Dizzy and nauseous from pain, Mercury began to fall, unable to spare any energy maintaining his altitude. He skittered to a stop on the slope above Christine and Finch, still focusing on deflecting the lava raining down all around them. The rain intensified, and his vision blurred, making it difficult to keep track of the two distant figures clambering down the mountain. Just a little farther, he thought. Just a little farther and you'll be safe. We'll be safe.

And then Christine slipped and fell. Mercury held his breath, waiting for the anti-bomb to go off. But a second passed, and then another, and they were all still around.

But then, of course they were. This had all happened before, hadn't it? Christine had told him how she and Finch had run down the side of Mbutuokoti, escaping safely from the lava and the lightning. If they hadn't, Finch never would have gotten the apple and Mercury would never have stolen it from him and imploded the moon. None of what was happening now couldn't be happening if it hadn't already happened.

Mercury shook his head dimly, trying to make sense of the situation with his addled brain. Down below, Finch was dragging Christine's limp body behind an outcropping that would offer some shelter. They were safe. Mercury smiled and passed out, tumbling like a ragdoll down the mountainside.

TWENTY-THREE

"All right," said Lubbers, trying to conceal his impatience. "How are we going to strike back against the BIOs?"

Lucifer smiled. He had no reason to delay any further. He had Lubbers and Babcock eating out of his hand. "I was thinking," he said, "that we would use Wormwood."

Travis paled at the word. Lubbers looked from Lucifer to the president, trying to figure out what he had missed. "Wormwood? What's Wormwood?"

"How do you know about that?" the president demanded, his voice betraying a combination of anger and fear.

"As I said," Lucifer replied calmly, "I have many contacts within your government. Little of importance happens without my knowledge. I would say that the development of a ten-kiloton nuclear device that can fit in a standard carry-on bag qualifies as important, wouldn't you?"

Lubbers's jaw dropped. Rumors of so-called "suitcase nukes" had circulated among conspiracy theorists for better than thirty years. While Lubbers knew that such a device was theoretically possible, it was generally agreed that any nuclear device small enough for a person to carry would have any number of practical problems. The main problem was that the explosive yield of a bomb was limited by the amount of fissile material used. For a suitcase-sized bomb, the yield would be less than one kiloton, given current technical limitations—less than a tenth the size of the of "Little Boy" bomb used by the Americans on Hiroshima. The other problem was that having a nuclear bomb in a suitcase required someone to *carry around a nuclear bomb in a suitcase.* The sort of person who would be willing to do that was the sort of person that in no case should be allowed to operate anything more dangerous than a belt sander.

But apparently someone in the government had decided that there was a need for such a device. Unbelievable. The potential for misuse if a portable nuclear weapon fell into the wrong hands was off the scale. No wonder Lubbers had been left out of the loop. His boss, FBI Director Keith Hansen, probably didn't even know.

"The thing must weigh a hundred pounds," said Lubbers.

Travis eyed Lubbers and then Rezon. Neither of them was cleared for this information. Project Wormwood was known about by only a few dozen people. Half of them were scientists and high-ranking military personnel and the other half were government officials—Travis, the vice president, a few cabinet members, and a handful of senators. Officially, the project did not exist.

"Look, Mr. President," said Lubbers. "We can play the security clearance game if you want, but clearly Mr. Rezon already knows about your super-top-secret project, and he's just told me about it. In any case, we're all on the same team here."

Travis nodded slowly. Lubbers was right. There was no point in standing on protocol now. "All told, the device weight is eighteen pounds," he said.

"Bullshit," said Lubbers. Then, remembering his place, said, "Sorry, Mr. President. In my opinion that statement sounds like bullshit, Mr. President."

"Ultra-grade plutonium-239," said Lucifer. "Ninety-nine point nine percent pure. Virtually no contamination from plutonium-240 or other isotopes. As far as most of the world knows, impossible to produce. With ultra-grade PU-239, you can build a ten-kiloton bomb that fits in an attaché case and emits less radiation than a typical microwave oven. The power to level a small city in a package that can fit in a backpack."

Travis nodded gravely. He didn't remember all the details, but Rezon's account sounded about right.

"Is that enough to take out the BIOs?" asked Lubbers. "Our intelligence isn't very specific about how many BIOs there are, or how spread out they are."

"We don't need to take them all out. Doing so would only be a temporary measure in any case. The important thing is that all of their technology, all of their power, is based on a form of trans-dimensional energy that is unknown to your scientists. They call it interplanar energy. The source of all of that energy is a pyramidal structure in the center of the city that they refer to as the Eye of Providence. If we can detonate Wormwood within a quarter mile of the Eye, the BIOs will be essentially helpless."

"So that's it?" asked Lubbers. "Blow up the pyramid, and the BIOS are done for? What about you? Won't it affect you as well?"

Lucifer nodded. "It won't kill the BIOs; it will merely remove the source of their power. The existing interplanar energy will continue to bounce around the Universe for a few thousand years, gradually dissipating until it is finally depleted. The other BIOs and I will continue to live, but with greatly diminished powers.

And most of our technology—notably the anti-bombs that took out Anaheim Stadium and the moon—will stop working. The attack won't hurt us; it will simply render us impotent. Think of it as neutering a dangerous animal."

"And you're OK with being neutered?" asked Travis.

"I will survive," Lucifer said enigmatically. He did not add that he had long ago built a miniature pyramid on the Infernal Plane that acted as a battery, soaking up stray energy and storing it for his own personal use. The battery would provide for his own needs over the next few thousand years. That was how he had been able to maintain his power despite being unable to return to Heaven. The destruction of the Eye of Providence would make him, by default, the most powerful being in the Universe. After all, in the country of the blind, the one-eyed man is king. By the time his own energy source was depleted, the Universe itself would have begun to fall apart. Without the power of the Eye to sustain it, reality would gradually disintegrate. And that was perfectly fine with Lucifer. He'd wreak havoc for as long as the party lasted.

"OK, so how do we get Wormwood that close to the Eye?" asked Travis. "They must have defenses against such things."

Lucifer smiled. "They have defenses, to be sure. It would be impossible, for instance, to get an anti-bomb anywhere near the Eye of Providence. But a nuclear weapon in a backpack? I doubt the idea has ever occurred to them."

Travis frowned. "Nuclear weapons have been around for seventy years. It's never occurred to them that someone might use one on them?"

"Airplanes have been around for a hundred years," answered Lucifer. "And yet it took you completely by surprise when someone flew one into the Pentagon."

"Point taken," said Travis dryly.

"I don't want to give you the impression that this will be easy," said Lucifer. "Not as easy as flying a 747 into a building, for sure. You will have to send a team of men through the portal to deliver the bomb. These men will have to traverse an intermediary location that we call a planeport in order to get to another portal, which leads to the BIO city. The planeport will be heavily defended. However, I have something that will even the odds between your troops and the BIOs."

"What is it?" asked Lubbers.

"An artifact called a Balderhaz Cube. Within a limited range, it makes it impossible for the BIOs to utilize interplanar energy. To conduct what you might call 'miracles.' Your soldiers will have the advantage, because they are used to fighting with conventional weaponry. And you will have one additional advantage."

"Which is what?" asked Travis.

"Me," said Lucifer. "I will be carrying the bomb."

TWENTY-FOUR

By the time Mercury regained consciousness, the thunderstorm had passed and the volcano was no longer spewing chunks of molten stone into the air. Some twenty feet away, a stream of lava was oozing down the mountainside past him.

Mercury got uneasily to his feet. His shoulder was stiff but had fully reattached itself, and only a mild ache remained to remind him of his previously shattered sternum. He climbed to the top of the mountain and surveyed the vista below. Christine and Finch were nowhere to be found. He remembered Christine saying something about escaping from the volcano in Finch's helicopter, but he had no idea where he had taken her. All he could remember was that Finch had somehow absconded with the apple and returned to Eden II. Christine had flown back to Los Angeles and taken the portal in her condo to warn Heaven about the anti-bomb.

The obvious thing to do would be to head straight to Eden II and try to get the anti-bomb back before Finch could activate the CCD. The problem with that idea was that Finch was in cahoots with Uzziel, which meant that Eden II was probably guarded by cherubim. Mercury would have a hard time getting past them. And even if he did somehow get into Eden II and find the apple, it would be crazy to try to sneak it past Finch's guards. The slightest jolt could set the anti-bomb off. If a bullet hit the apple, or Mercury dropped it, or any of a hundred other things went wrong, the anti-bomb would detonate and wipe out human civilization. No, it was better to leave the anti-bomb to Christine, Jacob, and the other Mercury. If everything transpired the way it had the first time around—and that seemed to be the way things were going—then by tomorrow night the other Mercury would be on his way to the moon with the glowing red apple in his hand.

It was too late to save the moon, but Mercury could still do something about Wormwood. Or could he? He still had no idea what Wormwood actually was. If he showed up in Heaven now, yammering about some ill-defined threat to Heaven, would anyone even listen? And without more specific information, what could they do about it? Not to mention the fact that the other Mercury was still in custody, so he'd first have to explain why there were two of him—and who knows how his presence in Heaven would affect the other Mercury's timestream. Maybe Uzziel would never send him to retrieve the Case of Pestilence. Then he'd never be captured by Gamaliel and brought to Eden II. He'd never be able to fly the anti-bomb to the moon. So by warning Heaven about Wormwood now, he might not only fail to prevent the destruction of Heaven, he might actually sabotage his own attempt to save the Earth.

Mercury let loose a scream of primal frustration. He wasn't used to having to deal with potentially catastrophic results of his decisions, let alone worrying about retroactively screwing up decisions he had already made. It was enough to drive a cherub bonkers.

Still feeling a bit sore, he floated gently into the sky, looking for any clue as to which direction Christine had gone. He saw nothing. Turning back toward the mountaintop, he surveyed the gruesome scene on the plateau. The charred bodies of the tribal elders lay in an eerie circle around the remains of the altar. The lava flow seemed to have bypassed them completely.

He noticed something odd among the remains and flew in closer. One of the bodies appeared lighter than the others—not only lighter skinned but also strangely uncharred by the lightning strike. Gamaliel! He was still unconscious!

Mercury landed next to Gamaliel and looked him over. He was bruised and burned, but already mostly healed. Mercury knew from direct experience that Gamaliel wouldn't be back to a hundred percent for several hours. Even an angelic nervous system took a while to recover from a hard reboot. Mercury realized what he needed to do.

He picked up Gamaliel and slung him over his shoulder, then leaped into the air, heading toward the Megiddo portal.

A few hours later, he reached the rocky promontory that marked the portal. Gamaliel flitted in and out of consciousness, mumbling incoherently. He couldn't seem to figure out where he was or what had happened. Mercury pulled the Sharpie from his pocket and wrote across Gamaliel's forehead:

A TOKEN

Then he wrote across his cheeks:

OF GOODWILL

Finally, he scrawled his signature across Gamaliel's chin:

~MERCURY

He dragged Gamaliel's limp body onto the portal. Within a few seconds, it had disappeared. Well, thought Mercury. That would keep Gamaliel out of trouble for a while. At least until that bastard Uzziel lets him go.

After disposing of Gamaliel, Mercury made his way to the port city of Haifa, where he knew of a charming bar that served some decent local beer. He needed to sit and think for a bit and plot his next move.

His next move turned out to be sixteen bottles of that very same local beer, which was better than he remembered. It was good to sit and rest for a while. He was still a little sore from his fight with Gamaliel, and lugging the big jerk a thousand miles on his shoulders hadn't helped any. He had been sitting at the bar for a good three hours when "L.A. Woman" by the Doors came on the radio.

Are you a lucky little lady in the city of light
Or just another lost angel...city of night
City of night, city of night, city of night, woo, c'mon

The lyrics triggered something in his memory. Hadn't Job said something about a lost angel? Yes, Mercury thought. He said something about a lost angel who somehow gains control over the Wormwood. Mercury had thought it was more metaphorical nonsense, but maybe there really was a lost angel somewhere who held the key to the mystery of Wormood.

An idea struck him. He made a call to Perpetiel via Angel Band.

Mercury! Perpetiel exclaimed. *I thought Uzziel had you in custody. What are you doing on the Mundane Plane?*

Perp still hadn't fully caught on to the whole time-travel thing, evidently.

No time to explain, replied Mercury. *Hey, do you remember that old story about the cherub who got misplaced by the MOC?*

Something of an urban legend, said Perp. *A bureaucratic snafu causes an MOC agent in Ireland to get assigned to report on the demise of the Ottoman Empire. His reports are never received, and for hundreds of years he languishes in Ireland, forgotten by his superiors. Eventually they realize the mistake that they've made and sweep the whole thing under the rug. The cherub is exiled on the Mundane Plane, and all records of his existence are expunged by the MOC. Officially, he no longer exists.*

Do you think there's any truth to it? asked Mercury.

Seems unlikely, although stranger things have happened, replied Perp.

Any idea where this cherub would be located, if he did exist?

According to the story, he was stationed in Cork, Ireland, said Perp. *He's known as Eddie, the Lost Cherub. That's about all I know. Oh, and that a three-inch tie never goes out of style.*

Thanks, Perp.

Eddie the Lost Cherub. Could he be the lost angel from Job's story? It was worth looking into, particularly since Mercury didn't have any other leads.

TWENTY-FIVE

Lucifer gazed out the window of his suite in the Watergate Hotel, smoking a cigar and sipping at a snifter of brandy. Far below him small boats moved almost imperceptibly along the glassy surface of the Potomac.

He could hardly believe how well things were going. His bet on Dirk Lubbers was paying off big-time. Lubbers had just the right combination of raw ambition and blind devotion to duty to make him the perfect agent for Lucifer's diabolical schemes. He was like G. Gordon Liddy all over again—minus the prostitutes on the houseboat.

Lucifer had also correctly calculated that President Babcock would accede to Lubbers's understanding of the situation. Babcock, like all dogmatists, feared more than anything else the possibility that someone was going to come along and pull out one of the bricks making up the fragile edifice of his belief system. It was far easier for Babcock to buy Lubbers's notion that the "BIOs" were just highly advanced alien creatures who posed a threat to national security than to rethink his conception of angels as benign spiritual beings who unquestioningly did the bidding of God Himself. The two men were practically stepping over each other to prove their devotion to the cause. Only one small matter remained to ensure the destruction of Heaven.

He heard the door open behind him. "Tiamat," said his servant Azrael. Lucifer smelled her honeysuckle perfume even before he saw her reflection in the glass. He turned to face the demoness, smiling cordially. "Would you care for a drink? Azrael will be happy to get you something."

"I'm fine," said Tiamat coolly. "I'm a very busy woman, Lucifer. Why don't you tell me why you called me here."

Lucifer nodded. "I apologize for making you come so far. I've got some pressing business in town that requires my constant attention. Business that I think may benefit you."

"Oh?" said Tiamat. "What's that?"

Lucifer took a drag from his cigar and blew a puff of smoke into the air. The smoke seemed to briefly form itself into a mushroom cloud before dissipating. "I'm launching an assault on Heaven," said Lucifer. "The Eye of Providence will fall."

Tiamat stared at him, her eyes wide. "You have finally lost it completely," she said. "You can't take out the Eye. You would be destroying the source of the angels' power. Not just the angels in Heaven, all of them. That includes you and me, Luce."

Lucifer shrugged. "I have a backup power supply. But what do you care?" asked Lucifer with a smile. "Weren't you going to be the absolute despot of time and space?"

"Hilarious, Lucifer," growled Tiamat. "Now if you're finished insulting me…"

"You misunderstand me!" protested Lucifer. "I'm not insulting you, I'm offering you a way to get your plan back on track. A way for you to retake Eden II, to get control over the Chrono-Collider Device. So you can run your little experiment to capture the…what were they called?"

"Chrotons," said Tiamat coldly. "Eden II is under constant guard by three hundred armed cherubim. If I get within twenty miles of that place, they'll string me up."

"How many demons do you have under your command?"

"All told? Around two hundred. It would be suicide to attack Eden II with those kind of odds."

"Hmm," replied Lucifer. "What if I could tip the odds in your favor ? Supplement your ranks a bit?"

Tiamat regarded him skeptically. "Just how many demons are we talking about?"

Lucifer downed the rest of his brandy. "I was thinking all of them," he said.

Tiamat was momentarily speechless. "*All* of them? But you must have—"

"Six-hundred and sixty-six combat-trained demons," Lucifer said. "Will that be enough?"

"I…I should certainly think so!" exclaimed Tiamat. "But why? Why would you give your entire legion? What's the catch?"

"No catch," replied Lucifer. "I won't be needing them for my assault. I'll be taking a more covert tack. What I need is a diversion. I want to draw the Eye's attention to Minas Tirith while I carry the Ring to the crack of Mount Doom."

"You want to do what with whose crack?" asked Tiamat, baffled.

Lucifer *tsk*ed. "You know, for the fake author of a line of books that rip off Tolkien left and right, you sure don't know much about *The Lord of the Rings*."

"Enlighten me."

"Frodo and Sam stealthily carry the One Ring to the crack of Mount Doom while Gandalf and the men of Gondor occupy the Nazgûl at Minas Tirith."

"Still not seeing the connection," said Tiamat impatiently.

Lucifer sighed in exasperation. "You distract Michael with an attack on Eden II while I sneak into Heaven and nuke the Eye."

"Oh!" replied Tiamat. "So you want me to take the brunt of Heaven's wrath, is that it?"

"Precisely," said Lucifer.

"Why would I do that?"

"Why wouldn't you?" asked Lucifer. "What difference does it make to you what I'm doing while you execute your assault? You said yourself that I'm crazy to think I can destroy the Eye. Which means that I will probably end up in prison, and you can keep my demonic horde for yourself. And even if I succeed, what is it to you? Once you've done your chroton thing, you'll possess the ultimate power in the Universe. You won't need the Eye anymore."

"You don't believe for a second that I'm going to succeed," said Tiamat.

"Of course not," said Lucifer matter-of-factly. "I think this whole thing with the Chrono-Collider Device is a colossal waste of time. Just like you think that I'm nuts for trying to destroy Heaven. But you need my demons, and I need a diversion. So what do you say?"

Tiamat threw her head back and laughed until tears rolled down her cheeks. "You really are the most cynical angel ever to fall out of Heaven," she said. "You're going to offer to help me even though you are certain I will fail, and you want me to help you even though I'm certain *you* will fail. All right, then. You'll have your diversion. When can I get the demons?"

TWENTY-SIX

Eddie spent the next several days after Cody's murder feverishly writing the second volume of his book, covering the events up to the destruction of the moon. He no longer felt like he had any choice in the matter. The story was unfinished, and it needed to be told. If finishing the story brought about the end of the world, then so be it. That was none of his concern.

It did bother him, though, that the world might end before anyone had any chance to read his masterpiece. Ideally, he would wait till the whole thing was finished before releasing it to the world, but if what Cody and Cain had said was true there might not be a world to release it to. He decided to hedge his bet by delivering the first two volumes of his saga to the Heavenly authorities before things got too far out of hand. He had them printed out at the Jiffy Print downstairs and then took a cab to Christine's condo. He walked up and knocked on the door, which was answered by the pleasant but dim-witted cherub Nisroc. Nisroc and his counterpart Ramiel had been assigned to guard the portal against any unauthorized intrusions.

"No visitors!" exclaimed Nisroc cheerfully as he opened the door and then slammed it in Eddie's face.

Eddie knocked again.

The door flew open again. "No visitors!" exclaimed Nisroc again. He made to slam the door shut but it caught on Eddie's foot.

"No visitors?" said Nisroc, confused.

"Who is it?" barked Ramiel from somewhere inside the condo.

"My name is Eddie," said Eddie. "Ederatz, actually. I work for the Mundane Observation Corps. Well, used to." He held up the six-hundred-page manuscript he was carrying—the first two volumes of his book on the Apocalypse.

"Ooh, literature!" exclaimed Nisroc, grabbing the stack of paper out of Eddie's hands. The Jehovah's Witnesses had stopped by earlier in the week, and Nisroc was anxiously waiting the next installment of *The Watchtower*. He hadn't expected it to be quite this heavy, though.

"Does this one explain how Earth becomes a paradise after Satan is imprisoned for a thousand years?" asked Nisroc, thumbing through the manuscript. "I had some questions about that."

"Er," said Eddie. "It doesn't actually go into that. But this is just the first two volumes. Maybe Satan is imprisoned in the third one."

"Maybe?" asked Nisroc doubtfully. This Jehovah's Witness didn't seem nearly as confident as the last pair.

"Who is it?" barked Ramiel again.

"Jehovah's Witness!" Nisroc called back. "Not a very good one though!" He continued thumbing through the manuscript. "Some bad language in here," he said, shaking his head. "And no pictures. Are you sure you're a real Jehovah's Witness? I'd like to see your badge, please."

"We don't carry..." Eddie started. "That is, I'm not a Jehovah's Witness. As I said, I'm with the MOC. I understand that you have an interplanar portal here, and I was hoping to make a delivery."

"Do we do deliveries?" Nisroc shouted.

"No!" barked Ramiel.

"No deliveries," said Nisroc, trying to hand the manuscript back to Eddie.

"Just listen for a minute, will you?" said Eddie. "This is a very important book. It's not quite finished, but it needs to be delivered to the Seraphic Senate now, in case...well, in case something happens."

"Something?" asked Nisroc. "Like what?"

"I'm not a hundred percent sure. Something that would prevent me from delivering the book. I won't know if it happens until I finish the book."

"Uh-huh," said Nisroc skeptically.

"Look, just send it through the portal. There's a note on the first page saying to deliver it to the Senate. OK?"

"I guess," said Nisroc. "Do you have anything with pictures?"

"Sorry," replied Eddie.

Nisroc sighed and slammed the door.

OK, thought Eddie. At least that's taken care of. It would probably take a few days for the manuscript to get delivered to the offices of the Senate, and there was a good chance that nobody would ever read it, but at least he had done his best to officially document the goings-on of the past few weeks. Maybe at some time in the distant future it would help someone to make sense of everything that had happened.

It was hard to believe that Heaven had put Ramiel and Nisroc in charge of preventing unauthorized access to the Glendale portal. Of course, anybody who did get past them would have to go through planeport security to get anywhere, so having angels guard the portal was really just a token gesture. Hell, there wasn't *anybody* watching the Megiddo portal. The Megiddo portal was pretty well hidden, though, and nearly impossible for anyone other than an angel to get to. Ramiel and Nisroc were presumably there to prevent random civilians from wandering onto Christine's linoleum and inadvertently transporting themselves to another plane of existence—something that wasn't a concern in the rocky wasteland of the Jezreel Valley.

Eddie took the cab back to his hotel. This was the last day of his Finch-sponsored stay at the Wilshire, so he would have to find another place to write. *Where* to write, however, was not as pressing a problem as *what* to write. It was unclear where the story went after the implosion of the moon. Most importantly, what had happened to Mercury? Was he really gone for good? It seemed like bad storytelling to have him just disappear to some unknown dimension, never to return.

Eddie was still fretting when he was stopped cold in the lobby by a tall, grinning man with silver hair.

"Hey, Eddie," said the man cheerfully. "Where are you off to this time?"

"Sweet baby carrots," Eddie gasped. "You're Mercury!"

"I am indeed. And you are the mysterious Eddie, the fabled Lost Cherub of the MOC, I take it."

Eddie nodded. *Fabled*. He liked that. "Where did you come from?" he asked. "I thought you disappeared after the thing with the moon."

"I did," said Mercury. "Now I'm back. I have a question for you. Does the name Wormwood mean anything to you?"

"Oh boy," said Eddie. "OK, I'll tell you everything I know about Wormwood, but I've got some questions for you first."

"Fair enough."

They took a seat at the hotel bar. Mercury told Eddie everything that had happened to him since the implosion of the moon. He had spent a day scouring Cork for the legendary Lost Cherub, eventually happening on a bartender who told him that Eddie was staying at the Wilshire Hotel in Los Angeles. Eddie frantically took notes while Mercury spoke.

"Incredible," remarked Eddie. "You lived the last two days over again, but from a completely different perspective. And somehow, without meaning to, you caused things to happen just like they did the first time around."

Mercury nodded. "It's like being a character in a book that's already been written. Unsettling."

"Tell me about it," agreed Eddie.

Eddie proceeded to tell Mercury everything he knew about Wormwood, which wasn't much.

"A portable nuclear bomb," said Mercury, impressed. "Beats curing cancer, I guess. What's Lucifer going to do, try to get it through the planeport into Heaven?"

"That would be my guess," said Eddie. "A conventional—that is, nonsupernatural—bomb wouldn't set off the automatic countermeasures in the planeport. If he can muscle his way through security, he could conceivably make it through the Heavenly portal. From there, it's a short walk to the Eye."

Mercury whistled. "So Lucifer is planning to take out the Eye of Providence. He's bold, I give him that much. Is Wormwood powerful enough to do it?"

"Ten kilotons," said Eddie. "A blast that size would vaporize anything within a half-mile radius. If he can get close to the pyramid, yeah, I'd say he could do it. Again, I'm just guessing, but it makes sense."

"And you didn't think it might be a good idea to warn your superiors?"

"I just found out about it," said Eddie. "And my superiors haven't really been listening to me for a while. In any case, I'm MOC, remember. I'm not supposed to get involved."

"OK, then," said Mercury, getting to his feet. "I guess it's up to me to warn them."

"Yep," said Eddie, watching Mercury leave. "Good luck."

And he meant it, even though he knew Mercury would fail. Wormwood couldn't be stopped. It was the end of everything.

TWENTY-SEVEN

Dirk Lubbers sat in an uncomfortable folding chair in a cramped, dark apartment that smelled like mildew and stale cigarettes, staring at a flat-panel monitor that was displaying what was perhaps the least interesting television program since *Diagnosis Murder*.

The monitor was split into six images, each of them a view from a camera that was aimed at Christine Temetri's condo building. The cameras were themselves marvelous works of twenty-first-century engineering, packing a high-resolution camera, a battery with a two-week charge, and a wireless transmitter into a package no larger than Lubbers's thumb. They had been hidden in various strategic locations around the condo building the previous days by FBI agents pretending to be cable repairmen and gardeners.

Lubbers took a sip of lukewarm instant coffee from a Styrofoam cup. As unpleasant as his current situation was, it still beat being at a three-man religious revival in the Oval Office. Lubbers had been through a lot in his fifty-nine years—notably a stint in Desert Storm, during which he had been part of an "enhanced interrogation team"—but there were some things that nobody should have to go through, chief among them holding hands with two other men. He shuddered at the memory. It had been an unspeakable relief when he had been shuttled off to Andrews Air Force Base to fly back to Los Angeles.

Lubbers told himself that it had been worth it. Mundane appearances to the contrary, this was the most important assignment of his career. He was going to oversee the delivery of a nuclear bomb to the headquarters of an alien race located in another dimension, eliminating a grave threat to the human race and ending thousands of years of interdimensional tyranny. The moment of truth for the human race was hours away, and Dirk Lubbers was its savior. He cracked his knuckles and gulped some more of the tepid coffee. "How's the gas leak coming?" he asked the gaggle of FBI agents huddled around a folding table in the next room, clacking away at laptop computers and yammering on cell phones.

"Everthing's set up, sir. We start going door-to-door in ten minutes," said one of the agents, whose last name was Gilbert. He pronounced it the French way, *Jheel-BAYR*. Lubbers called him "Joe-Bear." He knew that wasn't the right pronunciation, but nobody was going to make him say *Jheel-BAYR*. He'd rather hold hands with another man.

"Excellent. Good work, Joe-Bear."

Gilbert nodded curtly. They had planned a cover story about a natural-gas leak so that they could evacuate the condo complex before launching their assault. Civilians would only get in the way.

Uncomfortably warm in the cramped quarters, Lubbers stood up and removed his jacket, hanging it over the back of his chair. He had taken to wearing a black leather jacket with his FBI badge pinned to the left breast, which had raised some eyebrows among his peers and underlings. Poor bastards, thought Lubbers. They didn't know what it was like to have the King in your heart.

He walked to the window. The apartment Operation Righteous Anger had commandeered was on the third floor. Through the horizontal vinyl blinds he could see into the window of Christine's notorious breakfast nook. Not much was going on. He hadn't seen anything more interesting through the window than a man holding up a can of SpaghettiOs to the light so that he could read the label. After the twenty-sixth time this had happened, Lubbers had instructed his team not to record any further instances in the official report.

Christine's building was three stories and housed a total of twenty-four units. An open-air hallway ran the length of each floor. There were three other identical buildings nearby. The entire complex was surrounded by a metal fence.

"Sir, we've got somebody on monitor three."

Monitor three. That was the gate nearest Christine's condo. Ordinarily, a visitor would have to unlock the door with a card key to get in, but Rezon had warned Lubbers that the locks would be no barrier to a BIO, who could manipulate interdimensional energy to perform so-called "miracles." In fact, about an hour ago one did just that: the FBI had watched as the man brushed his hand over the lock and then pushed open the gate. Lubbers recognized that BIO as the same one who his agents had been tailing in Los Angeles, Ederatz—the one who had written the report that provided so much valuable intelligence. Ederatz had stopped at Christine's door and spoken briefly to one of the BIOS, the one Lubbers's team was calling SpaghettiO. Lubbers almost had his sharpshooters take him out, but he seemed only to want to deliver a stack of papers—probably a copy of the same report that the FBI had taken from him. There was nothing in that report that would compromise Operation Righteous Anger, and it was important to keep SpaghettiO and Spike (the other BIO inside the condo) ignorant of the FBI's presence as long as possible. Blowing Ederatz's head off outside their front door might just tip them off that there was a problem. In the end, Lubbers had made a judgment call, deciding that there probably wasn't anything in Ederatz's head worth blowing it off for. Ederatz didn't seem like a terribly important BIO. All he did was wander around the city and sit in his room at the Wilshire, banging away at a laptop.

Lubbers examined the feed from camera three. Whoever this fellow was, it wasn't Ederatz. This guy was a good six inches taller, for one thing, and he had silver hair. Silver hair! He passed his hand over the lock and opened the gate, walking toward Christine's condo.

"Sharpshooters ready, sir," said Gilbert.

Lubbers held his breath. What now? If he ordered his snipers to take out the BIO, he'd be firing the first shot in an interdimensional war. It might spook the BIOs inside, inciting them to warn their superiors that the humans were on to them. They might redouble their defenses, making it impossible for Rezon and the SEAL team to get through the planeport.

But what if this BIO was delivering a warning? What if he somehow knew about the plan to invade their home dimension? Then, if he got through, the BIOs might shut down the portal entirely or send a platoon of BIOs through the portal with those anti-bomb things to show the puny humans who was boss.

The worst possible scenario, though, would be firing at the silver-haired stranger and missing. Rezon had told them that a bullet through the skull would incapacitate a BIO for a few minutes. But if they couldn't get a clean shot, they would just piss him off. He might retaliate by calling down a pillar of fire to level the whole block. And that would be that for Operation Righteous Anger. It's now or never, he thought.

"They got a clean shot, Joe-Bear?"

"Yes, sir. He's about fifty feet from the front door, moving north. If we're going to take a shot, now would be the time."

Lubbers released his breath. "Take him out," he said.

TWENTY-EIGHT

Tiamat stood in front of a melamine and particleboard table in a conference room of the Nairobi Hilton, eyeing the black-hooded members of the Supreme Council of the Orders of the Pillars of Babylon. It was the best meeting spot she could find in the area on short notice. So as not to provoke suspicion, the Council members had kept their hoods in their jacket pockets before the meeting, only donning them once they were safely inside the conference room. Admittedly, this defeated the ostensible purpose of the hoods, but the OPB was big on ceremony. The assembled members represented a who's who of tycoons and political leaders from around the world. They didn't often meet in public, but these were special circumstances.

"Gentlemen," said Tiamat, "our time has come."

Grumbles went around the table. "*Your* time, you mean," muttered one man.

"Order!" barked Horace Finch, sitting next to Tiamat. An ill-fitting hood obscured his vision, requiring him to tilt his head back at a thirty-degree angle to see through the eyeholes.

After Finch's bungled attempt to master time and space by catching chrotons in a glass apple in Kenya, Tiamat had seized control of the organization. Finch had backed her bid to be the new leader, and in return she had allowed him to stay on as her second in command. It was either that or be cast out of the OPB entirely.

Tiamat evoked conflicting emotions among the members of the OPB. On the one hand, it had been her work in ancient Babylon that had formed the foundations of the OPB's efforts. On the other hand, she had basically ignored the OPB over most of the past four thousand years, laughing at their feeble efforts to uncover the secrets of the Universe. She offered some token support when they embarked upon their plan to build a particle collider beneath Los Angeles during the early twentieth century but abandoned them again when World War II broke out. She never really believed the CCD would work, and she had bigger things to worry about. There was so much suspicion about domestic spies during the war that the OPB had to suspend all of its operations for several years. And after the war, things were even worse: in the fifties and sixties, sneaking around and attending secret meetings was likely to get one shot for being a suspected Communist. By the time the OPB resumed active operations in the 1980s, the CCD was in disrepair, and areas of the Los Angeles suburbs that the OPB had intended to leave vacant had been overrun by theme parks. Even if they had gotten the CCD to work, they still had not solved the central technical problem: how to store the chrotons once they were generated. The CCD was mothballed.

When Horace Finch announced plans to build another collider, this time in Kenya, Tiamat once again offered token support. As the CCD-2 got close to completion, she had a few of her personal operatives look into its chances of success. She assumed that the OPB would once again be stuck when faced with the problem of how to capture the chrotons. But her spies learned that Finch had a contact in Heaven who had promised him a suitable receptacle for the chrotons. That contact turned out to be Uzziel, and the receptacle was an anti-bomb that had been hidden for millennia inside Mount Mbutuokoti. When Tiamat realized how close Finch was to succeeding, she belatedly offered her wholehearted support. It was not enough, as it turned out. Christine, Jacob, and Mercury had intervened, stealing the anti-bomb and rendering the CCD-2 impotent. Finch had fled the facility, which was then placed under guard by troops under the command of the archangel Michelle. All of the OPB's work on the CCD-2 over the past twenty years appeared to be for naught. Even if they could somehow retake the Eden II facility from Michelle's cherubic guard, without another anti-bomb to catch the chrotons the machine was useless. So while the Supreme Council resented Tiamat's involvement, there was no denying that they needed her. Putting her in charge was an act of desperation, a Hail Mary pass in the last two seconds of the game.

"As I say," said Tiamat, "*our* time has come. I have just spoken to one of my fellow demons, a gentleman by the name of Lucifer. Perhaps you have heard of him."

Another round of resentful, but impressed, grumbling. Tiamat had connections, that much was certain. Fortunately, most of the Council members weren't aware that Tiamat and Lucifer had been at each other's throats for most of the past seven thousand years.

"It seems that Lucifer is planning a major offensive against Heaven," Tiamat continued. "And we have agreed that it is better for both of our causes if we synchronize our attacks."

"Attack?" asked one of the hooded men. "What attack?"

Tiamat smiled. "Why, we're retaking Eden II, of course."

"Retaking Eden II? Why? The receptacle was destroyed! The CCD is useless without it!"

"Indeed," replied Tiamat, looking to the hooded man on her immediate right. "Horace, would you like to tell them?"

Finch tilted his head forward and spoke. The air was feeling very close inside the hood, and he was having difficulty breathing. "Before the interlopers took the apple, it shed a small piece of itself. Evidently the anti-bombs do this shortly before they are fully ripe. The remnant was a small, teardrop-shaped piece of glass. A glass apple seed."

Murmurs filled the room.

Finch went on: "I was forced to flee the facility, but before I did I dug a small hole in the ground inside Eden II and buried the seed."

"As you know," Tiamat said, "I now have in my employ a seraph by the name of Uzziel. Uzziel is something of an expert on these anti-bombs. I asked him about the glass remnant, and he said that it is indeed a seed. He said that the seeds grow very quickly. Plant one in any ordinary soil and a few days later you'll have a fully grown tree. By now, there should be at least one good-sized apple on the tree. Any apples would of course be practically worthless as anti-bombs; they need several hundred years to ripen before they are useful as munitions. But for our purposes, an unripe apple is as good as any."

"Fine," said another hooded man. "But Eden II is guarded by three hundred angels with flaming swords. How do you expect to get past them and into the CCD?"

"Lucifer has agreed to lend me six hundred and sixty-six of his best combat-trained demons," Tiamat replied. "Combined with my own forces, we will be unstoppable—assuming, of course, that our demons are armed with superior weaponry."

She smiled innocently, and there were more grumbles around the table. It was now clear why Tiamat had deigned to brief the

Supreme Council on her plans: she wanted access to the OPB's cache of weapons.

"You said we were going to synchronize attacks with Lucifer," said another man. "What kind of attack is Lucifer planning?" asked another man.

"Lucifer is launching an assault on Heaven," replied Tiamat. "My sources tell me that he plans to take out the Eye of Providence with a portable nuclear device."

Several of the hooded men gasped. The Eye of Providence was known to them as the near-legendary source of the mystical power of the gods. Destroying it seemed unthinkable.[10]

"Isn't the Eye of Providence the source of your power?"

Tiamat shrugged. "Of course," she said. "But the power of the Eye is nothing compared to the power we will hold when have used the CCD to harness chrotons. As I say, Lucifer's schemes are unimportant. I wish him the best of luck, but his success or failure will have no impact on our plan. Gentlemen, I resolve that the OPB throws its full support behind my plan to retake Eden II." There was a pause, and she jabbed Horace Finch in the ribs.

"Seconded!" yelped Finch, who was fighting off a bout of claustrophobia.

A muttered chorus of ayes went up from the group. What choice did they have? They knew Tiamat wasn't going to share the spoils with them, but the avowed purpose of the OPB was to uncover the hidden secrets of the Universe. Whether they were allowed to enter the Promised Land themselves was a secondary concern.

10 A representation of the Eye of Providence can be found on the US dollar bill, supposedly put there by wily Freemasons. Freemasonry has been the subject of much conspiracy theorizing, but in fact it is a completely benign and prosaic organization that was founded specifically to divert attention from the activities of the far more secretive and insidious Order of the Pillars of Babylon.

Tiamat's eyes flashed wickedly. "Gentlemen, we are on the verge of a new era. Once we have control over Eden II, all time and space will be ours!"

TWENTY-NINE

Eddie sat at a booth in the Charlie's Grill just down the street from Christine's condo, sipping coffee from a ceramic mug. He hadn't heard the gunshot, but he wasn't surprised to see Mercury fall. It was only a matter of time before the government put the condo under surveillance—or perhaps more accurately, under siege. Given what he knew about Wormwood and Lucifer's plans, Eddie had been a little surprised that he had been allowed to deliver his manuscript unmolested. Once again, being a little fish had paid off. Nobody gave a shit about Eddie Pratt.

Eddie told himself it wasn't his fault that Mercury had been taken. After all, he hadn't known about the snipers; he would only have been guessing. And what difference did it make in the end? Wormwood was unstoppable. Both Cody and Cain had told him so. If a sniper hadn't taken him down, something else would have. You couldn't fight destiny. Best to just get the whole thing over with.

While some small part of Eddie's brain continued to poke at his conscience like a man kicking a prostrate opossum, the rest of it focused on documenting the events of the past few days. He banged away at the laptop with a ferocity that elicited looks of concern from his fellow Charlie's Grill patrons. Mercury had given him a lot of material, what with his encounter with Job and Cain, his time traveling, and his epic battle with Gamaliel. This was good stuff, thought Eddie. Mercury made a pretty good hero. It really was too bad that the story had turned out to be a tragedy.

Eddie hit Save and regarded what he had written. The cursor sat blinking at the end of the last line, mocking him.

Nobody gave a shit about Eddie Pratt.|

Could just as well change that to present tense, Eddie thought. Nobody gives a shit about Eddie Pratt. He could imagine someone reading his report, impatiently skimming through the parts about this intolerably dull cherub, Eddie Pratt. Tough, thought Eddie. If I have to be part of this accursed story, then you have to read about it.

Eddie took another sip of coffee. He had added three artificial creamers to it already, but it was still too strong for his taste. He picked up another of the little plastic creamer cups, peeled back the lid, and poured it into his coffee. Then he stirred it with a spoon, set the spoon on the table, and took another sip. Not bad, he thought. He debated adding another one, but decided he didn't want to push it.

Paging through what he had written, he was satisfied that he had put together a compelling narrative about Mercury, but he felt like there were chapters missing. There was more to this story than what he had compiled so far. What had happened to Christine and Jacob, for instance? And what was Tiamat up to? It wasn't like her to just give up her diabolical scheming. Surely she was plotting something right now.

As he reflected on this, he stared out the window in the direction of the condo complex. There had been a flurry of activity after Mercury fell, with plainclothes agents dragging him to a parked SUV, which screeched away for some unknown destination. But now the scene was eerily placid.

While he watched, a bus pulled up to the curb, paused for a moment, and then pulled away. It had left behind a man and a woman who were engaged in an animated conversation. The man, who was short and dark-skinned, seemed particularly agitated, as if he could barely control his limbs. He grabbed the woman's wrist, but she wrested free and stalked off in the direction of the gate.

Great Scott, thought Eddie. It's Christine and Jacob. They were about to walk into the same trap that had just claimed Mercury. If the FBI hadn't spotted them already, they soon would. Eddie thought about warning them, but there was no time. By the time he had made it outside, Christine would be at the gate.

He breathed deeply, trying to make himself relax. It doesn't matter, he told himself. They're doomed to fail anyway. Just get it over with.

But something continued to bother him, a part of his brain that was less atrophied than his conscience: his sense of narrative. This was bad writing, pure and simple. You couldn't have the heroine fall into the same trap as the hero, only a few minutes later. What was the point? Why not just kill them all off at once, if that's what you're going to do? Why drag things out?

Christine continued to walk toward the trap, with Jacob following, pleading for her to stop. Did he sense the trap? Or did he, too, just feel like something was *wrong*?

"Damn it!" Eddie growled, jumping to his feet and knocking over his coffee. "Don't do it! It's terrible! The pacing is all off! It lacks unity and cohesion!"

The other patrons had fallen silent and were staring at Eddie. A waitress stopped by and flopped a towel down onto the table. Mopping up the coffee, she met Eddie's eyes and said, deadpan, "More coffee, sir?"

Eddie sat down. "Sorry," he offered meekly. The waitress shrugged, refilled his coffee cup, and walked away. Eddie turned to look out the window again.

Christine had stopped. She was facing Jacob, who was gesturing wildly. He seemed to point directly at Eddie. Christine looked in Eddie's direction and nodded her head, looking defeated. They crossed the street, headed toward Charlie's Grill.

Eddie froze. OK, play it cool, he thought. No need to panic.

Christine and Jacob took the booth behind him. In between bickering, they ordered a chicken salad sandwich and a French dip.

"I don't care," Christine was saying. "I have to try. There's no other way to warn them."

"And you think Lubbers doesn't know that? He's probably already here, parked in a van down the street, just waiting for you to show up. Lubbers may be single-minded, but he's not stupid. Daltrey is probably nearby, too. We were lucky to get away from him last time, Christine. He won't get fooled again."

Christine seemed to be suppressing a giggle, but Jacob continued, undeterred by her strange reaction.

"Not only will you fail to warn…whoever it is on the other side of that portal, you'll have played right into his hands. He's an expert on what they call 'enhanced interrogation,' you know.

They'll find out what you know. And once you're not worth anything to them anymore, they'll lock you up and throw away the key. Or worse. *Unck!*"

This last was a noise that Jacob made in his throat, startling Eddie so much that he almost spilled his coffee again.

"What would you have me do then? Nothing? You and I are the only ones on this plane—that is, this planet—who know what Lubbers is planning. We have a responsibility to do *something*."

Eddie sighed, realizing that it was up to him to resolve the stalemate. He got up and grabbed a chair from a nearby table, taking a seat at the end of Christine and Jacob's table.

"*Unck?*" said Jacob.

"I'm sorry to intrude," said Eddie, "but I couldn't help overhearing."

"Oh God," said Jacob. "We must sound like lunatics. *Unck*."

"This is a private conversation," said Christine curtly.

"Not as private as you might think," said Eddie. "Those guys in the cable repairman uniforms in the corner booth? Undercover FBI agents. Fortunately they seem to be more interested in their bacon cheeseburgers than in you, at present." Eddie had no idea who the guys were. Probably cable repairmen, judging by their outfits.

"So?" asked Christine, her hushed tone belying her nonchalance. "What do I care if those guys are…Anyway, who the hell are you?"

"My name is Ederatz. I used to work for the Mundane Observation Corps. You can call me Eddie."

"The MOC?" asked Christine. "You're…?"

"A cherub, yes," replied Eddie. "And Jacob is right. You can't go home to your condo. They're waiting for you. You'll never make it to the front door."

"How does he know my name?" asked Jacob. "*Unck*."

"How do you know they're watching my condo?" asked Christine.

"I observe. I document. It's what I do. And I just observed and documented your friend, Mercury, getting shot in the head and dragged away by federal agents."

Christine snorted. "You're a liar, Eddie, or whatever your name is. Mercury is gone, on some other plane, a billion miles away. He's never coming back."

"It would probably be better for him if he were," said Eddie. "But he came back. Somehow he traveled through time, returning to Earth before he left. He helped you escape from Mount Mbutuokoti, although you never saw him. He's the one who kept you from being pelted by chunks of molten lava."

"Time travel?" said Christine dubiously. "Really? You sound like you're making this up as you go along, Eddie."

Eddie shrugged. "All I know is what he told me." Eddie told her how Mercury had related everything that had happened over the past two days, including his scheme to convince the other Mercury, his past self, to turn himself in, and how he had delivered Gamaliel to Heaven as a token of goodwill.

Christine wanted to argue, but against all reason and logic what Eddie said made sense. He knew far too much about Mercury, down to the archangel's business card that he had been carrying in his pocket for centuries. And his story explained how Christine had managed to escape from the volcanic eruption, why Mercury had turned himself in, and why the Heavenly bureaucracy had gone so easy on him. There was no way around it: Eddie was telling the truth.

She said, "So you saw Mercury get shot while trying to get to my condo? Why didn't you stop him?"

Eddie made an effort not to betray any sense of guilt. "I didn't know," he said, which was technically true. "I didn't know the FBI had snipers set up until they took him out. I'm sorry." The words rang hollow in his ears.

"Well, that's that, then," said Jacob. "We can't go to the condo. *Unck.*"

"But we have to do something," said Christine. "We have to find Mercury. He can warn Heaven. Call them up on whatchamacallit, Angel Band."

"Maybe he already has," offered Jacob.

"I don't think so," said Eddie. "He wanted to warn them in person. He didn't think they'd believe him unless he went in person, and frankly I think he was right. He told me some pretty wacky stuff."

"What stuff?" asked Christine. "Damn it, Eddie, what aren't you telling us?"

"Are you familiar with something called Wormwood?"

Christine and Jacob shook their heads. "*Unck*," said Jacob.

"The short version: you're right to be worried. The US government is about to launch a preemptive strike against Heaven, and I have pretty good reason to believe that Lucifer is pulling the strings. In fact, I suspect Lucifer has taken Mercury prisoner."

"You mean the crazy blond guy in Kenya?" asked Jacob. "That's not his real name, is it? I mean, you're not saying he's actually—"

Christine cut him off. "Lucifer has Mercury? Where?"

Eddie sighed. "Look," he said. "I'll tell you everything I know. I may even be able to help you find Mercury. But I need you to do something for me first."

"What is it?" asked Christine.

"I need you to tell me everything that's happened to you since you left Eden II."

"Why?" demanded Christine. "Can't this wait? If what you're saying is true, the US government is about to launch an all-out war on Heaven."

Eddie shook his head. "I'm sorry. I have to document everything. The record has to be complete. Once you tell me your side of the story, I'll tell you how to find Mercury."

Christine was clearly furious, but she could see that Eddie wasn't going to budge. Every second she protested was going to be another second Mercury spent at the mercy of Lucifer. "Fine," she said, and launched into her account of everything that had happened to them over the past two days. With minimal interruptions from Eddie, she caught him up to the moment he and Jacob had gotten off the Covenant Holders bus less than an hour earlier. Eddie couldn't type fast enough to keep up, so he resorted to scribbling shorthand in a notepad.

"Now," Christine demanded, "where did Lucifer take Mercury?"

Eddie pointed at the floor. "Downstairs," he said ominously.

"Downstairs?" asked Jacob. "You mean, like, Hell?"

"No," said Eddie, shaking his head. "Downstairs. You know, the basement."

"What basement? You mean *here*, at Charlie's Grill?"

Eddie nodded. "Lucifer owns this whole chain, you know. Every store has a secret room in the basement. Lucifer uses them to store contraband and as impromptu meeting rooms. Or, you know, tort…that is, holding facilities." He hurriedly went on, "I saw them dragging Mercury into a food truck. Then, a little while later, I saw the same truck pull around back of this restaurant.

There's a door outside that leads to the basement. I suspect that's where they brought him."

"That's—*unck!*—ridiculous!" said Jacob. "They shot him in broad daylight and then brought him here, to a restaurant not more than a hundred yards away? I don't buy it."

Eddie shrugged. "They needed to get him someplace fast, before he regained consciousness. I doubt anybody saw anything. Mercury basically fell into the bushes, the truck pulled up, and he was gone. I only saw it because I was watching him. I'm telling you, he's downstairs. But you don't have to believe me if you don't want to."

"You bastard," Christine spat. "You made us sit here and tell you stories while Mercury is right downstairs, probably being tortured by Lucifer. All right, then. Show us where he is."

"Show you?" asked Eddie, taken aback. "I said I would tell you where he was, which I have done. I'm afraid that now I need to find someplace quiet to finish my book." He started to get up, but Christine gripped his forearm, fingernails digging into his flesh. "Ow!" Eddie exclaimed. "Don't make me—"

"Don't make you *what*, Eddie?" Christine growled. "Pull one of your so-called 'miracles'? Go ahead. Make it a big, flashy one. In fact, let me help you out." In a flash, Christine was standing on top of the table.

"Christine!" gasped Jacob. "What are you doing? Sit down! *Unck!*"

Eddie nodded, agreeing wholeheartedly with Jacob.

"Ladies and gentlemen!" exclaimed Christine. "I am pleased to announce that we have here at Charlie's Grill today a very special guest. His name is Eddie, and he's an *angel*!"

Every eye in the restaurant turned to Christine, and then to Eddie, at whom she was pointing.

"Don't be shy, Eddie!" Christine bellowed. "Wave to the nice people!"

"Stop, Christine," Eddie pleaded. "Please stop."

"Eddie works for something called the Mundane Observation Corps. His job is to remain completely unnoticed by the likes of you fine folks while observing everything you do. Under no circumstances is Eddie allowed to make a giant spectacle of himself. Isn't that right, Eddie?"

Jacob was now curled up in the fetal position under the table, trying to remain completely still and unseen. "*Unck!*" he yelled, in spite of himself. Eddie, meanwhile, had gone completely white and sat in his chair, paralyzed.

"Ladies and gentlemen," Christine went on. "Eddie has graciously agreed to perform a miracle for us today! Please put your hands together for the Fabulous Eddie, who will now disappear before your very eyes!"

If Eddie had any illusions about disappearing before, they had vanished. "All right!" he hissed at Christine. "I'll show you where he is. Just stop this!"

Christine smiled at the expectant crowd. "False alarm," she said, and hopped down to the floor, giving Eddie a shove and whispering in his ear, "Lead the way, Fabulous Eddie."

THIRTY

In one hand Lucifer held a lit cigar and in the other a wooden baseball bat. He stood in an unfurnished room with a concrete floor and cinder block walls lit by a single 100-watt lightbulb hanging from the ceiling. In front of him sat a tall figure tied to a chair, his head slumped forward and his silver hair obscuring his face. Presently Lucifer became aware that the figure was mumbling something.

"...ninety-eight, ninety-nine, one hundred!"

Mercury's head whipped upward, and his eyes fixed on Lucifer, standing in the center of the room. A look of profound disappointment swept over his face. "You know," he said, "I realize this is a small room, but you could put a little effort into it. OK, my turn to hide. I'll tie you to the chair."

Lucifer swung the bat at Mercury's face, knocking out three of his teeth.

"Ow!" Mercury howled, spitting blood on the floor. "What the hell? That hurt! Ow!"

"What, no more smart-ass remarks?" asked Lucifer. "I'm disappointed."

"Look," said Mercury, blood pouring down his chin. "I realize that I'm supposed to be the defiant, wise-cracking hero laughing in the face of adversity, but that fucking *hurt*. I mean, I'll do my best to play off the whole Hans Gruber thing you've got going, but I can't promise you a consistently high level of witty repartee if you're going to keep hitting me with a baseball bat. I'm liable to scream like a lovelorn howler monkey next time."

"Ah, Mercury," said Lucifer, twirling the bat in his hand and chomping on his cigar. "It's too bad we met so late. I could use somebody like you on my team."

"OK," said Mercury.

Lucifer scowled. "What do you mean, 'OK'?"

"I mean, 'OK, I accept.' You have full dental, right? I may need some work done."

"I wasn't actually offering you a job," said Lucifer.

"Oh," replied Mercury softly. "Yeah, I knew that." He strained against the twine that secured his wrists to the back of the chair. It wouldn't take much energy to weaken the molecular bonds of the twine…

"Don't even think about it," warned Lucifer. "You break the twine, I split your skull open."

Mercury relaxed his arms.

"Nothing personal," said Lucifer. "I kind of admire your style. Unfortunately, you keep screwing up my plans to wreak untold misery and destruction. So I have to keep you tied up down here for a while."

"Yeah, I heard about your plan to nuke Heaven. What's that all about?"

"Oh, just a little something I dreamed up while watching *O'Reilly*. Going to take out the Eye of Providence and eliminate the source of the energy that sustains the Universe."

Mercury nodded thoughtfully. "I'm curious, though, if you've thought through the ramifications of that," he said. "You see, you're not going to believe this, but I just got back from the distant future. I saw how it all ends. There's this creeping fog that gradually erases all of existence. It's frankly rather off-putting."

Lucifer shrugged. "If that's the way it ends, that's the way it ends. If God didn't want me to screw up His creation, maybe He shouldn't have created me."

"That seems like a bit of a cop-out," said Mercury. "I mean, take some responsibility, for Pete's sake."

"Responsibility!" growled Lucifer. "Why doesn't God take some responsibility, if He exists? Why doesn't He just step down from whatever cloud He's on and put a stop to my plans? I'll tell you why: either He doesn't exist or He doesn't care. I'm putting an end to the charade, once and for all."

"I still don't get it," said Mercury. "Why devote your life to trying to destroy the world just to prove that there is no God? I mean, you realize that if there is a God, He's probably having a good laugh at you right now, right? You've dedicated your life to Him just as fervently as a religious zealot. Everything you do revolves around a God that you claim doesn't exist. You don't find that a little ironic?"

Lucifer snorted. "This is who I am," he said. "I have an aversion to bullshit and a need to point it out. Hell, you saw what they tried to pull with Job, right?"

Mercury nodded. "Funny you should mention that…"

But Lucifer ignored him. "They set up Job as some kind of role model, as if all you had to do was go along with a few rules and everything would be hunky-dory. 'Follow these seven easy steps to guaranteed wealth and happiness!' Well, I called bullshit.

It doesn't work that way, and if Heaven had thought things through rather than patting themselves on the back, they'd have realized that. I was the one who pointed out their mistake, their arrogance. If there was any justice, I'd be recognized as the hero of that story!"

Mercury had to admit that Lucifer had a point. The seraphim could be arrogant, shortsighted micromanagers. Mercury had plenty of run-ins with Heavenly hubris himself. Still, what was the point of trying to blow shit up just to see if you could get away with it? Why not make the best of the situation?

There was a knock on the only door in the room, behind Mercury. "Come in!" Mercury yelled.

Lucifer shot a glare at Mercury and walked around him to the door. There was some whispering and then Lucifer returned. "We have a visitor," he said.

After him walked a wiry, compact man with a stern expression on his face.

"Cain!" Mercury gasped, blood dripping from his chin.

"You two have met?" asked Lucifer, raising an eyebrow.

Mercury nodded. Cain frowned and shook his head.

"That is, we *will* meet," Mercury explained. "In a few thousand years."

Cain shrugged at Lucifer, clearly puzzled.

"And you acted like you didn't know me, you bastard," said Mercury. "All part of your plan, I suppose. Make me come back here and play whatever part I'm supposed to play to make things turn out just the way they did last time."

"I have no idea what you're talking about," insisted Cain.

"Oh, I know you don't," said Mercury. "But you will, you infected nutsack."

"I hate to break this up, whatever it is," Lucifer said, "but I don't have a lot of time. Diabolical schemes to attend to. You have something to tell me, Cain?"

"I do," said Cain, grinning maliciously. "I've done it. The seventh book is nearly finished. Everything is unfolding according to plan!"

"Well, that's great," said Lucifer, without much enthusiasm. "Is that all, Cain?"

"*Is that all?*" echoed Cain in disbelief. "I'm bringing about the end of the world! Remember the whole ancient Sumerian manuscript deal? This was *your idea*!"

Lucifer shrugged. "I've got a lot of diabolical plans in motion at any given time. Right now I'm really focused on the whole nuking Heaven thing. But hey, that's not to take away from what you've accomplished. Really great work, Cain. Seriously." He put his hand on Cain's shoulder in a fatherly gesture that even made Mercury a little uncomfortable.

Cain glared daggers at Lucifer. "Do you have any idea what I sacrificed to make sure the final book is done properly? I killed my own daughter!"

"Really?" asked Lucifer. "That seems a bit excessive." He looked to Mercury, who nodded in agreement.

"All your scheming would come to nothing without me!" Cain snarled, prying himself away from Lucifer. "The only reason your plan to destroy the Eye of Providence has gotten this far is because of the work I've done! Why do you think all of your other schemes failed? The world can't end until the seventh book has been written! When everyone and everything else failed you, I did what needed to be done!"

Lucifer nodded, a condescending smile plastered on his face. He nodded surreptitiously at someone behind Cain.

"Goddamn you, Lucifer! You could at least say thank you!"

A muscle-bound demon strode forward and took Cain's arm.

"Thank you, Cain," oozed Lucifer. Then to the demon: "Get him out of here."

The demon dragged the grumbling and cursing Cain to the door. There was the sound of the door slamming, then silence.

"Man, I didn't think that guy was ever going to leave," said Mercury. "Doesn't he know we've got important stuff to talk about? Now, where were we?"

"I was about to blow up Heaven," said Lucifer. "But first, I need to make sure you won't interfere."

"I don't suppose that means you're going to make me sign a nondisclosure agreement?" asked Mercury.

"Sorry," said Lucifer, and brought the baseball bat down on his skull.

THIRTY-ONE

Eddie led Christine around to the back of the restaurant. Jacob, who was fairly shaken up by Christine's performance, trailed silently behind.

They rounded the corner of the building just in time to see a tall, blond man exiting from an unmarked door.

"Back!" hissed Eddie out of the corner of his mouth. Eddie kept walking, trying to appear nonchalant.

"Why, what..." started Christine. Then she saw him. Lucifer. The devil himself. Christine had met him twice before, and she didn't think he liked her much. Understandable, given that she had spoiled his two previous attempts to destroy the world. There was no doubt he would recognize her.

There wasn't time to get out of sight, so Christine did the only thing she could think to do: she spun 180 degrees and threw her arms around Jacob, planting a kiss right on his mouth. After a momentary start, Jacob fell into his part with ease. By unspoken agreement, they became Anonymous Couple Necking behind Charlie's Grill. After nearly knocking Eddie over, Lucifer strode past them, followed by two bulky demons. "Get a room," he sneered. The three demons got into a limousine, which squealed out of the lot.

Jacob and Christine kissed for a good three seconds longer than they needed to. At last Eddie cleared his throat.

Jacob pulled back slightly. "You OK?"

Christine smiled and nodded. "You?"

"Better," said Jacob, releasing his embrace. He was visibly calmer. "Let's go get your friend."

"Right," said Christine. She spun around again, walked to the door Lucifer had just exited, and tried the handle. "Locked."

"Hmph," said Eddie, waving his hand over the lock.

Christine tried again, and the door opened. Stairs led down into darkness. "After you," she said to Eddie.

"No way," Eddie replied. "I said I'd show you the door. I'm not going down there."

"Fine," said Christine. "Wait here and stand lookout. Let us know if anyone shows up."

Eddie shrugged, leaning against the stucco wall of the restaurant.

"Wait, Christine," protested Jacob. "You can't go down there. There could be…"

But she had already started down the stairs. Jacob reluctantly followed.

At the bottom of the stairs was another door, locked with a dead bolt from the outside. For locking someone in, thought Christine. Not that a simple dead bolt would hold an angel.

She turned the latch, releasing the dead bolt, and opened the door to find a bare concrete room lit by a single lightbulb. An unconscious man lay on his side, tied to a chair. His hair was matted with blood. Mercury.

"Is he…*unck?*" Jacob asked.

"Angels don't die," said Christine, rushing to Mercury. "Help me get him upright."

They righted the chair and started to untie Mercury's arms and legs. His eyes were closed and the left side of his face was covered with blood.

"Are you sure he's alive?" asked Jacob.

"He's been through worse than this," said Christine. As if in response, Mercury's head lolled from left to right and he groaned. By the time they had him untied, he was fully conscious.

"Early tarred all being Ed and Ed," mumbled Mercury.

"What did he say?" Jacob asked. "Is that some sort of code?"

Christine shrugged. "Mercury, what did you say?"

Mercury repeated, more slowly, "Really. Tired. Of. Being. Hit. In. The. Head."

"Understandable," said Christine, eyeing the baseball bat lying in the corner of the room. "Can you walk? We should get you out of here. There's an angel named Eddie upstairs standing guard, but I'm not sure I completely trust him."

Mercury started to laugh but it turned into a whimper. With Christine and Jacob's help, he got to his feet. "Eddie gummy shuttin' dead," he mumbled.

Jacob looked questioningly at Christine. She explained, "Eddie got him shot in the head."

"Ouch," said Jacob. "He's in remarkably good shape, considering. *Unck.*"

"He'll be fine in an hour or so," Christine said. "We just need to get him out of here before—" She stopped, realizing the doorway was blocked by a tall, well-built man.

"Before what?" asked the man, smiling. It was Gamaliel. He strolled into the room, followed by Izbazel. Two demons, one working for Tiamat and the other for Lucifer. This didn't bode well.

"Son of a bitch," Christine said. "Why didn't Eddie warn us?"

"Eddie?" asked Gamaliel. "Is that the guy who took off like a rabbit as soon as he saw us? You might want to pick a better lookout next time."

"Eddie...rabbit," mumbled Mercury, giggling to himself.

"Shut up, Mercury!" snapped Izbazel. "Gamaliel, seize Mercury. You two, upstairs, now."

Gamaliel shot Izbazel a bemused look. "I don't work for you, asshole," he said. But he grabbed Mercury by the arm, brushing Christine out of the way. He made his way upstairs, practically dragging the barely conscious Mercury with him. Christine and Jacob followed, with Izbazel prodding them from behind.

The three of them were forced into an unmarked van and their hands secured behind their backs with zip ties. Gamaliel got in the driver's seat and Izbazel in the front passenger's seat.

"Where are you taking us?" demanded Christine.

Izbazel smiled. "Where you can't cause any more trouble."

"Disneyland?" Mercury offered meekly.

THIRTY-TWO

While Christine, Jacob, and Mercury were being corralled into an unmarked van in Glendale, Tiamat stood stolidly surveying a horde of demons standing at attention on a remote plain in Kenya. The demons wore desert fatigues and carried assault rifles. A few of them also carried portable rocket launchers. Only the flaming swords hanging from their belts distinguished them from a brigade of human soldiers. Most of the demons belonged to Lucifer but they had sworn an oath of allegiance to Tiamat, and they were hers to command. Behind them, the sun slowly sank behind Mount Mbutuokoti. Ahead of them, barely visible in the distance, was the dome of the enclosed ecosystem known as Eden II, which concealed the world's largest particle accelerator—CCD-2, the key to total mastery of space and time.

The main object of the assault was simple: retake Eden II from Michelle's troops. Once the main assault started, Tiamat herself would lead a smaller force into the heart of Eden II, to the coordinates where Horace Finch had planted the apple seed. With any luck, the tree was already bearing fruit—and Michelle's troops hadn't noticed the peculiar tree growing in a secluded grove far inside the dome. Her bigger worry was that someone—either on her side or on Michelle's—would trample the little tree during the battle, destroying the apples before Tiamat could get to them. Barring that, once the facility was secure and she had plucked an apple from the tree, her team would proceed downstairs to the Chrono-Collider Device. She would then commence the execution sequence already programmed by Alastair Breem, causing a collision of subatomic particles that would release a batch of chrotons into the apple. Once she had control over the chrotons, she would control the space-time continuum itself.

Michelle's forces would have the advantage of cover, being dug under the dome of Eden II, but Tiamat had surprise and overwhelming numbers on her side. Given enough time, there was no way the Heavenly troops could hold out. Her greatest fear, though, was that Heaven would sense that they were losing and attempt to wipe out the whole facility with a Class 5 Pillar of Fire. Lucifer had assured her that he had agents in Heaven who could muck up the approval process for a while,[11] but that would buy her maybe an hour at most. She needed to get to the apple and head underground quickly, where even a Class 5 would be powerless to stop her.

"Alpha Team assemble!" she barked. Twenty demons came forth, standing at attention before her. She had selected these twenty from her own retinue of demons, picking them for their quickness, agility, and intelligence. This was the hand that was going to pluck the apple from the garden while the gardener was distracted, so they had better be quick.

"Teams Beta, Gamma, Delta, and Epsilon assemble!"

---

11 There is probably no single process in Heaven requiring more paperwork than a Class 5 Pillar of Fire. After several POF-related debacles early on (the worst being the incineration of Job's sheep by a misdirected Class 3), a considerable number of fail-safes were put in place to prevent future abuses and/or mistakes. Regulations became progressively more onerous over the course of the next few thousand years, culminating with the POFPAP (Pillar of Fire Paperwork Alleviation Protocol), which doubled the number of forms required.

The remaining demons sorted themselves into four groups of equal size. Each team would rally at a predetermined checkpoint and attack Eden II simultaneously from a different direction—north, south, east, and west. While the defenders were off-balance, Alpha Team would slip in from the southeast and head for the apple tree.

As the sun touched the tip of Mbutuokoti, Tiamat barked, "The time is at hand! Commence Operation Reclaim Paradise!"

The demons took flight, skimming low over the plain to avoid detection by the forces of Heaven. While teams Beta, Gamma, Delta, and Epsilon headed for their assigned checkpoints, Tiamat and her team took to the sky where they could observe the onslaught when it started.

Right on schedule, the teams assembled at the checkpoints. Team Delta, to the east of Eden II, was the last to assemble. Once it was in place, the four teams moved in unison toward the dome that was now glinting in the twilight. The blighted moon rose above the horizon.

By the time the sentries buzzing a few miles out from the dome knew what was happening, it was too late. The attack started with shoulder-fired missiles that tore gaping holes in the dome, massive chunks of concrete crumbling to the jungle floor below. The sentries managed to make nearly half the rockets detonate harmlessly in midair, but the dome was breached in a dozen places.

Angels poured out of the holes like angry wasps. At first they tried to create a repulsive barrier of energy around the dome, but this was a losing strategy. The attackers had expected this and easily neutralized the barrier, overwhelming the defenders with their sheer numbers. While half the attackers focused on dissolving the barrier, the other half hung in the air, picking off the defending angels with automatic rifles. The angels couldn't be killed, of course, but they could be knocked out of the game for a while with a few well-aimed shots. A few of the defenders had guns but most of them wielded only flaming swords, and in any case were too busy trying to keep up their barrier to put up much of a man-to-man defense. The angels fell from the sky in droves.

Mere minutes after the battle started, Tiamat and her team plummeted from above, unnoticed in the chaos. A few angels tried to bar her way but they were taken down by the rifle-toting sharpshooters in Team Alpha. Tiamat and her score of demons descended through a hole in the dome, landing on the floor of the jungle below. She pulled out a portable GPS unit into which had been programmed the coordinates where Horace Finch had planted the apple seed.

"This way!" she barked, and they headed down a path through the jungle.

THIRTY-THREE

Eddie sat alone at a bus stop in Glendale a few blocks down from Charlie's Grill, feeling sorry for himself. Why couldn't everyone just leave him alone? He was supposed to be a disinterested observer, not a character in the story. Certainly not some cowardly quisling, which is how his character seemed doomed to be written.

Yes, he had left Christine and Jacob to be shanghaied by Izbazel and Gamaliel, but it wasn't his job to play lookout. He had met his side of the bargain: their part of the story in exchange for Mercury's location. In fact, he had given them more than he was obligated to, leading them right to Mercury. Besides, what difference would it have made if Eddie had warned them? If he had stuck around, he'd probably have been taken captive along with them. And then who would write the story?

Eddie was aware, on some level, that he was going a little insane. He could no longer have offered any rational explanation for why the story had to be written. It had become an obsession, a reason unto itself. The story was all that there was. But if that were true, then who was Eddie? Just another character in the story, and not a particularly heroic one at that.

No! thought Eddie. I'm not just a character. I'm writing the story. I'm the author! But if that were true, why couldn't he get it to go where he wanted it to go? Why had he written himself as such a shiftless, craven twerp? Why couldn't he at least be the hero of the story? Just once Eddie would like to say something totally badass, like "Go ahead, make my day," "Yippie ki yay, motherfucker," or "Nobody puts Baby in the corner." Well, maybe not that last one.

Wormwood. It all came down to Wormwood. Cain and Cody had both told him so. And he could *feel* it. He could feel that Wormwood was going to bring about The End, with capital letters. There was no controlling it, no way around it. Whatever he did, whatever he wrote, the story came down to Wormwood. He couldn't stop it. No one could. So why drag things out by helping out Christine and Jacob? He wasn't doing them any favors by letting them run around for a little longer, trying to stuff troubles back into Pandora's box.

But try as he might to think of himself as an amoral agent of inevitability, he still felt like shit about letting Christine down. Christine had a sort of naïve confidence that made you want to root for her. She reminded him of Cody. Again Eddie became painfully aware of his humanity asserting itself and his angelic nature slipping away.

What was it that Cody had said? "Pull the switch." The phrase carried a sense of fatalism that was uncharacteristic of Cody. Pull the switch. Trigger Wormwood. End it all. What else could it possibly mean?

While he debated with himself, a very pregnant woman with thick, dark hair waddled up to the bench and took a seat next to him. She smiled shyly at Eddie and then looked away. She was young. Too young to be having a kid, thought Eddie. No ring on her finger. He wondered if she was all alone.

"Does this bus go to the mall?" she asked.

Eddie shrugged sheepishly, admitting that he had no idea where the bus was going.

She laughed. "Why are you here then?"

"Not sure," said Eddie.

"That's cool," she said, smiling charitably at him. "Sometimes it's good just to change things up a bit."

Eddie was about to reply when he became aware that they were no longer alone at the bus stop: a young man was now standing before the woman. He wore a backward baseball cap, a baggy sweatshirt, and jeans that hung off his midthigh, exposing a good five inches of his underpants.

"Yo, Maria," said the man. "Where's my money?"

Maria clutched her purse. "It's my money, Fernando. I need things for the baby."

"We agreed, we split your tips," said Fernando, regarding Eddie coldly. Eddie did his best to stare straight ahead. He didn't need to get involved in any more petty drama. This was all going to be over with soon enough.

"I need the money," pleaded Maria. "Please, Fernando. For the baby. For Ángel."

"Listen, *puta*," hissed Fernando. "Give me the money."

"See here, now," said Eddie, forgetting himself. "There's no call for that sort of language. Clearly Maria needs to buy some things for your baby. Maybe you could—"

"Not *my* baby," said Fernando. "I told her to get rid of it."

"It *is* your baby," insisted Maria.

"Regardless of whose baby it is," said Eddie diplomatically, "wouldn't you agree that—"

"Shit, man," said Fernando, turning to Eddie. "What are you, her guardian angel?"

Eddie considered this for a moment, then stood up and looked Fernando in the eye. "As a matter of fact," he said, "I am. We're stretched a little thin lately, as you can imagine, but I got a call that some *pendejo* was hassling Maria, so I came down to check it out."

"That right, *amigo*?" said Fernando, pulling up his sweatshirt to reveal the handle of a revolver tucked into his waistband.

"Fernando," said Eddie. "Please trust me on this. You do not want to do that."

Fernando grinned and pulled the gun, pointing it at Eddie. Eddie grabbed Fernando's wrist and pushed up, pointing the gun in the air. Fernando struggled, but Eddie—the least athletic of all the cherubim—was clearly stronger than he was. The more Fernando fought, the worse it went for him. Eddie's arm was now completely straight, holding the gun pointed straight up in the air, inches away from Fernando's right ear. And that's when the gun went off.

Fernando screamed and fell to his knees, clutching his ear. The gun slipped out of his hands and into Eddie's. Eddie carefully placed it next to Maria on the bench.

"*Mi oído!*" Fernando howled. "*No puedo escuchar!*"

"Calm down, you big baby," said Eddie, putting his hand to the side of Fernando's head.

"No! Leave me alone!"

"Will you move your hand?" Eddie said. "I'm going to fix your ear."

After a moment, Fernando reluctantly released his grip, letting Eddie cup his ear in his hand. Fernando's eyes lit up. "It's better," he gasped. "You fixed it!"

"*Sí*," replied Eddie. "Better?"

Fernando nodded, rubbing his ear. "I still hear ringing, though."

"Yeah, I left that as a reminder to you," said Eddie. "If you can avoid being an asshole for the next couple of days, it should go away on its own. You think you can do that?"

"*Sí*," said Fernando.

"Good. Now, Fernando, whose money is it?"

"Maria's," Fernando said sheepishly. "For the baby."

"And whose gun is it?"

Fernando glanced at Maria, who was sitting with her hand on the revolver, a look of sheer amazement on her face.

"Maria's gun," he said.

"Damn straight," said Eddie. "I'm not going to ask you whose baby it is. I'll let you two work that out." Eddie got to his feet. "I apologize for leaving so abruptly, but I have some important revisions to make to a report I'm working on. But Fernando, you'd better treat Maria with respect or I'll come back. And next time, I won't be as forgiving. *Entiendes?*"

Fernando nodded.

"Good," said Eddie, picking up his bag and starting to walk away. After a moment, he stopped and turned. "Hey, Fernando," he said.

"Yeah?"

"That ringing you hear?"

"Yeah?"

"That's an angel getting his wings, *amigo*."

THIRTY-FOUR

"Did I ever thank you guys for rescuing me that time?" Mercury asked. "You remember, that time I was tied up under that restaurant?"

"That was like an hour ago, Mercury," said Christine humorlessly.

"Is that all? I guess time flies when you're enjoying your freedom."

"Shut up, Mercury. And you're welcome."

Christine, Mercury, and Jacob had been blindfolded, driven around for a while, and then brought inside some sort of building. It had a vaguely corporate smell, like coffee, cleaning products, and cubicles. They took an elevator several floors up and then were prodded into a room where they had been made to sit in chairs facing each other. Izbazel had tied them together for good measure and then the two demons had left the room.

"Shhh!" said Jacob. "I can hear them talking."

Indeed, murmurs could be heard on the other side of the door.

Before Jacob could make any sense of what was being said or who was saying it, though, he heard the door opening, followed by footsteps. After a moment, their blindfolds were removed. The room was nondescript and windowless, illuminated only by fluorescent panels in the ceiling. Izbazel was standing in front of Jacob with a cruel look on his face. Gamaliel stood a few feet away, speaking softly into a cell phone and fiddling with something on a chair in the corner of the room. "Yep, he's right here," said Gamaliel. He stood up and walked to Jacob.

"Horace Finch has something to say to you," said Gamaliel, holding the cell phone in front of Jacob's face.

"Jacob Slater!" said Finch's voice. "Let me say first of all how sorry I am that I can't be there to see you and your friends killed. Terribly rude of me, considering that you took the time to come to Kenya in person and sabotage my multibillion-dollar particle collider. Unfortunately, I have business to attend to at the moment. Yes, you'll be delighted to learn that despite your meddling, my plan to gain complete mastery over time and space is about to come to fruition. How do you like them apples?"

"You're a lunatic, Finch," said Jacob. "Get professional help. *Unck*."

High-pitched laughter could be heard through the phone. "I'll take your psychiatric diagnosis under advisement. Did you see the present I left for you?"

Gamaliel took a step to the side, revealing what he had been working on in the corner. Sitting on the chair was a fist-sized lump of putty. A timer stuck to the putty was counting down the seconds: *9:16...9:15...9:14...*

"What?" Christine asked. "What is it?" From where she was seated, she couldn't see the bomb.

"Half a kilogram of C4," said Finch. "Enough to blow all three of you to kingdom come. You should thank me, really. It's a completely painless way to die. I mean, except for the ten minutes of agony while you reflect on where you went wrong in life. After that, though, completely painless."

"Screw you, Finch," growled Christine.

"Clever," said Finch. "You should be a writer. Well, I'd love to stay and chat, but I've got some chrotons to catch. Enjoy your last minutes on Earth!"

Gamaliel put the phone to his ear. "Hey, Finch," he said. "Can you put Tiamat back on? I wanted to ask her…" He trailed off uncertainly, and then said, "Um, all right then. In that case, I'll call her back. Good talking to you." He snapped the phone shut and slid it into his pocket.

"He hung up already, huh?" said Mercury.

"Shut up, Mercury!" Gamaliel growled, kicking Mercury in the shin. He turned to Izbazel. "Let's go."

The two demons stalked out, slamming the door behind them.

"Is there a timer?" Christine asked. "What does it say?"

"Eight minutes," said Jacob.

"Eight minutes to live," said Christine. "And I'm not even sure who is killing us or why."

"I thought Finch was pretty clear on the phone just now," said Mercury.

"Right, but I thought it was Lucifer who captured you. Then Izbazel and Gamaliel come to retrieve you, and I know that Izbazel works for Lucifer, but I thought that Gamaliel worked for Tiamat. And how the hell does Finch fit into any of this?"

"I think they're all in it together," said Mercury. "They've reached some kind of truce so they can attack Heaven on two fronts at once. Tiamat must be planning to take Eden II from the angels while Lucifer takes out the Eye. Finch is dreaming if he thinks Tiamat is doing this to help him and his buddies in the

Order of the Pillars of Babylon, though. Once she's got that apple stuffed full of tasty croutons, she's not giving it up for anything."

"Hang on," said Christine. "What's this 'eye' you're talking about? Eddie said something about it too, but I didn't really understand what he meant."

"The Eye of Providence," said Mercury. "You've seen it. It's that big, pyramid-shaped thing that's just down the street from the Apocalypse Bureau. It's the source of all the interplanar energy, what angels use to cause miracles. It's also what ultimately sustains the Universe, keeps it from falling apart. Lucifer wants to blow up the Eye to cripple Heaven and ultimately to bring about the destruction of the Universe."

Jacob snorted. "You're saying that there's some magical pyramid that—*unck*—gives off mystical energy that holds the Universe together?"

"Well," said Mercury. "I'd have said that it's a mystical pyramid that—*unck*—gives off magical energy that holds the Universe together, but yes."

Ignoring Mercury's mockery, Jacob pressed him further. "Look, I'll acknowledge that you...*angels*," he said, somehow managing to convey air quotes despite the fact that his hands were tied, "have access to some pretty advanced technology. But don't try to bullshit me with your mystical hocus-pocus. I've seen a lot of strange stuff, but I've never seen anything to make me believe there's one all-powerful force controlling everything."

Mercury nodded. "It generally hides from scientists," he said. "You see, what you call the 'laws of physics' are really just guidelines. It's the interplanar energy that keeps those guidelines working. You don't notice it because it's always there, the way a fish doesn't notice that he's in water. Miracles are just a matter of tweaking the energy flow a bit to bend the laws of physics in a certain direction. Of course, miracles are very rare, especially when you're specifically looking for them, so for all practical purposes the laws of physics are reliable. Except when they aren't."

"Sounds like nonsense to me," said Jacob.

Mercury shrugged.

"So the Whore of Babylon and the devil himself are teaming up to kill us," said Christine.

"Yep," said Mercury. "The fact that Lucifer, Tiamat, and Horace Finch are all cooperating to kill you speaks quite highly of you. If there is an afterlife, make sure you mention that to the Man Upstairs."

They sat in silence for a moment, reflecting on their situation.

"Could you defuse it, Jacob?" Christine asked. "I mean, if you could get to it?"

"Probably," said Jacob. "And I could fly if I had wings. *Unck*. Hey, Mercury, can't you, um, do one of your tricks or whatever?" asked Jacob.

"You mean miracles?" Mercury asked.

"Call it what you like," said Jacob, trying to be patient. "Break the ropes and get us out of here."

"Call it a miracle, or I'm not doing anything."

"Seriously, Mercury?" asked Christine. "You're going to pick this moment to be an asshole?"

"No," replied Mercury. "I'm going to pick this moment to not stop being an asshole. Seriously, ask me nicely to perform a miracle, or I'm not doing it."

"Fine," said Christine. "Mercury, can you please perform a miracle and get us the hell out of here?"

"Not you, him," said Mercury. "Captain Unck."

"Why is it—*unck*—so important to you that I call it a miracle?" Jacob asked, growing more irritable.

"Why is it so important to you that you don't?"

"Whatever," grumbled Jacob. "Mercury, could you please perform a miracle, and get us out of here?"

"Wish I could," said Mercury. "They've got a Balderhaz Cube somewhere nearby. Can't get a fix on the energy channels."

"You son of a—*unck*—bitch," growled Jacob. "You mean you can't do anything?"

"I can do plenty," said Mercury. "Just no miracles."

"Damn it, what is that?" asked Jacob.

"A Balderhaz Cube is a device specially constructed to interfere with the interplanar energy channels, preventing—"

"Not that," said Jacob. "Water. Dripping on my head. *Unck!* It's like Chinese water torture."

"How can you tell what kind of water it is?" asked Mercury.

"This is going to drive me insane," said Jacob.

"Hey, you're not exactly my top choice for the sack race either, Rain Man," said Mercury.

"I was talking about the water," growled Jacob. "And don't call me…Hey, is it raining?"

"Holy crap, enough about the water dripping on your head." said Mercury. "Can we talk about something else, like how dry and comfortable I am?"

"Mercury," hissed Jacob through clenched teeth. "Shut up. I am asking a serious question. Was it raining when they brought us into this building?"

"I don't think so," said Christine. "But it may have just started. It did feel like the pressure was dropping. Why?"

"I think I know where we are," said Jacob. "*Unck*. I think we're at the top of the Beacon Building."

"Finch's building?" asked Mercury. "What makes you think that?"

"Other than the fact that I just got off the phone with him? I've been here before. It seemed familiar, the way it smelled, and the elevator. Did you notice—*unck*—they punched some kind of code into the elevator. The Beacon Building has a hidden floor at the top. I tried to find it the last time I was here. But it was the water that clinched it."

"What do you mean?" asked Christine.

"Well, we're inside a building. If that's rainwater dripping on my head, then we must be on the top floor. But why is it only dripping on my head? Well, the other thing about the Beacon Building is that it's not a perfect pyramid. There's a little flat area at the top, just a couple feet wide, for antennas and lightning rods and stuff. I think there's a hole in the roof right at the top of the pyramid. Right above my head. After all, the rain comes from above. *Unck*."

At this, Mercury started to chuckle. The chuckle turned into a full-blown laugh, and the laugh turned into guffaws. Soon he was gasping for air.

"What's up with Miracle Man?" asked Jacob.

"Beats me," said Christine.

"The rain..." wheezed Mercury, "comes...from *above*."

Thunder rumbled somewhere in the distance.

"See?" said Jacob. "Thunder. It is raining."

"Yeah," said Christine. "So you have any ideas for getting out of here?"

"Sorry," said Jacob.

Mercury continued to giggle uncontrollably.

"You want to let us in on the joke?" asked Christine irritably.

"That was the message...I got from Michelle," said Mercury. "About the flood."

"What flood?" asked Jacob.

"I think he means *the* flood," said Christine. "You know, in Genesis."

"Oh," said Jacob. "Wait. Are you saying there's going to be another flood? Like in the Bible?"

"I'm not saying anything," said Mercury, who was starting to regain his composure. "It's just a stupid note I got from Michelle when I was trying to figure out who sent the flood. At the time I thought maybe it had some deep meaning, but I'm pretty sure it was just a red herring to keep me from sticking my nose where it didn't belong. When you said it, I realized how pointless this all is. It was like the Universe's final 'fuck you' to me."

Thunder rumbled again, closer this time. The timer read *5:03*.

"Wish I had learned to control the weather," Mercury said wistfully. "I always meant to. Not that it would matter with the Balderhaz Cube here. Sort of a Catch-18."

"What the hell are you talking about, Mercury?" asked Christine.

"Oh, the thing about Balderhaz Cubes is that they aren't a hundred percent reliable. Energy surges, like lightning strikes, can knock them out briefly."

"For how long?"

"Maybe two, three seconds."

"Long enough for you to break these ropes?"

"Sure," Mercury said with a shrug. "If I was concentrating."

"So if the Beacon were hit by lightning?" Christine asked. "Jacob, didn't you say that there were lightning rods at the top of the building?"

"Yeah," said Jacob. "*Unck*. There are lightning rods atop most large buildings. But the chances that a particular building will get hit by lightning in any given storm, even if the storm passes right overhead...well, I wouldn't hold your breath."

"Is there anything we can do to increase the odds?"

"Well, like I said," replied Mercury, "I could theoretically make lightning strike the building. Except that, number one, I'm lousy at controlling the weather and, number two, the Balderhaz Cube is preventing me from using interplanar energy. If it weren't, we wouldn't need the lightning to take it out. Catch-18."

"It's a Catch-22, Mercury," said Christine. "It's from a book."

"What book?"

"*Catch-22*."

"Well, maybe I'm thinking of a different book."

"Oh? And what book would that be?"

"I believe it was called *Catch-18*," Mercury sniffed.

"Of course," replied Christine dryly. "So to sum up, you could deactivate the Balderhaz Cube if the Balderhaz Cube weren't preventing you from deactivating it?"

"Exactly. Maybe. Assuming I could get lightning to strike us."

"I don't get it," said Jacob. "I thought miracles were supposed to be, you know, *miraculous*."

Mercury snorted. "Says Mr. I-Won't-Say-the-Word-Miracle."

"You understand my—*unck*—point. If you're going to throw around the word *miracle*, it should mean something. If you can't do your miracles because of some stupid magic cube, then maybe they weren't miracles to begin with. I mean, it's like me saying, 'Well, I could miraculously untie us if I just had my miracle pocket knife with me.' "

"Do you?" asked Mercury excitedly.

"No," said Jacob. "That was just an example."

"Oh," said Mercury. "That was a bit of an oversight, wasn't it? If I had a miracle pocket knife, I'd take it with me everywhere."

"I don't have—*unck!* Never mind. The point is that miracles are by definition inexplicable. If you can say, 'Oh, I can't perform miracles right now because of phenomenon *x*, then you're fitting miracles into a rational, scientific schema. And once you do that, they aren't miracles anymore. And they probably never were. That's why I don't like using the word."

After a moment of silence, Mercury muttered, "They are too miracles."

"Prove it," said Jacob.

"How?"

"Make one happen—*unck*—despite your Balderdash Cube."

"Balderhaz. I told you, I can't."

"Then they aren't miracles."

"Hmph."

Thunder boomed again, still closer.

"Jacob, are you sure you could defuse the bomb?" asked Christine.

"Pretty sure, yeah. It looks like an N27 trigger. Nothing fancy. Just pull the green wire. But this is all—*unck*—academic. I can't get to the bomb."

"How much time do we have?" asked Christine.

"Three minutes, ten seconds."

"Get ready," Christine said.

"Ready for what?" asked Jacob.

"Mercury, you too. When the Balderhaz Cube shuts off, you need to be ready to break through the ropes."

"Am I missing something?" asked Jacob.

Mercury shrugged.

"Lightning is going to strike," said Christine.

"You can't predict a lightning strike," said Jacob.

"Actually..." began Mercury.

"Trust me," said Christine. "Lightning will strike. Now shut up and concentrate."

"Concentrate on *what*?" asked Jacob, bewildered. "On a one-in-a-million chance that lightning is going to strike this building in the next two minutes?"

"Yes!" shouted Christine. "Yes! Concentrate on that. For two minutes, concentrate on something that probably isn't going to happen. What are you afraid of? That you're going to be wrong? That you're going to waste the last two minutes of your life hoping that somehow, despite all evidence to the contrary, that things are going to be OK? I happen to think that there's a reason that all this stuff is happening. I think that as chaotic and crazy and hopeless as things seem right now, there's someone in charge who knows what's going on and is keeping things from going too far off track. And yes, I do happen to believe in miracles. I think there are signs all around us, if we care to pay attention. Like that message from Michelle—'The rain comes from above.' What if that's God's way of telling us, 'Hey, don't give up. I've gotten you through worse shit that this'? I suppose that makes me naïve and childish, and I'm sorry if it violates your sense of scientific integrity, and I will totally be respectful of your right to go to your grave insisting that there are no such things as miracles. I'm not asking you to believe in God or angels or Heaven or anything else, even though you've seen a hell of a lot more evidence than most people. But for the love of whatever it is that you do believe in, could you at least *shut the fuck up for two minutes*?"

Jacob shut up.

Whatever he did for the next minute and fifty-two seconds, he was not going to spend it pissing off Christine. If they did somehow make it through this, she'd never let him live it down. Mercury, remaining conspicuously silent, had presumably come to a similar conclusion. Although if what Christine had told him about the "angels" was true, Mercury had little to fear from a conventional explosive device. He would simply "reincorporate" eventually. Must be nice.

What about me? Jacob wondered. Will I "reincorporate" in some other dimension or plane or whatever? There's no reason to think so. The human mind is a biochemical system. Blow it to smithereens and that's the end of it. Consciousness couldn't exist outside of the physical system. Still, it's a nice thought. Maybe God will put me together right next time.

When the hair on Jacob's arms stood up, he momentarily wondered if he was having a religious experience. The deafening roar that filled his ears a second later knocked that thought—along with every other thought hanging out in the area—right out of his head. It felt like his teeth were going to rattle out of his skull. If he hadn't experienced it, he wouldn't have believed it. A lightning strike, right when they needed it. Absurd! The fluorescent lights flickered and went dark. Other than the dim glow remaining in the fluorescent tubes, the only light in the room was the digital timer on the bomb, which now read *00:17*.

Jacob strained reflexively against the rope and it bit into the flesh of his arms. Wonderful. Mercury hadn't been ready, hadn't been concentrating. A one-in-a-million chance, and they were still going to die because Mercury had the attention span of a gnat.

Then the rope unexpectedly gave way, disintegrating like it had suddenly aged a thousand years in a second. Jacob tumbled out of his chair, landing headfirst on the carpet. His hands and feet were still tied. His left elbow brushed up against someone in the dark, and he rolled onto his left side.

"Mercury! My hands!"

After an agonizing moment of groping in the dark, Mercury's hand touched the bonds around Jacob's wrists, and the ropes fell apart. Not bothering with his feet, Jacob threw his body forward, moving like a drunken inchworm across the carpet.

00:13.

When he reached the bomb, he came to a sickening realization: in the darkened room, he couldn't see the green wire. He felt under the timer, his fingers feeling two wires traveling from the timer to the detonator. One of them was red and the other green. On an N27 trigger, pulling the green wire would defuse the detonator. Pulling the red wire would collapse the circuit that was being kept open by the timer, triggering the detonator.

00:09.

Shit! Which one was it? Why weren't the lights going back on? If he could just see the wires, just for half a second, he'd know which one to pull. It occurred to him, though, that even if he knew which wire was the right one, he might not be able to pull it out with his fingers. It would be crimped down, and once the wires were attached, they were meant to stay attached. *Where's my miracle pocket knife when I need it?*

00:06.

Screw it. Pick a wire and pull. He wrapped his finger around a wire at random, trying to get as much leverage as possible, and then pulled. The wire remained securely attached.

He pulled harder, his whole body straining against the stubborn thread of copper. It felt like it was going to slice his finger in half. How did the saying go? "Better to enter the Kingdom of Heaven with half a finger..."

Pull, man, pull!

The wire let go, sending Jacob sprawling backward across the room. As his head hit the floor, the lights overhead flickered on. The timer read *00:03*. When it remained on that number for a few seconds, Jacob let out a laugh of relief. "Three seconds to spare," he said. He lay back on the carpet, his whole body shaking with adrenaline.

"YES!" exclaimed Mercury, leaping awkwardly to his feet, which were still bound. "Didn't I tell you? Lightning! KAPOW!" He lost his balance and fell over, crashing into the chairs.

The Balderhaz Cube having silently reclaimed its hold on the interplanar energy channels, Mercury was helpless to do anything but pick at the knots with his fingers until they loosened. Christine turned out to be far more proficient at this. While Mercury was still cursing the ropes around his ankles, Christine walked over to the bomb resting on the chair.

"I thought you said you were going to pull the green wire," she said.

Jacob, who had managed to get his feet untied, walked to the bomb and examined his handiwork. The red wire stuck out like a stray hair while the green wire remained firmly attached.

"Yeah," he said, swallowing hard. "They, um, reversed the wires. Luckily I—*unck*—figured it out."

"Uh-huh," said Christine, smirking at him.

"Got it!" Mercury exclaimed, holding up the rope triumphantly. "I'm like freaking Henry Houdini. What are you guys talking about?"

THIRTY-FIVE

As Lucifer's limo glided to the curb in front of Christine's condo building, he pulled a cell phone from his pocket. "Call Ramiel," he said.

"Did you say, 'Call Hugo Chavez?' " the phone asked.

"Call *Ramiel*," repeated Lucifer.

"Did you say, 'Call Vladimir Putin?' " the phone asked.

"Call *RA-mee-el*," shouted Lucifer into the phone.

"Did you say, 'Call Nancy Pelosi?' " the phone asked.

"Useless fucking piece of shit!" Lucifer snarled.

"Calling Ramiel," replied the phone.

Lucifer saw a figure through the window of Christine's apartment tossing refuse to and fro. While he was waiting, the door of the limo opened and Dirk Lubbers slipped into the seat next to him, carrying a heavy metal briefcase. Lucifer held a finger up and pointed to the phone.

After several rings, Ramiel finally located the cell phone and picked it up.

"Hello?" he said uncertainly.

"Ramiel," said Lucifer.

Ramiel's voice dropped to a whisper. "Master? Is that you?"

"It's time, Ramiel."

"So you want me to..."

Lucifer hung up.

Through the window, he saw the silhouette of a man walking up to another man from behind and pounding him on the head with a can of SpaghettiOs. The second man fell over, disappearing from view. Ramiel went to the kitchen and returned with a long serrated knife, then knelt down where Nisroc had fallen.

"Damn," murmured Lubbers, observing the scene.

"Decapitation will ensure that Nisroc doesn't alert his superiors. The element of surprise is crucial. Is that what I think it is?"

Lubbers nodded. He slid his thumb along a pad on the top of the case. A red light turned green. He pulled at a catch on either side of the handle and the case popped open. Nestled in foam padding was an object about the size and shape of an Oxford Dictionary. The components were encased in thick brownish-green plastic, but Lucifer could see the outline of a cylindrical object running diagonally across the device, with several other squarish components filling out its bulk. On top of one of the squarish components was a small timer. The cylinder was where the chunks of plutonium would be smashed together to create critical mass, resulting in a nuclear explosion. The other components were neutron generators and batteries, presumably. It certainly didn't look like much, but the name fit: the drab plastic covering made it look like a rotting hunk of wood.

"Ordinarily, it would be detonated remotely," said Lubbers. "But my understanding is that you are going to detonate the device personally."

"That is correct."

"And you realize that's suicide, right?"

"If suicide were an option, I wouldn't be here right now," said Lucifer. "I appreciate your concern, Director Lubbers, but I'll be fine. I'll reincorporate a few hours after the blast, as strong as ever."

"It's your funeral," said Lubbers. "We did attach a timer, though. That way you can arm the device before you get into the thick of the action. Just pull this switch here to arm it. Once it's armed, it's difficult to disarm, so don't pull the switch until you're ready. It's set for five minutes. Will that give you enough time?"

"It will be fine," said Lucifer. "Are your men in place?"

"Yep. The SEALs are ready to go. Twenty of the best men we have. Are they going to make it back in one piece?"

Lucifer didn't reply.

"Oh well," said Lubbers. "Acceptable losses. Ready?"

"You have no idea," said Lucifer.

Lubbers closed the briefcase, and they exited the limo, heading toward two military personnel carriers parked just down the street. "It's go time," barked Lubbers, slamming the side of the first carrier. Ten men in combat gear poured out of each carrier.

"Men, this is Mr. Rezon," said Lubbers. "He will be leading the assault. Commander Levin, you've got something for Mr. Rezon?"

One of the men leaned into the carrier and pulled out a bulky black backpack. "Kevlar," he said handing it to Lucifer. "It'll protect the package from stray bullets."

Lubbers set the briefcase down on the floor of the van and extracted Wormwood, gently sliding it into the backpack. Lucifer picked up the pack and slipped a small black cube into it. He zipped the backpack shut, slung it on his back, and turned toward the condo building.

"All right, then," he said. "Let's do this."

"Godspeed, men," said Lubbers. "Give 'em hell."

Lucifer shot him a wicked smile and strode toward Christine's condo, followed by the twenty SEALs.

Lubbers was so excited that he fell into a karate stance, executing several kicks in the air. Then, having pulled a hamstring, he hobbled to a canvas director's chair that read FBI and sat down. The spirit was willing, but the flesh was weak.

THIRTY-SIX

"And you're sure you got the timer right this time?" asked Christine.

"I'm sure," said Jacob coldly. "I do know what I'm doing. I just couldn't tell that the wires were switched from across the room. *Unck*." He wasn't actually sure it would have made a difference if he could have seen the detonator up close, but there was no point in mentioning that.

He, Christine, and Mercury were hiding behind the building next to Christine's condo. From their vantage point, they could see a group of FBI and military men standing around in front of Christine's condo, smoking cigarettes and engaged in hushed, anxious conversation, not far from an unmarked white van and several other military and civilian vehicles. Dirk Lubbers sat alone in a folding chair, eyeing the building and anxiously checking his watch. They were the only people within a hundred yards, a perimeter of barriers and police officers serving to keep the evacuated citizens out of the ersatz war zone.

Mercury, antsy with excitement, was occupying himself with a bizarre variety of calisthenics. "How much time do we have?"

Jacob looked at his watch. "Five seconds."

"OK, let's do this!" exclaimed Mercury, springing to his feet from a push-up pose. He took off running toward Christine's building.

"Dammit, Mercury!" Christine spat.

The report of automatic weapon fire rattled between the buildings, but Mercury kept moving. He was either dodging the bullets or repulsing them before they hit him.

"Cover your ears," urged Jacob. Christine, seeing that Jacob had gone into a crouch with his hands clamped firmly over his ears, did the same.

When Mercury was almost to the front door, an explosion erupted underneath the white van, lifting it several feet straight in the air. The shockwave knocked Lubbers and his men to the ground. Mercury, who was farther away, stumbled to one knee.

Christine got to her feet and ran toward Mercury, Jacob following closely behind.

Lubbers's men mostly remained on the ground, dazed or unconscious. Two men in military garb were getting slowly to their feet but were too preoccupied to notice the three intruders.

By the time Christine and Jacob had nearly caught up to him, Mercury was back on his feet, shaking his head and working his jaw. "NEXT TIME WE SHOULD WAIT UNTIL AFTER THE BOMB GOES OFF TO START RUNNING," he yelled.

The military men glanced their way, pointing and chattering amongst themselves.

"Let's go!" Christine snapped.

Mercury sprang forward, launching himself at the door to the condo. It swung open, and he ran inside. Christine followed, with Jacob bringing up the rear.

In the living room stood a very bewildered-looking Ramiel, cradling Nisroc's severed head under his right arm. The rest of Nisroc lay on the floor, bleeding profusely into the carpet.

Christine stopped and screamed in terror at the scene.

Mercury, however, didn't even slow down. When he got to Ramiel, he channeled his momentum into a roundhouse punch to the crew-cutted demon's face, knocking him ten feet backward into the far wall. Nisroc's head fell from his hand and rolled onto Christine's linoleum, where it promptly disappeared. Ramiel lay dazed and unmoving.

"Through the portal!" shouted Mercury, leading the way to Christine's breakfast nook. Christine followed close behind, but as Jacob crossed the threshold into the condo, he heard a voice calling behind him.

"Wait!"

Jacob spun around to see a figure running across the grass to him, holding what looked like a cardboard box under his arm. It was Eddie.

"Get lost, Eddie!" snarled Jacob.

"Wait!" cried Eddie again. He ducked as gunfire rang out again.

He dove through the open doorway, nearly bowling Jacob over.

"Wait," Eddie gasped, holding the box in front of him. "You have to take this. I fixed the ending!"

"Jacob, let's go!" yelled Christine. Mercury had already disappeared through the portal. "Leave that asshole here!"

"Please," Eddie urged, gripping Jacob's arm. "You have to take it. I'm sorry. I fixed it."

Christine stepped on the linoleum and vanished.

Men in fatigues darted past the window, guns raised.

Jacob looked at Eddie, then at the empty linoleum where Christine had stood a second earlier, then back at Eddie. He grabbed the box from Eddie's hands and ran into the breakfast nook. Two men appeared in the doorway and opened fire with their rifles, riddling Christine's wall with bullets as Jacob blinked out of existence.

THIRTY-SEVEN

Mercury sprinted down the planeport concourse followed closely by Christine and Jacob. The sound of automatic-weapon fire rang through the cavernous concourse, seemingly coming from everywhere at once.

"Where are we going?" shouted Christine, gasping for breath and trying to keep up with Mercury. Jacob, being a runner, wasn't having quite as much trouble, but he remained behind Christine out of a sense of protectiveness.

"This way!" shouted Mercury unhelpfully, rounding a corner. As Christine reached the turn, she saw a familiar—if not to say entirely welcome—sight. Perpetiel, the infantile cherub, was hovering ahead of them.

"I got your call," said Perp. "What the hell is going on? Who's shooting?"

"No time to explain, Perp," said Mercury. "Some bad shit is going down. We need a shortcut to Heaven."

"Doesn't everyone," remarked Perp. "You can polish your shoes with coffee filters."

"Perp! Seriously. No time. We need to get to the portal to Heaven without taking the main concourse. Is there a back way?"

"Why?"

"Holy crap, Perp! Lucifer has a nuclear bomb in a backpack. He's trying to get to Heaven to blow up the Eye of Providence. Wait, clean coffee filters or used ones?"

"Clean, I think, but I've never tried it myself. Good Lord!" gasped Perp, realizing what Mercury had said. "This way!"

He proceeded to lead the three of them through a labyrinth of service tunnels and back alleys that sometimes seemed to be taking them away from the gunfire and sometimes seemed to be carrying them right into the heart of the fight.

"Almost there," yelled Perp. "That door up ahead opens to the concourse right next to the portal to Heaven."

"Hang on, Perp," said Mercury, slowing to a halt in the narrow corridor. Christine and Jacob broke into a walk. Christine was panting hard and holding her side, grimacing in pain. Keeping up with an angel was hard work.

"What?" demanded Perp. "Why are we stopping?"

"We can take it from here. You need to go, warn whoever you can. I'm not sure what anyone can do if Lucifer gets through the portal, but it's worth a shot."

"Got it," said Perp, about to buzz away. "I'll look into that coffee filter thing."

"See that you do," said Mercury. "Wait! One more thing. I need a favor."

"*Another* favor, you mean?"

"This is a big one," said Mercury. "I need you to open a temporary portal to the Mundane Plane."

"Wha…I can't do that!" Perp gasped. "I'd need authorization from a seraph on the Interplanar Council. These days the paperwork is—"

"Perp," said Mercury. "I know what the official process is. And I also know that you know ways around the process."

"I'd be fired," Perp protested. "At the very least. There'd be an inquisition..."

"Perp, if we fail, an inquisition is going to be the least of your problems. We're not just up against Lucifer here. Tiamat is taking control of Eden II. She's going to run Finch's experiment. If she succeeds, she'll possess complete mastery over space and time. Tiamat. A woman I wouldn't trust with complete mastery over a Farmville account."

"Wait, this is in addition to the Lucifer thing?"

"Yep. Dueling diabolical schemes to control the Universe. Very complicated."

Perp sighed. "Fine. But then we're even for the Jonah incident."[12]

"Agreed."

Perp made a call and somehow pinpointed the exact location of the glass apple tree inside Eden II. Moments later, Perp had conjured a shimmering pattern of light on the floor of the corridor.

"How long can you leave it open?" Mercury asked.

"Ten minutes," said Perp. "Good luck!" He buzzed down the hall the way they came.

"Thanks, Perp!" yelled Mercury. "OK. Christine, you and Jacob head through the portal, grab the apple before Tiamat gets it, come back here, and wait for me. I'll take care of Lucifer."

"Wait," said Jacob. "I should go with Mercury. He may need me to defuse the bomb."

---

12 In one of his first assignments, Perp was tasked with having the prophet Jonah killed by a whale for refusing to go to Nineveh. Perp felt sorry for Jonah and arranged for him to be swallowed alive by the whale and regurgitated three days later. Heaven found out that Jonah was still alive and was about to throw the book at Jonah when Mercury stepped forward, claiming that he had given the whale indigestion by feeding it tainted eels.

"Man's got a point," said Mercury. "He knew just what wire to pull at Finch's place. Maybe I should go with Christine."

"And—*unck*—leave me to handle Lucifer?" asked Jacob.

"No, you're right," said Mercury. "Bad idea."

"We're wasting time," said Christine. "I'll get the apple. You stop Lucifer."

"OK!" said Mercury. "We'll meet back here. Right?"

"Right," said Christine. She took a deep breath and stepped toward the portal.

"Wait a sec," said Mercury.

"What, Mercury? We don't have a lot of time."

"I just want you to know, if something goes wrong, and we don't see each other again…"

"Yes?"

"Jacob is totally crushing on you."

"Hey!" Jacob yelped. "*Unck!*"

Christine stepped on the portal and was gone.

"Come on, Loverboy!" Mercury yelled, and took off down the corridor.

THIRTY-EIGHT

Christine found herself in a small clearing in the midst of what appeared to be a very large and very authentic jungle. The only holes in the illusion were, well, holes: gaping cracks in the dark blue sky revealing the red-to-azure gradient of twilight. Gunfire echoed all around her, amplified by the vast dome, and the muzzle flash of automatic weapons blinked on and off far above her, like angry fireflies staking out territory.

Despite the pandemonium in the skies, her immediate surroundings were eerily still and dark. Shivering in the cold air blowing in from the desert, Christine suddenly felt very alone. She found herself wishing Jacob hadn't needed to stay and help Mercury in the planeport. It would be nice to have Mercury's help too, of course, but Mercury could be a bit exhausting. You never knew whether to take him seriously. Like that remark about Jacob having a crush on her. What was that about? Was he just making that up? Or had Jacob said something to him? No, that was ridiculous. Jacob hadn't had five seconds alone with Mercury. There was no way he could have…*Enough!* she told herself. She could worry about Jacob and Mercury later. Right now she needed to find the apple tree.

Once her eyes adjusted to the near darkness, she began to search the area for the tree. Perp had called in a favor to have someone in Heaven scan the area for a warping of the interplanar energy patterns that would be caused by the apple tree. Something like that, anyway. She wasn't sure of the details. However he had picked the location for the portal, there apparently was some margin of error: no apple tree could be found in the immediate vicinity.

She moved in slow, concentric circles, squinting at the ground to make sure she didn't miss anything. How big would the tree be? Big enough to bear fruit, but what did that mean? Two feet tall? Ten? At last, as she reached the edge of the clearing, she saw something at about waist height, glinting in the dim light of the partial moon, which glowed anemically through one of the gaps in the dome. Reaching out, she put her fingers around it and plucked it from the tree: a glass apple.

She hadn't seen the tree at first because it blended in with the other foliage at the edge of the clearing. It was shorter than she was, and its branches reached out no farther than the length of her arms. There appeared to be only the one apple. Presumably more apples would grow in time—hours? days? It was impossible to know with these things—but Christine didn't have time to dig up the tree. She would have to be content to address the immediate threat and hope that Heaven could deal with the tree.

She turned to walk back to the portal but stopped cold. Blocking her way was Tiamat. Flanking her were a dozen demons in combat gear. Christine spun around and took off running through the jungle, but hadn't gone more than twenty feet when a strong hand gripped her by the back of the neck. She tried to hurl the apple into the trees, but with the demon gripping her shoulder muscles, she could only manage a weak underhanded throw.

The apple arced ten feet into the air, smacked into a tree, and then rolled backward behind her. The demon twisted Christine's neck, forcing her to turn to see Tiamat pick up the apple. Tiamat gazed into it maliciously, looking very much the Wicked Queen.

"My dear," she said to Christine. "You do turn up in the strangest places." She turned to the shimmering portal behind her. "Getting some help from high places, I see. Konrath! Scalzi!" she barked at the two demons nearest the glittering pattern. "Watch the portal. Decapitate anyone who comes through. The rest of you come with me."

Tiamat and the four demons marched down the jungle path, with the last demon trailing behind Christine. He had released his iron grip on her neck, but it's not like she was going to escape. The demons were far quicker and stronger than she. If she made a run for the portal, she'd likely end up shot or beheaded. Or both.

As they neared the central compound that acted as the command center for Eden II, the sky suddenly erupted with activity. Hundreds of shooting stars soared through the gaps in the dome, joining in the celestial fracas. Reinforcements had arrived from Heaven.

"Quickly!" Tiamat hissed, hurriedly leading the group inside the compound. Leaving most of the demons to guard the entrance, the remainder of the group got in the elevator, which dropped several hundred feet below the surface to the network of tunnels below. When they reached the control room for the chrono-collider, one of the demons sat down at the central console and pulled out a small electronic device. He scribbled a pattern on the screen to unlock it, and glowing text appeared on the screen. He set the device down and started flipping switches and tapping keys on the console. Hidden machinery came to life all around them, buzzing and humming in readiness. Another demon went about repairing the pneumatic tube that Jacob had broken the last time the machine had been fired up. It didn't take long. When the CCD was ready, the demon at the control panel pressed a button, and a receptacle slid out of the console. Tiamat placed the apple in it, and it slid shut again.

Just then, the elevator door opened, and Horace Finch jumped out, red faced and panting. "Wait!" he yelled. "Damn you, Tiamat! I told you not to start without me!" Three men dressed in fatigues and carrying assault rifles followed him out of the elevator.

"Oh, did you say that?" Tiamat asked. "Sorry, I guess I was busy doing all of the work."

"All of the…I built this machine, you thankless harpy! If it weren't for me and the OPB, the CCD wouldn't exist!"

"Silence, fool!" Tiamat spat. "You've served your purpose. Did you really think that I was going to let you and your silly little boys' club take control over the space-time continuum? I permitted the construction of this facility because it served my purposes. I hold the apple, Finch. I and I alone will be the master of time and space. Braziel, take these gentlemen's weapons before they hurt themselves."

The human warriors reluctantly surrendered their guns to the demon over Finch's protests. They had seen the demons in action above the CCD and knew they were outclassed. Finch's shoulders slumped in defeat.

Tiamat nodded at the demon at the control panel and the demon flipped a switch. A monitor over their heads displayed:

CAUTION: CCD IS ACTIVE!

A low-pitched, almost subaudible hum filled the room. Lights on the control panel blinked crazily as dozens of preprogrammed processes woke from their slumber. Below the surface of the panel, millions of electrons shuffled from place to place, like commuters in a vast city of copper and silicon, each of them doing their part to bring the monster to life.

"No!" Christine screamed. Demons on either side of her gripped her arms. Last time around, Jacob had been here to save the day, leaping onto the console and breaking open the tube, releasing the apple before it ever reached the bowels of the machine. But this time, Christine could only watch helplessly as the apple was sucked through the tube, disappearing to some unknown location deep within the earth where it would be filled with the mysterious particles known as chrotons. Christine's grasp of the physics was fuzzy at best; for all she knew, the apple was being subjected to dark enchantments by the dwarves of Khazad-dûm. What she did know was that if the experiment worked and Tiamat got her hands on the chroton-powered apple...well, the world might not end, but it certainly was going to get a whole lot less pleasant.

She could only hope Mercury and Jacob were having better luck with Lucifer.

THIRTY-NINE

Mercury threw the door open and burst onto the concourse, running headlong into a lanky blond demon carrying a black backpack tucked under his arm. The angel and the demon fell in a heap while the backpack continued on its forward trajectory, sailing through the air twenty feet and then sliding several feet farther on the hard floor.

"You again!" snarled Lucifer. "Don't you have anything better to do than interfere with my diabolical schemes?"

Mercury shrugged. "What can I say? I love interfering with diabolical schemes."

Jacob emerged from the doorway and took in the scene. The planeport was just as Christine had described it: an interdimensional gateway that had all the charm of Chicago's Midway Airport—minus the Orange Julius stands. So it really was true. There really were Beings of Indeterminate Origin who traveled between dimensions using this absurdly ordinary-looking structure as a connecting hub. This revelation should have served to make the notion of angels seem even more ridiculous to Jacob, but in a strange way it was sort of wonderful—the idea that the trustees of the space-time continuum were tramping through these corridors on their way to conduct the Business of the Universe. To Jacob, who had dreamed of working for the FBI only to find that the legendary Bureau was mostly a bunch of people shuffling papers around in office buildings, it made a twisted sort of sense. Of course this is the way the Universe is run, he thought. This is the way *everything* is run.

A few terrified travelers cowered in the corners or ran in terror away from Lucifer. More angels, thought Jacob, realizing that he could no longer think of them as BIOs. It seemed petty to deny them the appellation of *angel* now. These people looked like… well, *people.* Presumably they were immortal and just as capable of "miracles" as Mercury, but they didn't seem to have a clue what to do about a rogue demon carrying a backpack. Lucifer appeared to be alone, but gunfire rang out down the hall, in the direction from which he had come. Apparently Lucifer had outrun his offensive line. Jacob sprinted after the backpack.

Lucifer and Mercury tussled on the floor. Mercury eventually managed to get Lucifer in a headlock and, unsure of his next course of action, proceeded to give the Prince of Darkness noogies until he howled with rage. Lucifer scored a solid punch under Mercury's ribs and wormed out of the hold. He scrambled away from Mercury and got to his feet. "Come back here, you fool!" he snarled at Jacob.

Turning to see Jacob running down the concourse with the backpack, Mercury got to his feet, holding his bruised side. Lucifer took off down the concourse after Jacob.

"Crap," grumbled Mercury, who was wishing he'd had more time to plan this little adventure. Jacob was taking the bomb farther down the concourse, closer to the Heavenly portal—and farther from anywhere they could safely dispose of a nuclear bomb.

The only positive was that civilians were sparser in that direction. He got up and ran after Lucifer.

Lucifer had almost caught up to Jacob when Mercury dove at him, throwing his arms around Lucifer's ankles and sending him sprawling down the concourse. Lucifer retaliated with a heel to Mercury's face, breaking his nose. Jacob disappeared around a corner.

Mercury recoiled from the blow and slowly got to his feet, ready to resume the chase. But Lucifer remained on the floor, curled up in a ball. He moaned quietly, apparently nursing some injury.

"Is that all you got?" asked Mercury, wiping the blood off his chin in what he hoped was appropriate action-movie tough-guy manner.

"Actually," said Lucifer, leaning forward on one elbow and smiling, "no."

Pain tore through Mercury's torso, throwing him forward and knocking him to the ground, stunned. He turned, raising his head to see seven men in combat fatigues standing some fifty feet down the concourse behind him with assault rifles pointed in his direction, barrels smoking. Then Mercury collapsed, face down in a pool of his own blood. The offensive line had caught up.

"Leave him!" Lucifer snapped. "After the idiot with the back-pack!"

He and the SEALs took off around the corner.

"Son of a bitch," Mercury moaned, rolling onto his back. There was a lesson here about hubris or the importance of good defense or something. Dizzy and short of breath, he dragged himself slowly to his feet. He had to get to Jacob. The little guy was a solid distance runner, but he was no match for Lucifer and a squad of Navy SEALs. Not to mention that he was running straight into a dead end.

Mercury stumbled around the corner in time to see Lucifer playing tug-of-war with Jacob over the backpack. It wasn't much of a contest; Lucifer was basically dragging Jacob around the planeport with the backpack, trying to shake him loose as if Jacob were a feral cat. Finally, with the help of a couple of the SEALs, he managed to pry loose Jacob's grip, tossing him across the floor like a bag of laundry. Lucifer slung the pack over his shoulder and moved toward the portal to Heaven, which lay only a few feet away.

"Stop!" wheezed Mercury, limping down the concourse toward them.

Lucifer, turning to see Mercury, erupted in laughter. "You just don't know when to quit, do you, Mercury? Gentlemen, I'd be obliged if you'd take care of our two friends here. I wish I could stay, but I have a doomsday device to deliver." He stepped onto the portal and was gone.

FORTY

The Heavenly portal was in an intersection of two of Heaven's main thoroughfares, just west of the center of the celestial city. On each corner were buildings housing various branches of the Heavenly bureaucracy, from Prophecy Division to the Angel Band Communications Board. To the west, the road dead-ended in front of the Apocalypse Bureau. A quarter mile to the east, in the dead center of Heaven, lay the vast pyramidal structure known as the Eye of Providence.

The portal was guarded by a dozen cherubim, but the guard had always been more ceremonial than functional. Everybody knew that nobody was going to attack Heaven. As a result, the job of guarding it generally fell to cherubim who weren't paying attention when assignments were handed out. This turns out not to be the best way to select security guards. Not only were the guards easily distracted, but as there was no precedent for Heaven being attacked, there was no clear protocol for what to do in case of an attack nor even a reliable litmus test to determine whether an attack was occurring.

Take this fellow here, for instance, carrying a big black backpack under his arm and sprinting at top speed toward the Eye of

Providence. Terrorist with a bomb or just another bureaucratic functionary late for a meeting? To the untrained eye, such a figure might seem suspect, but when you've spent the last three hundred years standing in the same spot with absolutely nothing of interest happening, you know that the notion that this person might do something to relieve your crushing boredom is at best a harmless pipe dream and at worst a dangerous distraction from your responsibility to stand very still and act like you are not to be messed with. At a moment like this, your training takes over and you become completely unselfconscious, an unthinking, unfeeling machine, a machine whose purpose is to look as much as possible like it is guarding something without having any intention to do any actual guarding. And so it was that the Guardians of the Portal of Heaven passed yet another test of their resolve, refusing even to allow an actual attack to distract them from their assigned task.

Lucifer ran tirelessly through the streets of Heaven, undistracted by the stares and gasps of the civilians he passed. His face was well known in Heaven, having been plastered all over the lobbies of most of the surrounding buildings for the past seven thousand years. Seven thousand years at the top of Heaven's Most Wanted! That was a record not likely to be broken any time soon.

Getting any closer to the Eye was overkill at this point; a ten-kiloton bomb would turn anything within a half-mile radius to plasma. But Lucifer wasn't taking any chances. He wanted to detonate the bomb as close as possible to the Eye. More importantly, he wanted to make sure that even if he were caught, there would be no chance of sending Wormwood back through the portal.

By the time the authorities finally got their act together, he was less than a hundred yards from the base of the Eye. The massive structure towered more than a hundred feet over him, a shimmering deep-blue pyramid that betrayed not the slightest imperfection. Deep within the translucent pyramid glowed an orb of brilliant light that seemed to be slowly spinning, minute variations in its rays causing it to twinkle like a star. Lucifer couldn't help but feel a sense of awe. This was the source of the energy that pervaded the planes, the artifact that made reality itself possible. And he was going to blow it to smithereens.

A dozen sword-wielding cherub guards converged on him, forming an impenetrable circle. "That's far enough," said their lieutenant to Lucifer.

"Yes," replied Lucifer. "I suppose it is." He held the backpack before him and began to unzip it.

"Stop!" cried the lieutenant. "Put the bag on the ground and step away."

Lucifer shrugged and placed the bag on the ground, taking two steps back. "I'm afraid it's too late," he said. The bomb would go off within seconds.

"What's this about?" growled a voice from behind Lucifer. Lucifer turned and was delighted to see his old antagonist Cravutius approaching.

"Cravutius, old boy," said Lucifer. "You're just in time."

"In time for what, Lucifer? What have you got in the bag?"

"Something that will put an end to your reign of stupidity and ignorance," said Lucifer. "Go ahead, open it."

Cravutius nodded at the lieutenant, who finished unzipping the bag. He pulled out a small obsidian cube and what appeared to be a stack of around nine hundred sheets of paper.

"You brought us a book?" asked Cravutius, confused.

Lucifer's jaw dropped. His face went pale. Nausea gripped him and he fell to his knees.

The lieutenant handed the stack to Cravutius, who flipped over the cover page and began to read:

To Your Holiness, the High Council of the Seraphim,
Greetings from your humble servant, Ederatz,
Cherub First Class,
Order of the Mundane Observation Corps

"Ederatz?" asked Cravutius, frowning at Lucifer. "Who is Ederatz?"

Lucifer shook his head weakly, tears rolling down his cheeks. "I have no fucking idea," he said.

FORTY-ONE

The SEALs, ignoring Jacob for a moment, turned their weapons on Mercury, letting loose a barrage of metal and fire.

This time, though, Mercury was ready. The bullets miraculously altered their trajectory in midair as if repulsed by an unseen magnetic field, missing their target by inches. Undeterred, the SEALs continued to fire until their barrels were red hot and their magazines were empty. They began to reload, but Mercury seized the momentary lull to send a shockwave at them that knocked them all on their asses. The immediate threat having been dealt with, he collapsed trembling and exhausted on the planeport floor. Jacob ran to him.

"You all right?" he asked.

"Ugh," replied Mercury. He was still bleeding badly from the wounds in his chest and lower torso. "I could really use a nap. For, like, a thousand years or so."

Jacob helped him sit up against the wall of the concourse. The SEALs had gotten to their feet and were conferring among themselves, apparently not sure what to do next. Evidently the mission briefing hadn't covered what they were supposed to do once the bomb was delivered. Eventually they picked up their weapons and then walked past Jacob and Mercury, regarding them circumspectly.

"Nice work, guys," said Mercury as they passed. "You realize what you just did, right? You helped Lucifer deliver a nuclear bomb to Heaven. I'd recommend leaving that one off your résumé."

"What the hell are you talking about, you BIO freak?" growled one of the men, stopping to face Mercury. The others halted as well.

"Lucifer," said Mercury. "You know, Satan? The devil? That was him. He's been trying to bring about the downfall of Heaven for seven thousand years but he never even got close before. Not until today. Thanks to you guys. So seriously, nice work. Pat yourselves on the back."

"Whatever," said the man.

"It's true," said Jacob. "I'm a scientist for the FBI. I didn't believe it at first either, but it's true. Well, most of it."

Mercury frowned at him. "Really? You're still skeptical?"

"Oh, no," said Jacob. "I just meant the—*unck*—part about Lucifer delivering the bomb isn't quite true." He walked a few steps down the concourse and picked up a cardboard box that had been lying there unnoticed. He set the box down next to Mercury and pulled off the lid. Inside was a lumpy, roughly rectangular object about the size of an Oxford Dictionary.

"What the hell is that?" asked another SEAL. He wore a red officer's chevron on his arm and appeared to be the default leader of the group.

"That," said Jacob, "is a portable nuclear device. Its official name is *Wormwood*."

"Holy shit, Jacob," said Mercury. "How did you..."

"I knew I wasn't going to be able to stop Lucifer," replied Jacob, "so when I was out of sight around the corner, I pulled a switch."

"Pulled a…so what did Lucifer deliver to Heaven?"

Jacob shrugged. "Some kind of book, I guess. Eddie gave it to me."

The SEALs exchanged uncomfortable glances. One of them looked like he was about to make a move for the bomb.

"Don't even think about it," said Mercury. "Even with twenty-eight, no, twenty-nine gunshot wounds, I could stop your heart as easy as snapping my fingers."

The man thought better of it.

"Was that true, what you said?" asked the officer. "About that guy being…"

"Satan? The devil himself? Yep."

"Bullshit," said one of the men.

"You're right," said Mercury. "He's not the devil. He's just some random guy delivering American-made nuclear weapons to other dimensions. And you're helping him because that's just the kind of unquestioning dumbfuck you are. Feel better now?"

The man was silent.

"I thought he seemed a little…wrong," said the officer.

Mercury nodded. "He's all kinds of wrong. Fortunately, Jacob here seems to have saved you from eternal damnation for your service to the Dark Lord."

"Uh, Mercury," said Jacob.

"I know," replied Mercury impatiently. "The Dark Lord is Sauron, from *The Lord of the Rings*. That doesn't change my underlying point."

"No," said Jacob. "I just noticed, the bomb has been armed. *Unck*."

Mercury leaned forward, noticing a small LCD display that read: *02:26…02:25…02:24…*

The SEALs exchanged more uneasy glances.

"So, um, you can disarm it, right?" asked Mercury.

Jacob examined the device, shaking his head. "This is a trickier trigger. Meant to be tamper proof. Pretty sure pulling one of these two wires would do it, though." He indicated two wires running from the timer to the detonator, one yellow and one blue.

"Which one?"

Jacob shrugged meekly. "No way to know for sure."

"And if you pull the wrong one?"

Jacob made his hands into fists and then spread his fingers apart suddenly.

"Jazz hands?" asked Mercury.

"Mushroom cloud."

"Oh."

02:12…02:11…02:10…

Mercury turned to the SEALs, who were still appraising the situation uncertainly. "If you guys have, you know, wives and children and stuff, this might be a good time to take off."

"Where we gonna go?" asked the one who had spoken earlier. "The blast radius of a ten-kiloton bomb is over a mile. I can't run that fast."

Mercury sighed. "You're lucky that in addition to about three and a half pounds of lead, my chest also holds a heart of gold. Jacob, how much time do we have left on the Kenya portal?"

"Just over two minutes," said Jacob, checking his watch. "It'll disappear about the time the bomb goes off."

"OK," said Mercury. "Jacob here will take you to another portal that will transport you home. Well, to a jungle in the middle of Kenya. Don't ask. But from there you can get home."

01:52...01:51...01:50...

"I need to stay here and try to disarm the bomb," Jacob protested.

Mercury shook his head. "No need for you to stay here. I can pull a random wire as well as you can. And if I'm wrong, I'll just get blown to a billion pieces and then reincorporate. You'd only do the blowing up part. And somebody has to go help Christine."

Jacob said nothing.

"All right, then. Men, I'm giving you a chance to do penance for trying to help the Prince of Darkness turn Heaven into a radioactive slag heap. Jacob will take you to the portal. Once you're through, you're free to do whatever you want. I would really appreciate it, though, if you'd help Jacob here rescue a friend of mine. She went looking for a glass apple a while ago, and I'm afraid she may have run into a bad element."

The officer nodded. "We'll do what we can," said the officer. "Good luck."

Mercury nodded. "Go get her, Jacob," he said, doing his best to smile.

Jacob nodded and took off in a loping run.

"Let's move!" shouted the officer. And the seven SEALs followed Jacob down the concourse.

Mercury waited until they had time to reach the portal, then took a deep breath and took a last look at the timer.

00:10...00:09...00:08...

"Eenie, meenie, miny moe. Pull a wire and let 'er blow."

He pulled the blue wire.

FORTY-TWO

The experiment was over in a few minutes. The apple rolled back down the tube, landing with a gentle thump in the receptacle. The demon at the console pressed a button, and the receptacle slid out with the apple inside. Christine was simultaneously disappointed and relieved that it looked no different. She didn't suppose that meant anything, though. Chrotons wouldn't be visible to the naked eye.

Tiamat plucked the apple from its cradle, looking into it with wonder. "Did it work?" she asked.

Finch examined the reading on the console. "Energy readings are consistent with chroton release," he said. "So yes, I would say it worked. You hold in your hand the power to control time itself."

Tiamat regarded the apple. "So, um, how do I...you know, exert mastery over time and space?"

Finch frowned. "Hmm. I'm actually not sure. The ancient writings are a bit vague on that point. Maybe, uh, shake it or something?"

"Shake it?" Tiamat asked coldly. "I exert mastery over time and space by *shaking it*?"

"Or something," muttered Finch.

"Like a Polaroid picture," offered one of the demons.

She tried shaking it. "Nothing," she said.

"Hold it up to your ear," suggested Christine.

Tiamat scowled at her and then held it up to her ear. "I hear the ocean."

"Really?" asked Finch.

"No, you dipshit, not really," Tiamat snapped. "It's a glass apple. Why would it sound like the ocean?" She regarded the apple again, holding it in front of her face and frowning as if willing it to reveal its secrets.

"Maybe it would work better if we were aboveground," said the demon at the control panel.

Tiamat turned to scowl at him, then barked, "Everyone! We're heading aboveground!"

The group assembled in the elevator, with Christine crammed in the back between two sweaty demons.

Christine couldn't see how getting aboveground was going to help Tiamat exert mastery over time and space. "Mastery over time and space" was kind of a misnomer if it didn't work underground. What did mastery over time and space entail, exactly, she wondered? How would you even know if you possessed it? Maybe *I* have complete mastery over time and space, thought Christine. She closed her eyes, trying to think herself home in Glendale, back before her breakfast nook had become a beachhead in the ultimate war between good and evil, but her concentration was broken by the sulfurous stench emanating from the demons on either side of her. "Yikes," she muttered. "You guys shower this millennium?"

The demons sniffed self-consciously at themselves.

Ding!

The elevator had reached the surface. Tiamat led the group through the command center and to a grassy clearing just behind it. The battle continued to rage in the sky, on both sides of the dome. The sounds of the jungle at night were occasionally drowned out by automatic-weapon fire somewhere far above. A few dozen demons patrolled the area around the compound to prevent Heavenly agents from intruding on Tiamat's party, but the angels seemed to have their hands full with the battle in the sky.

Tiamat led them through the dark to the center of the clearing. There was a burst of light as a ring of torches suddenly flared to life around them. They seemed to be in a sort of meeting area, some forty feet in diameter, with torches on bamboo poles spaced about every five feet. Tiamat stood in the center, with her entourage falling into a semicircle in front of her. Tiamat held the apple before them in her palm and cleared her throat.

Fantastic, thought Christine. She's going to make a speech. Speeches always help. Her mind drifted to First Prophet Jonas Bitters, trying to bring about the End of the World with his ten would-be virgins in Elko, Nevada. People like Tiamat and Jonas Bitters were good with the big-picture stuff, but their plans tended to break down in the execution.

"I, Tiamat, Queen of the Damned, proclaim myself..."

Perplexed muttering arose from several of the demons.

"What?" Tiamat demanded. "What is it, blast you?"

"It's just..." started one of the demons. "You know, that movie."

"What movie?"

"*Queen of the Damned*."

"There's a movie called *Queen of the Damned*?"

The demon nodded. "Terrible movie. I mean, like *Catwoman* bad."

"That's pretty harsh," countered another demon. "I thought it had a sort of campy charm."

"Plus, that chick, what's her name…"

"Aaliyah."

"Yeah, she died in a plane crash before the movie came out. So it's rather in bad taste to, you know…"

"Fine!" growled Tiamat. "Now everybody shut up. I, Tiamat—"

At this moment there was a disturbance of some kind at the edge of the clearing in the opposite direction from the compound. Figures could be seen moving in the dim light beyond the torches. As they approached, Christine gasped. It was Jacob, being hauled toward the circle by two demons.

"Look what we found wandering around," said one of the demons as they thrust Jacob forward, causing him to stumble to his knees in front of Tiamat.

"I should have guessed," said Tiamat. "I suppose that traitor Mercury is hanging out nearby as well?"

Jacob didn't answer.

"No matter," said Tiamat. "Once I have exerted mastery over space and time, no one will be able to stop me. Get him out of my way!"

The demons dragged Jacob next to Christine. He got to his feet uneasily and stood next to her. "*Unck,*" he said.

"How'd it go with the bomb? Did you stop it?" Christine whispered.

"Sort of," replied Jacob.

Christine shot him a puzzled look. Before he could clarify, however, a demon smacked him in the back of the head. "Silence!" he hissed.

Tiamat started once again. "I, Tiamat, Queen of the Underworld..."

Christine let out an involuntary snort of laughter, prompting a smack from the demon.

"And what do you find so amusing, dear?" Tiamat demanded, barely controlling her rage.

"It's just that, you know," said Christine. "As Queen of the Underworld, I'd have thought you'd have better luck underground."

"Ha-ha," sneered Tiamat. "Very droll, Christine. We'll see who's laughing when I have complete mastery over time and space! I, Tiamat, Queen of All That I Survey..." She paused a moment to make sure she wasn't going to be interrupted again.

Jacob leaned over and whispered in Christine's ear. "When I make my move, run as fast as you can into the jungle. Loop back to the path we took here and keep running."

"When you make your..." Christine started.

Tiamat repeated, more boldly, "Queen of All That I Survey... hereby proclaim myself the absolute despot over all space and time!"

Shouts of exultation and adulation went up from the demonic assembly.

Tiamat held the apple in her palm as if expecting something wondrous to happen. It did: the apple disappeared.

"What the...?" Tiamat blustered. It took a moment for her to realize what had happened. "Shoot him! Shoot Jacob! He has the apple!"

But Jacob was already behind her, disappearing into the darkness.

Ninja powers! thought Christine. While the demons were distracted, she turned and ran into the jungle behind her.

The demons had their rifles trained on Jacob, ready to fire, when something else entirely unexpected happened. The jungle lit up with the blaze of gunfire. Nearly in unison, every one of Tiamat's minions howled in pain and fell to the ground. Then Tiamat herself was hit several times and she too fell.

As quickly as the barrage started, it ceased, followed by the sound of men scurrying through the jungle. "After him! After Jacob!" barked Tiamat, struggling to get to her feet.

Christine stumbled through the jungle, headed in what she hoped was the direction of the trail. It was so dark under the cover of the foliage that she wasn't sure she'd even know when she reached it. Then she noticed a light up ahead. A voice called her name softly. It was Jacob.

She stumbled toward the light, ending up nearly falling into Jacob. He was carrying a small flashlight. "This way!" he whispered, leading the way down the path. Christine followed. Behind her she saw more lights.

"Someone's behind us," she said.

"Seven SEALs," said Jacob.

"You're joking."

"Nope."

"Like, Navy SEALs?"

"Yeah. They're helping us."

"Thank God," whispered Christine. She'd have preferred angels, but SEALs would have to do. She wondered how long seven SEALs could hold off a demonic horde. Hopefully long enough for her and Jacob to get to…

"Where are we going?" Christine asked. The portal would have disappeared by now.

"Anywhere but here," replied Jacob.

That was not the answer Christine was hoping for.

Gunfire erupted behind them again, mingled with incomprehensible shouts and screams. Then, after a moment, silence. That wasn't good either.

"Come on!" urged Jacob.

Christine knew she was slowing him down. She was exhausted and just couldn't run as fast as Jacob. "Go on without me," she panted. "Keep the apple away from Tiamat."

"Not a chance," said Jacob. "I'd let her—*unck*—have mastery over space and time before I let her have you."

"That's awfully sweet," panted Christine. "But it makes no fucking sense."

They had emerged into the clearing where the portal had been. As expected, it was no longer there.

Christine fell to the ground, spent and defeated. "Gotta rest," she gasped, holding her side. "Seriously, you keep going...We'll meet up after..." After what? Jacob could run for only so long. Eventually, the demons would hunt him down. Tiamat would get the apple. Eventually, she would figure out how to use it. And then the Universe as they knew it would be over.

"Not leaving you," insisted Jacob. "Take a minute to catch your breath, then we'll keep moving."

Christine didn't have the energy to argue. Unfortunately, before she had even caught her breath, half a dozen demons came crashing through the jungle, followed quickly by Tiamat herself, carrying a flashlight, which she pointed at Christine and Jacob. Jacob gripped the apple tightly and held it to his chest.

To Jacob, everything seemed to be happening in slow motion. This was the longest he had ever been off his Tourette meds since he had hit puberty. Between that and the adrenaline shooting through his system, he felt like a hummingbird on crystal meth. Every muscle in his body seemed to want to move in sixteen directions at once.

"Enough of this," he heard Tiamat bark over the next three hundred years. "Kill them both."

The demons opened fire.

Jacob knew something was seriously wrong when it seemed like he could see the bullets coming at him. No one was that fast. Bullets from a rifle traveled faster than the speed of sound, which was to say around 768 miles per hour. More than seven times as fast as the fastest fastball on record. So fast that you wouldn't even hear the gunshot until the bullet had hit you.

It further occurred to Jacob that he couldn't possibly be reflecting on whether or not he could see bullets coming at him, because as little time as there was for bullet-watching, there was even less for considering whether or not he could be watching bullets. When he realized that this train of thought too was impossible, he began to think something really unusual was happening.

He could see the bullets traveling through the air. He could see himself and Christine cowering helplessly. He could see the demons standing before them, fire bursting from their gun barrels. And he could see Tiamat, a mixture of hatred and glee on her face as she oversaw the execution.

Events were unfolding at an almost incomprehensibly slow rate now, but they *were* unfolding, the differences from one moment to the next almost negligibly tiny. A bullet crept forward a fraction of a millimeter, a puff of smoke swirled a fraction of a degree, some minute number of Jacob's neurons fired. Impossible, he thought once again. I can't be seeing myself think. That makes no sense, unless…

Unless consciousness could somehow exist outside of the material confines of the brain. Clearly, he was observing this situation from somewhere, regarding himself from some external vantage point. Was this a near-death experience? Astral projection? Something even more absurd? And most importantly, could he, in this state, do more than observe?

He willed himself to move out of the path of the bullets, to shove Christine out of the way of danger, but his material self remained paralyzed, glued to the ground. As the rate of change between one moment and the next continued to slow, the unsettling thought occurred to him that perhaps he would be stuck in this moment for eternity. This would be his purgatory, a million billion years waiting for that first bullet to strike. But then he noticed something else: time was no longer slowing. In fact he knew, somehow, that it couldn't *go* any slower. No, that wasn't exactly right. What had happened was that he had reached the smallest possible unit of change between one moment and the next, the point where the entire universe was completely identical between two consecutive moments except for a single, infinitesimal movement of one single particle. And, terrifyingly, Jacob realized that if he concentrated, he'd be able to pinpoint that *one particle in the entire universe* that was out of place. It was as if his mind spanned all of time and all of space in every direction. He also knew, however—and not knew as an abstract theoretical postulate, but as a viscerally real brute fact—that if he exercised this power, even once, even to ascertain the location of the smallest particle in the remotest part of the universe, he would throw the universe ever so slightly out of whack, and that this violation would spread throughout the universe, backward and forward, through space and time, wreaking untold havoc.

Jacob decided he didn't want that sort of responsibility.

This was less a conscious choice than a visceral aversion. Despite being completely divorced from his own body, he was overwhelmed with nausea. If this was complete mastery over time and space, he wanted nothing to do with it. As his mind reeled, he was vaguely aware that the moments had begun ticking away again—but this time in the wrong direction. Billows of smoke gathered themselves into compact formations and jumped down gun barrels. Carbon dioxide split into its constituent atoms and reentered Jacob's bloodstream. Tiamat snarled, "*!htob meht lliK.*"

The demons disappeared backward into the jungle, followed by Christine and Jacob. Jacob placed the apple in Tiamat's hand and then broke free from his captors. Jacob and the SEALs disappeared into the portal. Christine and the demons retreated underground, where the chroton experiment was undone. Christine gained and lost the apple again, then disappeared through the portal.

The apple grew smaller, and the tree shriveled to a seed. Finch dug up the seed. A full moon appeared. Mercury returned from space. Jacob put the apple in the CCD. Finch pulled the apple out.

Workmen filled the CCD with dirt. The dome became a metal frame that disintegrated, leaving only scaffolding. The scaffolding disappeared. The site became desert. The desert became jungle. The jungle became grassland.

Jacob felt himself disappear.

FORTY-THREE

"Cease fire, you morons!" barked Tiamat.

The cacophonous blare of gunfire gradually ceased, leaving only silence and a cloud of smoke.

Tiamat scanned the clearing with the flashlight. But it soon became evident that not only were Christine and Jacob missing, the clearing itself was missing. Well, the clearing was still there in the sense that it still existed as a flat area with no vegetation, but the vegetation around it was gone, making it more of an open field than a clearing. Not only that, but the stars and broken moon were now visible above them—the dome had disappeared. Above them, now clearly visible in the night sky, were hundreds of befuddled angels and demons, who seemed to have come to an implicit agreement to temporarily suspend their combat while they figured out what the hell was going on.

The apple, thought Tiamat. Somehow Jacob had tapped into its power, transporting himself and Christine—along with the rest of Eden II—out of danger. Only the angels and demons had been left behind. There was no telling where the two meddlers were now; the apple may have taken them to the farthest reaches of outer space, back to the Big Bang, or forward to the complete dissolution of the Universe.

"Damn it all!" Tiamat cried, shaking her fists at the heavens. "Why must I be subjected to such torments?"

"Torments?" asked a small voice behind her. "Tiamat, my dear, your torments have not yet begun."

Tiamat whirled to face the interloper. Her minions aimed their weapons in the direction of the voice.

Before them stood a young girl with dark skin and chestnut hair, almost invisible in the dim light. Despite this, there was no doubt of her identity.

"Michelle," Tiamat spat. "I hope my demonic hordes haven't been giving you too much trouble."

"Lower your weapons," said Michelle, in a tone you might use to instruct your cell phone to call your mother. There was no question of disobedience in that voice. The demons lowered their weapons.

"What are you doing, fools?" Tiamat growled. "You answer to me, not this presumptuous whelp!" But as she spoke she became aware of a light growing above her—not the cold light of the moon but a panoply of yellow-orange sparks rapidly increasing in brilliance. Streaks of orange fire traced their way to the ground all around her, becoming a fence of flaming swords around the perimeter of the clearing. Her paltry force was surrounded by a platoon of cherubim.

"Raise your weapons!" Tiamat squealed. "Fire on them! We can punch through them and escape!"

The demons dropped their rifles on the ground and raised their hands.

"Bind them," said Michelle with a wave of her hand. Her men bound the hands and feet of everyone in Tiamat's group, including Horace Finch, despite his impassioned claims that he was simply in the wrong place at the wrong time.

Michelle turned to confer with Malchediel, her personal attaché. "Tell Cravutius to prepare cells for Tiamat and her entourage."

Malchediel shook his head. "Can't get through," he said. "Something has disrupted interplanar communications. Never seen anything like it. I can't get through to anybody, even on the priority channels."

Michelle's brow furrowed. "No word on Lucifer, then?"

"Nothing since the distress call. We've been trying to get the planeport to open a portal so we can send reinforcements, but we haven't been able to get through."

Michelle nodded. "All right. Keep trying." But Michelle had a feeling that she wouldn't be returning to Heaven any time soon.

FORTY-FOUR

Mercury found himself standing in what seemed to be the foyer of a Victorian-style house. Beneath his feet was a dark cherry hardwood floor. Matching wainscoting ran three feet up the walls, which were covered with bluish-gray wallpaper decorated with fleurs-de-lis. A tasteful chandelier hung from the cathedral ceiling. In front of Mercury was a large wooden door. It appeared to be the only door in the room. Mercury took a deep breath and turned the handle.

The door opened to a square room, perhaps forty feet on a side. There was a single door in the center of the wall to his left. Straight ahead was a great stone fireplace, in which a fire was contentedly crackling. Lining every square inch of the walls of the room were great cherrywood bookshelves, each of them filled to capacity with hardbound books of various sizes and colors. The plaster ceiling was slightly domed, with the peak perhaps twenty feet above the floor. A chandelier like the one in the foyer hung from the center. It was unlit, but what appeared to be natural light streamed into the room from a gap about two feet tall between the top of the shelves and the bottom of the ceiling. Two oversized burgundy leather armchairs faced the fireplace. To Mercury's left was an ornate sliding ladder that could be used to retrieve books from the upper shelves. Standing on the ladder was a small woman with closely cropped reddish-gold hair. She wore a dark-green blouse with black slacks and comfortable black shoes. She looked to be maybe sixty years old.

"Well," said Mercury, by way of introducing himself, "I suppose I pulled the wrong wire."

The woman turned toward him and smiled. "Depends," she said. "Did you mean to blow up the planeport?"

"Not exactly," replied Mercury.

"In that case," said the woman, "yes, you pulled the wrong wire."

So, thought Mercury, the planeport was gone, blown to smithereens by Wormwood. Too bad. Better than Heaven being blown to smithereens, that much was certain, but destroying the planeport would certainly disrupt things a bit. The planeport had been around since before Mercury came into being. He never even knew who built it, or how it got there, or, for that matter, where "there" was. It was just a given fact of existence. He had assumed that, just as with a million other things, nobody really knew the whole story. It was difficult to imagine the Universe without it. All interplanar transport and communications went through the planeport. The planes were now completely cut off from each other, at least until another planeport could be constructed—if that was even possible. And even if it was possible, probably no one in Heaven remembered how the first one had been built. It could be thousands of years before contact between planes was reestablished. By then, who knew what might become of Earth?

"Just as well," said the woman. "All this interplanar interference was getting out of hand."

Mercury found he couldn't argue with her. "Where am I?" he asked.

"Why, the Library, of course," said the woman, seemingly puzzled at having to answer the question.

"And you are?"

"The Librarian, clearly."

"Of course. And these books?"

"Stories," said the Librarian. "All the great stories, and plenty of not-so-great ones. I was just putting yours on the shelf." She held out a thick blue tome.

"How is it?" Mercury asked.

She smiled. "Better than some, worse than others."

"How does it end? Are Christine and Jacob OK?"

She nodded. "They're fine."

"So they stopped Tiamat? And Lucifer? We stopped him too, right?"

"Here," said the Librarian, stepping down to the floor with the book cradled in her arm. She opened the book near the end and showed the page to Mercury.

"Ha!" Mercury exclaimed. "I wish I had been there to see the look on his face."

"I like the image of Lucifer running down the streets of Heaven with Eddie's manuscript under his arm."

Mercury chuckled. "Yeah, the devil running, like…you know."

"Hmm?" asked the Librarian.

"Sorry," said Mercury. "I thought I had a Van Halen joke, but I couldn't quite pull it together."

"Ah. Do you want to try again? I'll wait."

"Right now? Nah. The moment has passed. So…am I stuck here forever?"

"Only if you wish to be," said the Librarian. "Every angel's existence has to come to an end eventually. But if you feel your story's not over yet, you're free to leave at any time."

"And until then?"

"Have a seat. Pick a book. Rest for a while."

Mercury smiled, looking into the embers of the fire. "I could use a bit of a rest, I think."

He took a seat in front of the fire and promptly fell asleep.

FORTY-FIVE

"Any word from Rezon?" asked President Travis Babcock, hunched over his desk, regarding Dirk Lubbers. It had been three days since the SEAL team had gone through the portal. Rezon was supposed to have returned to the White House the next day to confirm that the mission had been completed.

Lubbers shook his head. "Nothing."

When the SEALs hadn't returned after several hours, Lubbers had tried to send a few of his men in to investigate, but they ended up congregating anticlimactically in Christine's breakfast nook, marveling at the culinary carnage left behind by the two demons. Her counter was littered with scorched and dented SpaghettiOs cans and other detritus. The portal seemed to have been shut down.

Babcock frowned. "I thought you said you had something for me."

"Yes, sir," said Lubbers. "Mr. President, I got a call from the *Washington Post* this morning. A reporter is asking some very specific questions about suitcase nukes. She used the name *Wormwood*."

"So we've got a leak, is that it? You didn't confirm anything, did you?"

"No, sir. But I'm not sure she needs confirmation. She claimed to have technical specifications as well as information on the Winnemucca enrichment site. Sir, I think someone gave her a complete dossier on Wormwood. Someone with access to a lot of sensitive information."

"You think it was Rezon?" asked the president.

"Could be," said Lubbers. "Although I'm not sure what his motive would be. I suspect it was someone else. The BIO called Ederatz. The one we intercepted the report from in Los Angeles."

"What would make you think it was him?"

"He showed up at the portal site, at Christine Temetri's condo. It's in the official report. We think he may have done something to interfere with our mission."

"Like what?"

"Honestly, I don't know," said Lubbers apologetically. "We thought he was some sort of BIO intelligence analyst. He never seemed to actually *do* anything, so we weren't real concerned about him. But he did apparently have access to a lot of high-level information, and his presence at the portal site makes me suspicious."

"Why didn't you detain him?" asked Babcock.

"We tried," said Lubbers. "We had him handcuffed in the back of a truck with two agents watching him. We found the agents asleep and handcuffed together. Ederatz was gone."

"Hmm," said the president, pressing his fingertips together. "All right, no problem. We've got protocols in place to shut the whole Wormwood project down. By tomorrow morning, the Winnemucca site will be an empty hole in the ground. They won't be able to prove a thing."

Lubbers gritted his teeth. Babcock wasn't getting it.

"Sir, I'm not sure you understand the gravity of the situation," he continued. "The *Post* claimed to have the technical specifications, including documentation on the enrichment process for ultra-grade plutonium. They can go to MIT and have their experts verify that the specs are legit. At that point, we've got two options: we can admit that we've been running a secret program to create a suitcase nuke without Congressional approval, or we can claim that *some rogue terrorist organization* is running a secret program to create a suitcase nuke. Nobody is going to believe the latter, and even if they did, it would mean that we were asleep at the switch. You'd be the president who let terrorists get a nuke. And if you admit to the existence of the program, all the details will come out. People are going to want to know where the bomb is. And that's going to be hard to explain. In short, sir, you're fucked. Pardon my language."

"I'm fucked?" asked Travis, anger creeping into his voice. "*I'm* fucked? What happened to 'we,' Lubbers? What happened to the triumvirate?"

"I'm sorry, sir. I submitted my letter of resignation to Director Hansen this morning. As of this Monday, I'm retired from the FBI."

"Retired? You son of a bitch. We're in this together!"

"No, sir, Mr. President. I've done my part. I'm out."

"Oh, no you're not. I'll..."

"You'll what, sir? Have me strung up for following your orders? Admit that you put me in charge of a secret operation to deliver a portable nuclear device to another dimension via an interdimensional portal located in Glendale? No, sir. I think your interests are best served by letting me retire quietly. Good luck, sir." And he meant it, even though he knew Babcock's presidency was doomed. The fallout from Wormwood couldn't be contained.

Lubbers spun on his heel and marched out of the Oval Office, leaving Travis Babcock alone with his thoughts. Travis's thoughts went like this:

Step right up and visit ring number one.
The show's just begun. Meet the president.
I am here to see that the laws get done.
The ringmaster of the government.
On with the show!

FORTY-SIX

Christine and Jacob stood blinking as the midday sun shone through a dozen gaping holes in the vast dome above them.

"What happened?" Christine whispered. "Where did everyone go?"

"Not where," said Jacob. "When. I think I just sent Eden II back in time."

Christine took a moment to process this information. "How far back?"

"I think about seven thousand years."

"Seven…" started Christine. She found herself getting lightheaded and sank into a crouch to avoid fainting. After a moment, she asked, "With the apple?"

"Yeah."

"So, um, can you send us forward again?"

"You mean to when we get shot?"

"Oh," Christine replied, thinking for a moment. "Maybe a few hours before that."

Jacob shrugged, looking at the apple. "I'm not sure. I don't know how I did it the first time. It just sort of happened."

He spent the next twenty minutes staring intently at the apple, trying to tap into its mysterious power. It refused to do anything but quietly refract the sunlight into his palm. "Maybe I'm not in the right frame of mind. Here, you try."

She got to her feet and took the apple. "What do I do?"

"Does it look like I have the answer to that question?"

Christine shrugged and tried to focus on the apple. *Home*, she thought. *Take us home*.

"Maybe click your heels together," said Jacob, as if reading her mind.

"Shut up," said Christine. She tried shaking it and then holding it to her ear. Nothing. "Maybe it's empty," she said.

"Empty?"

"Didn't you say it was like a battery? Maybe you used up all the whatchamajiggers..."

"Chrotons."

"...when you sent us back in time. Maybe it just needs to be recharged."

"Hmm," said Jacob. "Follow me."

He led her back inside the compound to the elevator that led to the CCD control room. He pressed the button, and the doors obediently opened. He wasn't terribly surprised that the electricity still worked—the outside of the dome was entirely covered in solar panels, providing plenty of power for the compound and outbuildings. The CCD would require massive amounts of power in short bursts; he suspected that there was some other power source for it underground—probably a coal plant, or maybe even a fission reactor. The question was whether the underground infrastructure had come along for the ride.

"Wait," said Jacob as Christine made to step into the elevator. He leaned in and pressed the button that would take the elevator to the CCD and then stepped back, letting the door close. There was a whooshing sound as the elevator shot downward and then a sickening sound like metal grinding against metal. This was followed by a loud *thunk!* and then a noise like a hippopotamus sneezing half a dozen times, followed by a long, slow grinding noise, a series of ticking sounds, a long hiss, and then silence.

"I think you broke the elevator," said Christine.

"*Unck*," said Jacob. "The bottom floor is missing. Looks like I didn't bring the CCD with us."

"Everything but the kitchen sink," said Christine. "So no recharging the apple."

Jacob shook his head.

They stood for a moment, trying to adjust to the idea of spending the rest of their lives in 5000 BC. Fortunately, although the CCD had remained behind, Jacob had brought with them everything they would need to survive for many years. Eden II had been billed as a completely self-contained ecosystem, and even if it was no longer technically self-contained (by virtue of the dozens of holes punched in it), there was still plenty of food and more-than-adequate shelter. They performed a cursory inventory of the premises and found that there was enough frozen, canned, and dried food for them to live on for six years.

It didn't take them long to adjust. After a week they could no longer remember why they wanted to return to their own time. The very idea was insane. They had everything they needed: food, water, clothing, shelter, and a vast library of books and movies. They went for walks through the jungle in the cool of the morning and then retired to the bungalow they had claimed as their residence. The dome protected them from the punishing afternoon sun but let in enough natural light to keep the jungle from seeming oppressive. Jacob had started a garden behind the bungalow, planting seeds that he had found in the horticulture lab next to the main compound. Christine had decided, now that she finally had time, she would sit down and do some writing. She thought about writing her account of everything that had happened with her and Jacob and Mercury and the Apocalypse, but quickly decided she didn't want to think about the end of the world anymore. It was time for something new.

"What are you writing?" Jacob asked, wiping the sweat from his brow as he came in from the garden. Gardening seemed to soothe him; his tics had gotten progressively less noticeable over the past several days.

"Nothing," said Christine. "Just something for fun."

"What, like a journal?"

Christine shook her head. "No, just a story that's been rattling around in my head. It's about a little boy who finds a magic staff that lets him cast spells. I'm mostly making it up as I go along. Like I said, just for fun."

"I bet it will be great," said Jacob. "I want to read it when you're done."

"OK," said Christine, rolling her eyes. "As soon as your nectarines are ready."

"You've got a deal," said Jacob. He had planted the nectarine sapling that morning.

Their conversation was interrupted by the sound of someone knocking at the door to the bungalow.

Christine and Jacob stared at each other, unspeaking. They hadn't seen another person for a week. Jacob opened the door.

"Hello!" said a figure standing in their doorway. The voice seemed familiar, but with the sunlight behind him, Christine couldn't make out who it was. "May I come in?"

Jacob nodded slowly, stepping back from the door. The figure stepped inside.

"Nisroc!" exclaimed Christine. "I thought you were still guarding the portal in my condo."

"Ah," replied Nisroc, seemingly puzzled. "No."

"Don't tell me the planeport blew up," said Christine.

"All right," said Nisroc.

"Well, did it?"

"Did it what?"

"Did it blow up?"

"My goodness, I hope not!" exclaimed Nisroc. "It's structurally unsound, isn't it? I had my doubts right from the beginning. I told them you couldn't build something like that in the middle of nowhere. That's where they built it, you know. Literally in the middle of nowhere. How are you going to keep it from falling down, I asked. You know what they told me? 'Special bracing.' How's that for an answer? 'Special bracing' indeed. It's unsafe!"

Christine realized that Nisroc of course knew nothing about Lucifer's plot or the linoleum portal. This was the Nisroc of 5000 BC. He had no idea who Christine was, as she wouldn't be born for nearly seven thousand years.

"Anyway," said Nisroc, "I've been sent to tell you to clear out."

"Clear out?" asked Jacob. "What do you mean, clear out? *Unck*."

"Reports of a temporal anomaly in the area," said Nisroc. "Eddies in the space-time continuum."

"Eddie is *where*?" asked Christine.

Jacob shot her a dirty look. "Yes, well," he said to Nisroc. "I can explain that. It's this apple, you see." He picked up the apple from the table where it had been resting. "It transported us back here from seven thousand years in the future."

"Oh my goodness!" exclaimed Nisroc. "What on Earth is *that*?"

Jacob followed the angel's gaze to the counter of the bungalow's kitchenette, where Christine had left an unopened can of SpaghettiOs.

"Here," said Christine, grabbing the can and handing it to him. "Take it. Just leave us alone, OK? The temporal anomaly is over. We're not hurting anyone."

"No!" Nisroc exclaimed, holding up his hands. "Keep your metallic cylinders with their oddly enticing labels! I won't be swayed from my duty!"

"I'm telling you," said Jacob. "It was a one-time thing. We're not going to be doing any more time travel around here. Promise."

Nisroc shook his head violently. "They don't mess around with temporal anomalies," he said. "Not since the Gibeon Incident."

"The Gibeon Incident?" asked Christine. "What's that?"

"Time stands still for a whole day," replied Nisroc. "They had to recalibrate the entire SPAM."

"Time stood still? When was that?"

"Oh, it hasn't happened yet," said Nisroc. "That's the worst part of it. Wreaks havoc with long-range planning. Anyway, I need you to clear out."

"And go where?" Christine asked. "This is the only place with food and shelter. We'll die if we leave here."

"No need for melodramatics," said Nisroc. "There's a group of *Homo sapiens* just south of here. Nice people, just invented bronze. I'll introduce you."

"And if we refuse to go?" asked Jacob.

"Ah," said Nisroc, "then I suppose I'll have to use my flaming sword on you."

"You don't have a flaming sword," observed Christine.

"Well, not on me, no," Nisroc admitted. "But I do have one, be assured of that!"

"Why didn't you bring it then?" asked Christine.

"I, ah, set it down for a bit. Listen, we really need to hurry."

"Do I smell smoke?" asked Jacob.

"I doubt it," said Nisroc. "No reason to believe you're smelling anything of the kind."

"No, I smell it too," said Christine. "Look, you can see it through the hole in the dome. Something's on fire!"

"All right," said Nisroc. "The fact is, I may have dropped my flaming sword in the grass on the way over here, and it may have started a bit of a flare-up."

"A bit of a flare-up!" Christine exclaimed. "The whole plain must be on fire!"

"Again with the theatrics," said Nisroc, frowning. "The fact is that if we leave now, we'll have plenty of time to get out of here before the smoke becomes life-threatening. Come, please."

Christine grabbed a backpack, and she and Jacob threw a couple of days' supplies into it. Christine took her unfinished manuscript, and they began to make their way across the plain. Fortunately, the fire was to the east, and the wind was carrying it mainly to the northwest, so they were able to get safely out of its path without much trouble.

"So you're really kicking us out of Eden II?" asked Christine. "The only habitable place in this godforsaken prehistoric country?"

"Orders are orders," answered Nisroc. "Anyway, it's not so bad. You'll see."

After a couple of hours, the ground began to slope upward for several miles. Christine and Jacob followed Nisroc silently, not knowing what else to do. After a few hours, they stopped to rest at the peak of a hill overlooking a muddy creek bed at the bottom of a valley. Sheep grazed on the side of the valley, and at the bottom were several dozen small grass huts nestled among a stand of deciduous trees. A handful of people were visible milling about the huts.

"See?" Nisroc exclaimed proudly. "Civilization!"

"Looks nice enough, I suppose," said Christine, shivering as a cool breeze picked up. The sun was about to set, and the temperature would soon drop precipitously. The bonfire at the center of the village began to look rather welcoming. But was she really going to spend the rest of her life here? It didn't seem like she had much of a choice. At least she had Jacob to keep her company.

"What did I tell you?" asked Nisroc. "Nice people. Getting the hang of agriculture, but they still make time to do the hunting and gathering thing. Good balance of work and home life."

Jacob shrugged. "We'll manage," he said. "Assuming they don't kill us on sight."

"Nah," said Nisroc. "They're pretty easygoing. You'll be all right."

"Oh shit!" Christine exclaimed suddenly. "We left the apple!"

It was true. In their haste, they had left the glass apple on the table in the bungalow.

"I'll have to go get it," said Nisroc. "Heaven wouldn't want something like that to fall into the wrong hands. I have to go back for my sword anyway. You'll be all right without me?"

Jacob put his hand on Christine's shoulder and smiled. "Yeah," he said. "I think we'll be OK."

"OK, good luck!" said Nisroc, and leaped into the air, soaring across the darkening sky back the way they had come.

Nisroc didn't have any trouble finding his sword; it lay smoldering at the edge of several hundred acres of blackened ground.

The fire continued to blaze in the distance; fortunately it was traveling away from the village. Presumably it would burn itself out eventually; Nisroc didn't really know how that worked, but he figured that he couldn't be the first one to accidentally drop a flaming sword in a highly combustible area. Damn things were hard to hold on to.

The glass apple presented more difficulty: it wasn't on the table. He searched the entire bungalow, but it was nowhere to be found. This wasn't good. He had heard about those apples; they had started out as an experiment to create instant temporary portals, but they were too unstable to be of any practical use. The apple wasn't terribly dangerous at present, but it would gradually absorb more and more interplanar energy until it eventually imploded, sucking all nearby matter into another plane. It would probably be thousands of years before the apple imploded on its own, but still—that wasn't the sort of thing you'd want just lying around unaccounted for. Nisroc would be in a lot of trouble if they found out he had lost it.

As he rifled through the bungalow, tearing out couch cushions and looking under rugs, he heard someone clearing her throat behind him. He turned to see what appeared to be a young, dark-skinned girl standing before him. Behind her were several very serious-looking cherubim standing at attention.

"Looking for something?" she asked sternly.

"No," said Nisroc nervously. "That is, these temporal anomalies…they can be tricky devils. Sometimes they hide in the couch cushions. Can I, ah, help you?"

"We're on assignment from Michael, the archangel," said the girl. "Tracking a fugitive. Have you seen any other angels around? We've lost a marketing director."

Nisroc shook his head. "Just a couple of humans. I was told to escort them out of the area, because of the temporal anomaly."

The girl nodded, looking around at the disheveled bungalow. "We'll take it from here," she said. "Good work, uh…"

"Nisroc. Thank you, sir. Ma'am." He stood for a moment, looking at the girl.

"Anything else, Nisroc?"

Nisroc opened his mouth and then closed it. "No, ma'am."

"Be on your way, then."

Nisroc nodded and left. He felt a little bad about not telling the girl about the apple, but that wasn't really his job. He had done what he had been instructed to do, and he couldn't worry about problems that might not surface for several thousand years.

Besides, he thought, these things had a way of working themselves out.

FORTY-SEVEN

Job watched as the fog rolled in, enveloping a stop sign not more than thirty feet from where he stood. He could no longer see even the nearest buildings; the horizon was nearly an unbroken blur of gray. All that remained was this little patch of concrete, and soon that would be gone as well. Reality itself was at its end.

"Quit stalling," said the voice of Cain behind him.

Job smiled and turned. "Not stalling, just thinking."

"What's there to think about?" Cain sneered. "It's over. Soon there will be nothing left. Admit it, Job. You were wrong. There's no point, no purpose, no meaning. It's just game over, that's it. Since the Eye of Providence was destroyed, the Universe has been living on borrowed energy, and now it's gasping its last breath."

"Hmm," said Job thoughtfully. "Aren't you supposed to be the skeptic?"

"What do you mean?"

"You keep saying that the Eye of Providence was destroyed. But what evidence do you have?"

"What evidence?" asked Cain. "Are you serious? Look around you, Job. Reality is disintegrating before your eyes. The sustaining energy of the Eye is gone."

"Maybe," admitted Job. "Or maybe this plane has just been cut off from the energy somehow. Just because things are ending for us, that doesn't mean that reality itself is done for. I just have this feeling that the Eye is still out there somewhere, and that its energy is still radiating out into the void, maybe creating whole new universes as we speak. For that matter, even if the Eye is gone, who's to say that there isn't something greater than the Eye, something completely beyond our understanding, that somehow imbues all of this with meaning, even when it seems like everything is falling apart?"

"Unbelievable," Cain grumbled. "I've got to listen to this bullshit right up to the last moments of my existence. Just shut up and serve the damn ball, would you?"

Job smiled. "Twenty-five to twenty-four," he said. "Game point."

He tossed the ball into the air.

WITH THANKS TO:

- Joel Bezaire, Jeff Ellis, Mark Fitzgerald, Nicklaus Louis, Jocelyn Pihlaja, Medeia Sharif, Michele Smith, and Charity VanDeBerg for their invaluable feedback on the manuscript;
- The Amazon Publishing team for taking a chance on a silly book about an angel and for their continued support and general awesomeness;
- All my Facebook friends and Twitter followers, especially those of you who have been around since the Mattress Police days, for your words of support and encouragement;
- And of course my wife, Julia, for putting up with me.

ABOUT THE AUTHOR

Robert Kroese's sense of irony was honed growing up in Grand Rapids, Michigan—home of the Amway Corporation and the Gerald R. Ford Museum, and the first city in the United States to fluoridate its water supply. In the second grade he wrote his first novel—the saga of Captain Bill and his spaceship, Thee Eagle. This turned out to be the high point of his academic career. After barely graduating from Calvin College in 1992 with a philosophy degree, he was fired from a variety of jobs before moving to California, where he stumbled into software development. As this job required neither punctuality nor a sense of direction, he excelled at it. In 2009 he called upon his extensive knowledge of useless information and love of explosions to write his first novel, *Mercury Falls*. *Mercury Rests*, his third book, concludes the trilogy.